Binding Rails

Bruce Goeser

Jerome
Best of luck in the future and keep of the good work
Bruce Goeser

PUBLISH AMERICA

PublishAmerica
Baltimore

First printing

ISBN: 1-4241-7443-0
PUBLISHED BY PUBLISHAMERICA, LLLP
www.publishamerica.com
Baltimore

Printed in the United States of America

Dedicated to my wife, Lorie, for her patience and help while writing this book

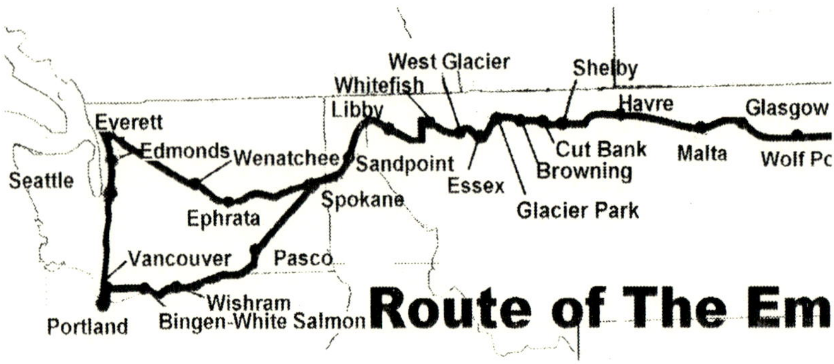
West Glacier
Shelby
Whitefish
Libby
Havre
Glasgow
Everett
Edmonds
Wenatchee
Sandpoint
Cut Bank
Malta
Wolf Pc
Seattle
Browning
Essex
Spokane
Glacier Park
Ephrata
Vancouver
Pasco
Wishram
Portland
Bingen-White Salmon
Route of The Em

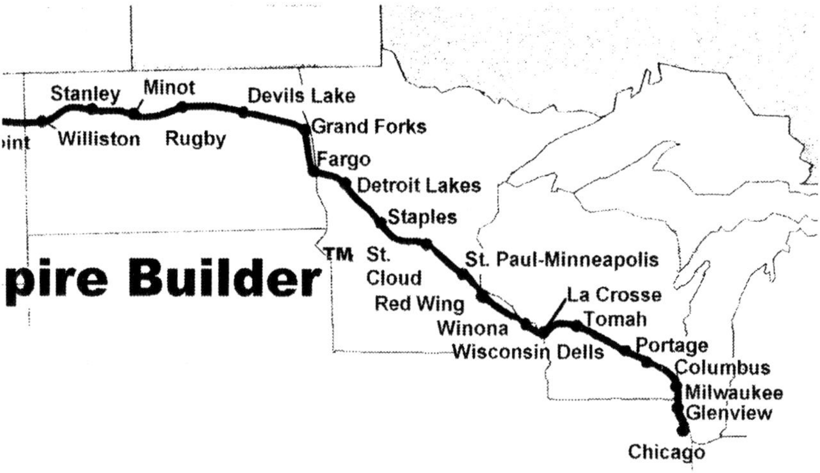

pire Builder
TM
Stanley
Minot
Devils Lake
Williston
Rugby
Grand Forks
Fargo
Detroit Lakes
Staples
St.
Cloud
St. Paul-Minneapolis
Red Wing
Winona
La Crosse
Tomah
Wisconsin Dells
Portage
Columbus
Milwaukee
Glenview
Chicago

Chapter 1
Ski Trip in Idaho

There was an orange glow permeating Brett's bedroom as the winter sun was poking through the dawn clouds over Seattle: The phone rang five times before Brett realized what was happening. He awoke just enough to roll over, grab his cell phone off of the night stand beside his bed, flip it open and mumble a faint, "Hello?"

The voice on the other end pierced through his eardrum like an arrow, "Hey, Dingleberry, where the hell are you? The train is about ready to leave!" Brett jolted upright, rubbed his eyes and squinted to see the red LED of his alarm clock—8:32—he looked once again before the time registered in his brain—at that point he just yelled back into the phone, "You asshole, Margo." Margo, who loved playing tricks like this on Brett, just howled and screamed with laughter. "I got you again, Dingleberry"

Brett retorted as he flopped back down onto his bed, "Ya, well screw you. I almost had a heart attack, you asshole."

"Well at least I'd know you have a heart. Hey, anyway, what time you picking me up today?" Margo inquired as she finally stopped laughing

"I don't know, maybe I'll just leave you home after what you just did to me," Brett responded with a sting in his voice.

Margo just chided back knowing full well that it would never happen "Oh, quit your pouting and get your ass ready. I'll be ready by noon—so pick me up then. We can have some lunch before getting on the train."

Brett replied, "Noon sounds fine to me. I know you won't believe it, but I am actually ready to go. I just have to stop at the ATM and I'll be set—I'll be there at noon—Lunch sounds great." Brett closed his phone and just lay there staring at the ceiling. He was really looking forward to a week of skiing up in Idaho. *Seattle is so gloomy in December,* he thought. *Hopefully it will be sunny and cold up at Schweitzer Mountain.* But more importantly he was also looking forward to spending time with Margo; the two had met two years ago when attending a ski club outing. Although he and Margo were not romantically involved, they were close friends. In fact, he thought Margo was semi-seriously dating some guy for the past four months. Brett enjoyed his relationship with Margo because there were no strings attached. He thought that he could be himself and not worry about the baggage that comes with a formal relationship. And besides he was free to date other women, which he never did.

On the other end of town, Margo jumped up from her bed after hanging up the phone, still chuckling from the prank she pulled on Brett. "God, I love it when a plan comes together,"she said aloud to herself. "I'll bet he nearly peed his pants." She was also looking forward to the time away, although more to the time away from the city, than to the actual skiing. Her job as an injection mold designer kept her in front of the computer for more hours than she cared for. But the bills had to be paid, and time is money. She was also looking forward to the time with Brett. Something might come of this she thought: The guy has potential.

The twenty-three-year-old Margo Endres walked quickly into the bathroom, dropped her nightgown onto the floor, and as she turned on the water, she admired herself in the mirror next to the tub. She was a half an inch short of six feet tall, thin, and sported a head of thick red hair that she kept cut short in a bob-type style. *Not bad,* she thought as she ran her hands down over her breasts and thighs, *it won't be too many more years before things begin to sag and wrinkle, but not yet.* She turned sideways to the mirror, shook her head with a smile and said aloud, "Yes, I'm cool." She then flipped aside the shower curtain and stepped in.

By the time she got out of the shower, ate a yogurt and a bowl of Fruit Loops it was already ten o'clock. Margo figured she had better get her act together and be ready, because if Brett showed up and had to wait—there would be hell to pay. She went over and turned on the stereo and got to work. As Kurt Cobain was singing about his addiction, she packed enough cloths in her duffel bag for the five day trip. Then as Green Day criticized the war in Iraq, she collected her skis and boots to put them next to the door. With that accomplished she just had to pack her toilet kit, which was only a two-minute job.

Gosh, I'm like a little kid before going to Grandma's house, she thought as she plopped herself down across the arm of the sofa. She couldn't believe how excited she was. Maybe it was because it was the train ride, or maybe it was just because she just needed a break. In any case she was flying. Margo got up to change the stereo. She wasn't in the mood for that old fashioned music so she found a System of a Down CD, put it in the player and turned it up. She looked around the small three room apartment and realized she probably should clean it up a bit. She knew Brett wouldn't care, but no sense in giving the wrong impression. The rotund snowman on her coffee table looked so much better without the crumpled Hershey Kisses wrappers half burying it—the Christmas cards sure looked more impressive when stacked as opposed to helter-skelter around the living room and the pizza box under the coffee table really didn't go with the decor of the season. Once straightened up, the living room actually looked like the Christmas season was upon them.

As she finished straightening the living room, Margo glanced at her watch—11:15—A few dishes to do and she would be done. She dug into them with the a clear purpose to be finished before Brett showed up. The stereo blared "Fuck the System" as she put the last dish away. *In a few minutes the wait would be over and she would be officially on vacation,* she thought, as she grabbed a beer from the refrigerator, and looked around for anything she might have forgotten.

She took a few slugs off the bottle just as the doorbell rang.

Brett stayed in bed for another hour before he got up, showered, shaved and dressed. As he grabbed the bagel from the toaster, he ran through the check list in his Franklin Planner, "Train tickets—breast pocket, hotel confirmation—wallet, wallet—pocket, skis and suitcase—in the car. It looked like he was ready, and one last check of the house proved it. As the graphics arts manager for Northwest Printing Company, Brett had become accustomed to check lists and their efficacy, so he carried his Franklin wherever he went. Last year his brother gave him a Palm Pilot for Christmas but it still sat in his dresser drawer—it just didn't have the same feel as his faithful leather binder. Brett thought that one wouldn't think a guy 25 years old would be so set in his ways. He wondered what he'd be like at 75.

It was normally a 45-minute drive to Margo's apartment, but today it seemed to take hours. Brett guessed everyone must be out shopping—It was December twenty-third and the clouds were taking a break from the continuous rain of the last week. Finally he turned the corner and pulled up to the curb in front of the two-story brick building, where Margo rented the second-floor apartment. He took a deep breath to relax, looked in the rearview mirror, ran his fingers through his short black hair, smiled contentedly with the results and then took another deep breath. After the preparations, he glanced down at his watch and muttered, "Oh shit, it's already 12:05." He quickly jumped out of the car, raced across the lawn, through the front door and up the stairs. He'd waited months for this vacation and now it was officially here. He rang the doorbell.

"Dingleberry! You're late. Come on in, I am pretty much ready to go," Margo said, as she flung open the door. Margo had given Brett the Dingleberry nickname from his Newbury last name.

Brett stepped through the open door and watched intently as the redhead pulled a maroon and gold *University of Minnesota* sweatshirt over her tee shirt. He quickly asked, "How are you doing? You know you damn near killed me this morning. And it is only five after twelve. Traffic was a bitch. Every old fart and their brother is out shopping."

"Oh quit with the excuses," Margo replied from the kitchen area as she poured the rest of her beer down the drain. She then walked over to the bathroom, grabbed her small toilet bag, closed the bathroom door behind her and walked back toward the door and Brett. "I thought my phone call was kind of funny," she continued.

"You should wake up earlier you know. Hey, seriously, if you really don't like the pranks I can stop."

Brett quickly replied, "Oh, I don't really mind; it keeps my heart healthy. I will get you back one of these days. You wait."

"I'll be waiting." Margo smirked as she put her skis over her shoulder and grabbed her backpack. "Let's go, Dingleberry," she said as she bounded down the steps, skipping every other one. "Hey, lock the door for me, will you? Just pull it shut," she yelled back up the stairs to Brett, who was a bit lost with the speed with which Margo grabbed her stuff and flew down the stairs. "Come on, let's get going," Margo insisted. "I'm on vacation, no time to waste."

Brett pulled the door shut and half ran down the stairs himself. "I'm coming, I'm coming. You sure you've got everything?" he asked as they reached the car. "It doesn't seem like very much stuff for five days."

"I'll be fine," Margo answered as she was sliding her skis into the back seat of Brett's Honda. "Where do you want to eat?" she asked

"How about Bill's? It's close to the station and they have pretty good food," Brett replied

"Sounds fine to me. I'll buy, since you're driving," Margo said as she got into the front seat.

About the time Brett and Margo were leaving the apartment George Hanover looked out the front door of the hotel at the clearing Seattle sky and longed for his wife and children back in Chicago. Three more days and he would be home to spend five glorious days of holiday spirit with his family. It had been four days since he'd seen his kids and he missed the excitement they exuded to everyone in the house this time of year. Strange as it seemed, he also missed the cold and snow. Not the shoveling and traffic hazards, but the crispness and the cleanliness a fresh coat of snow gave the earth. Like a fresh paint job on an old and worn house, it gave everyone, even the occupants a new perspective on life. George wondered if feelings like that could be aroused in a climate like this, where snow is uncommon and the rain doesn't seem to wash away the gloom but only appears to make it worse.

Just then the taxi pulled up in front of the hotel and honked once. George picked up his overnight bag and stepped out into the damp afternoon air. "Howdy, George," greeted the driver. "Merry Christmas to ya. I missed you the last time through. How are you doing?"

George replied, "Merry Christmas, Petie. I'm doing fine, you?

"I'm doing just wonderful," Petie said with a big smile, as he put George's bag in the trunk of the yellow cab, walked around and opened the door for George. "Here you go." The tall dark-skinned driver then quickly crossed around the front of the car and got in.

"Thanks, Petie. What did you get the Misses for Christmas this year?" George inquired as the taxi pulled away from the curb. He had gotten to know Petie pretty well during his frequent taxi rides back and forth to King Street Station over the last six years. Petie and him had spent more than one night in the hotel bar drinking scotch whiskey and telling passenger stories. George's were Amtrak passengers and Petie's were Yellow taxi passengers. It seemed to George that people were the same whether riding the train or a taxi. Some were glad for the service, some were nondescript and then there were the few who were just plain pains in the ass. Fortunately the latter were the most rare.

"I got Karen a pearl necklace with three diamond pendants. I got a deal from this customer of mine who owns a jewelry store down in the harbor district," responded Petie.

George was amazed and expressed his shock, "Holy shit, Petie, you must be doing well driving this taxi."

Petie replied, "My aunt died and left me some money and I did get a good deal. I figure Karen deserves something for putting up with me for these twenty-two years. I know she'll be pissed that I spent the money on her, but I know that she'll love it, and show off to all her friends," Petie added. "What'd you get for Alice?" Petie asked George.

"Nothing like you got, just some earrings, a book she wanted and a day at a spa in the city," George replied.

The rest of the fifteen-minute ride was spent on small talk and passenger stories.

"Here you go, George," Petie said as they pulled up in front of King Street Station. "Wish everyone a Merry Christmas from me."

"Thanks, same here, I hope Karen likes the necklace," George said as he got out of the taxi and walked around the back to where Petie had already gotten his baggage out. "Merry Christmas and happy New Year, Petie," George said as he shook the taxi driver's hand and gave him a twenty for the $11.95 fare. "I'll see you next year. Keep the change; you'll need it for the necklace."

"Thanks, buddy. Have a good trip," Petie replied and got back into his cab and drove off.

George walked into the front doors of the dark brick station, with its signature steeple-like tower rising above Jackson Street. He walked across the waiting room and directly to the waiting Empire Builder, where he boarded the fourth car back from the locomotive. This was to be his sleeper car, where he would be the passenger attendant for the three-day trip. George walked down the aisle and turned right into his berth, hung up his jacket and changed into his "Amtrak" clothes. The dark blue vest, blue tie, white shirt and matching pants were the mainstay of George's wardrobe, but he didn't mind; he was comfortable in his routine.

After he was changed and settled into his berth, George put on his cap and walked down the aisle looking at the car that would be his life for the next days. The train was still bustling with activity as the crew was getting ready for the passengers to board. Although the cleaning crew had thoroughly cleaned the entire train, there were still the incidentals to be finished, making sure the rooms were made up properly, that there were towels in the showers and bathrooms, making sure bottled water was available for passengers and that the passenger list was prepared. George took a quick glance at his watch, which revealed it was 3:45, and the passengers would begin boarding any minute, so the porter stepped outside the door to begin his greeting ritual. As he looked down the length of the train he waved to the other car attendants waiting outside their respective cars. Some were smoking their cigarettes before they entered the smoke-free train; others were just milling about waiting for the onrush of passengers.

Being Christmas meant the train would be filled to capacity, and the problems with the crowd would be foremost on everyone's mind.

After a quick lunch at Bill's Bistro, Brett and Margo drove the four miles to the station and parked in the adjacent lot. Although they still had 45 minutes before departure, they both jumped out of the Honda, grabbed the luggage, skis and coats, and raced across the parking lot into the waiting area.

Inside the waiting area the low winter sun displayed its wares through the huge west windows The rising dust illuminated by the glow appeared as bars of light reaching down from the heavens to pull together this cross section of the Northwest's human population. This sea of humanity mingled together in their collective yet separate worlds: There were those procrastinators who nervously went about dealing with their last-minute travel preparations; there were young lovers saying tearful goodbyes with hugs and passionate kisses; there were old friends and families wishing *Merry Christmas's* with handshakes and formal hugs; there was a lone passenger slogging through the station with, what looked like, no definite goal. Three small children were playing a game of running back and forth, and then falling to slide across the marble floor giggling with laughter. Against the far wall an old man in an old ratty tee shirt played the same monotonous song on his harmonica, hoping some compassionate passer-by would drop some spare change into his hat.

Margo and Brett reeled in the scene, entered into this cross section, integrating into this swirl of excitement, ready to witness a 75-year-old tradition—the departure of the Empire Builder.

As Margo entered the waiting area, she exclaimed, "This is going to be so much fun; I am so pumped!"

They set their luggage on the nearest available bench and began filling out those annoying little paper tags Amtrak uses to identify their things. "You know, I've never ridden the Empire Builder. I think the trip will be as much fun as the skiing," Margo continued

Brett replied equally as excited, but trying hard to hide it, "I've never ridden the train at all. I've heard some not very good things about Amtrak. I hope we don't have a crappy ride," he continued with a bit of pessimism.

"Oh quit being so negative; we're going to have a blast. We'll make it whatever we want. If you start nitpicking everything and get negative, I'll leave you, go sit in the lounge and get drunk," she reprimanded with a giggle.

"I won't screw things up for you, I promise." He waited a second and then continued, "I'm not like that, am I?"

As Margo pressed her way through the crowd toward the check-in counter, she was buffeted about and almost dropped her skis when a six- or seven-year-old boy ran between her legs. Brett caught her arm and helped while she carried her things to the counter and began checking in, she thanked him thoughtfully and then continued the previous conversation. "I don't think you are pessimistic, but you might have that tendency to gravitate toward that end of the spectrum. But don't worry it'll be a great trip."

Brett followed the check-in procedure in silence and went over and sat down next to Margo, who had taken a seat on one of the long benches in the waiting room. He remained quiet until Margo broke the spell.

"Come on Dingelberry, don't be so introspective," she said. "We're on vacation." She was cut short by the announcement that came over the P.A. system. "You may begin boarding the Empire Builder bound for Spokane, Whitefish, Havre, St. Paul, Milwaukee and a final destination, Chicago. Thank you for choosing Amtrak."

Brett stood up, grabbed his Franklin, pulled out the tickets and stuffed the planner back inside his duffel bag, but by the time he looked, Margo was halfway to the platform.

The bright, silver-colored, stainless steel, Amtrak Superliner cars were lined along the platform with their doors open waiting to accept the passengers. Each car had its own smell, and noise emanating from the coach. As the couple passed each car, their nostrils were tickled with the smell of burned diesel fuel, the odor of old grease from the mechanical components of the undercarriage, the stinging smells of the cleaning solvents used to clean the train between runs and finally the sweet smells of humanity.

Brett had run to catch up to Margo. "Hey,wait!" he yelled. "Where are you going? Our car is right here."

Margo turned, but kept walking, saying, "Let's go check out the engines. I've read some stuff about trains and want to check them out." She continued, "Hey, did you bring the camera? It might be cool to take our picture in front of the engines."

"I've got the camera, but I don't want to get in trouble," Brett said reservedly.

"We won't get in trouble by just taking a photo alongside the train," Margo said as she rolled her eyes and continued down toward the far end of the covered platform and the front of the train. The crowd thinned as they approached the locomotives so the high-pitched whine of the diesels mixed with fumes to provide the sense of power.

Once up to the front of the of the train, Margo stepped over, put her hand on the side of the sleek, silver and blue locomotive and posed as if she were modeling a blouse for LL Bean. "What do you think of this?" she giggled, "or how about this?" she asked as she turned and put her head against the side of the locomotive, as if she were hugging the giant machine.

Brett cracked up. "Oh ya! That's nice," he said as he quickly reached into his pocket, grabbed the camera, flipped it on and took a shot.

Margo then turned, put her back against the side of the locomotive, raised her right arm above her head and put her left foot up on the edge of the front cowl.

Brett laughed again and in his best Austin Powers imitation shouted, "Yeah, baby! Yeah! Give it to me, baby! Give it to me, baby!" He took four more photos as he moved in a semi circle around the hamming–it–up Margo. Both Margo and Brett nearly jumped right of their skin when the tall thin man dressed in a dark blue suit asked, "Can I have a copy when you get one?"

Neither one of the travelers had noticed as the engineer approached. With a flush of red in her cheeks Margo apologized, "Sorry, we didn't mean any harm,"

"No need to apologize," Mark Hatfield—the Amtrak engineer—said. "I am serious. I'd like a copy of the photo. I don't believe that I've ever seen a pose so striking as that with one of my units."

"Are you the engineer?" asked Margo as some of the color eased from face.

"Yes, my name is Mark Hatfield. Where are you traveling to on this fine winter day?" the engineer asked the young couple.

"We're going to Sandpoint to do some skiing," Brett replied. "My name's Brett and this soon-to-be-famous model is Margo."

"Nice to meet you both," Mark said. "I would appreciate if, in the future, you would keep your feet off my engines," he chided with a smile.

"Sorry," Margo replied. "Hey, would it be possible to get a ride in the cab?" she continued with the approach of a sales pro. "I've read some stories of guys that ride along in the cab. We wouldn't touch anything."

"Sorry," Mark replied, "insurance regs say no. I wouldn't mind the company, but Amtrak would have my head." After a couple of seconds he continued, "I will let you take a look inside if you like."

"I'd love it!" blurted Margo, practically jumping up and down like a grade-schooler, while Brett just stood back in amazement.

"Here," Mark said, "I'll open the door and step in. You can come up the ladder and look in."

About six feet back from the front of the engine was a ladder leading upward to the door entering the engineer's compartment. Mark hopped up onto the first rung, opened the door inward and stepped inside the belly of the purring locomotive.

Brett didn't have to tell Margo she could go first; in fact he would have been knocked out of the way if he had moved in front of her. She quickly lifted her long left leg and put her foot on the bottom rung. With a slight jump she was halfway up the ladder. She used both hands to hold on to the grab bars on each side of the door and poke her head into the cab. Mark stood halfway behind the door and said, "What do you think? There's not much to see is there?"

The inside of the operators compartment resembled a small home office. Across the front, underneath the windshield, was a full-length, padded, dashboard-type desk, with three small computer screens, two telephone handsets and a various assortment of buttons and switches. The desk and chairs were appointed in brown leatherette while the ceiling and walls were painted a bright white. Mark pointed to the seat and desk right next to the door. "That's my seat, and controls. That lever is the throttle and the other one is the brake," he explained. "Everything is computerized so there aren't a lot of gauges, knobs and handles like in the old days."

Margo looked around the compartment. "What's with the number 238 all over the walls and ceiling?" she asked pointing out the black stenciled number printed three times on the front and once on each of the side walls.

"Oh, that's Amtrak's way of making sure we don't forget which locomotive we are driving," Mark explained. "A bit redundant, wouldn't you say?"

"Thanks for letting me see," Margo said. "I'd better get going so Brett can have a look. I don't want to be responsible for making Amtrak run late." She then thanked the engineer once more and said, "Sometime if you wouldn't get in trouble, I would love to ride up here on a trip." And then she quickly backed down the ladder.

Brett quickly climbed the ladder poked his head in the doorway and climbed back down without saying a word. Margo had quickly dug through her fanny pack and come up with one of her business cards. She instructed Brett to take a photo of her with the engineer framed by the cab door. She climbed the ladder once more, handed the card to Mark and asked if he would pose for a photo saying, "Would you mind a photo?

Mark replied with a smile, " I'd love to be in a photo shoot with an up-and-coming model." He winked at Brett who was steadying the camera for the shot.

"I'm serious about the cab ride. Give me a call if the opportunity arises," Margo stated as she climbed down for the second time. She again thanked Mark, who replied that he was serious about the photo and would indeed call her. He then waved and closed the door to begin his duties as the engineer on Amtrak Train number 8 heading from Seattle to Chicago.

After the engineer closed the door Brett and Margo started back towards their assigned coach. After a few steps Brett turned and asked Margo, "I didn't know you were so interested in trains. How did this come about?"

"My Dad is a rail fan," the redhead responded. "My family used to go watch trains at every opportunity. We spent most vacations somewhere near a set of train tracks: weekends we drove along the mainlines between Minneapolis and wherever they took us." Margo glanced at the coach number they passed and then continued, "My mother, bless her soul, just went along for the ride. I think she just felt fortunate that she could spend time with my father, even if it was divided between her and the trains. I learned a lot from my father on those trips—Not all of it was railroading."

As she approached the next open doorway Brett interrupted saying, "Here's our car. Don't stop, I want to hear all about these trips."

As the tall, red-haired woman and her male companion approached, George asked, "Can I help you?"

Brett handed George the tickets and responded, "I believe this is our coach."

"Sure is," George said as he pointed the couple inside of the car. "Keep the rest of your tickets for your return trip," instructed the porter, as he tore the stubs off of the first two tickets and handed the remainder back. "Please watch you step as you board the train."

Margo and Brett stepped through the wide doorway as George instructed them, "Up the stairs on your right, seats 22 and 23."

"Thanks," Brett replied as he followed Margo up the narrow stairway.

Margo was immediately impressed by the cleanliness and modernity of the coach. "Wow, this isn't what I was expecting," she exclaimed. "This is a lot different than the commuter and excursion trains I've been on."

Brett replied as he strolled down the aisle looking at the seat numbers, "Ya, this is pretty neat," and as he sat down in the seat assigned, he continued, "Comfortable too! I'll bet you'll even have enough leg room."

Brett sat next to the window and watched as the tall redhead settled into her seat and adjusted the back angle. "You're right, these aren't too bad. As long as the person in front doesn't lean the seat all the way back, I'll be fine," she said.

Brett just nodded. He was watching the other travelers as they walked up and down the platform. Noticing that from what he could tell, there were basically three types of travelers boarding the train: those with families, who looked like they were using the train for travel to visit other family members, those who were alone or not so well off, used Amtrak as their main means of long distance transportation, and finally, those like Margo and himself, who were using train travel as form of vacation. He enjoyed watching people, but didn't want to make a poor showing while trying to impress his travel companion.

"Hey," Brett said as he stood up. "I'm going to go to the bathroom before we start moving. All that coffee at Bill's is taking its toll on the kidneys. You want to take a quick walk?"

"No thanks, I'm fine," Margo replied.

"Ok, I'll be right back," Brett said as he climbed over Margo and out into the aisle. He looked toward both ends of the car in puzzlement.

Margo noticed and piped up, "I think they are downstairs, seems to me I saw a sign."

"Thanks," Brett replied as he headed for the stairs.

Margo opened her fanny pack and pulled out her iPod and the Empire Builder schedule card she had picked up at the station. She put on the headphones and selected a couple of old Creed songs and settled into the music as she studied the timetable. "Let's see," she said aloud to no one, "how does this thing work? Oh, I see, you read it from the bottom up. Clever."

In a few minutes Brett came back and Margo started in a loud voice, "We should be in Spokane at 12:32 in the morning, and Sandpoint at 2:47."

Brett began laughing and pointed to his ears, gesturing for Margo to remove the headset. "Sorry," she whispered in embarrassment.

"Do you know how to read this thing?" she continued, but this time in a normal tone, "the right column is for when you are traveling east. See?" she said, as she showed the card to Brett. "We are supposed to leave here at 4:45. We should get to Spokane at 12:32 in the morning, and finally to Sandpoint at 2:47 tomorrow morning. If we kept going we'd get to St. Paul at 7:05 in the morning, the day after tomorrow."

Brett studied the card in Margo's hands. "Oh, I see, and the westbound you read the other way."

As several more passengers filed past, Brett noticed that the coach was filling up. He nudged Margo and began, "Wow, there are a lot of people on here. It's good to see so many people using the train as mass transit. Just think, if they were all driving their cars, there would be more global warming."

Margo replied, "I wish there were more trains like this; I'd like to be able to use them, but I guess the powers-that-be are so short sighted and selfish that they don't care what is best for the world; they just care for their own pockets," she continued, as she was getting riled up now. "It's amazing how people can be so self-centered. Do you think we will become that way as we grow older?" she asked earnestly.

"I don't think so," Brett responded. "You don't seem to be self centered like some of my other friends. They are already into status, and having more money than each other. Sometimes, I think, it takes a scientific mind to see the whole picture and to assess the situation—not to be concerned about just yourself, but how an act will affect the whole picture."

"Sure does seem that way sometimes. I'm not sure if it is science, or just upbringing. Kind of goes back to that nature-nurture thing that people have been studying for years. But wouldn't you think education would affect people somehow?" Margo asked, and then answered her own question, "I guess people just hear what they want to. Look at the evidence for global warming, and yet some people still don't believe it is happening."

"Yeah, it's pretty sad," Brett said with a hint of depression. "When are people going to respect each other and each other's things?"

There was a slight shudder as the train started to move and then a thud as George slammed the heavy steel door shut down below them. Both Brett and Margo turned quickly to watch out the window as the train pulled away from the platform and started on its 2200-mile, 47-hour trip from the Pacific Ocean to Lake Michigan—halfway across the country.

Margo was the first to speak, "Well, Sandpoint, here we come. No more depressing talk of the world's problems."

"Alright, we're on our way. Let's have fun," Brett added. But nothing more was added for the next several minutes as they stared out the window and watched as the familiar scenery of Seattle passed outside the window.

Brett was the first to break the silence, "This is so cool. Listen, you can hear the whistle and then the grade crossing bells as we pass. And check out, that all the cars have to stop and let us go by."

Margo was practically sitting sideways in her seat and leaning all the way across Brett as she watched and replied, "Ya, it's kind of like a power trip."

Again silence as they were transfixed on the passing scenery. Finally Brett offered, "Do you want to sit next to the window? I think I'll read for a bit, and you seem to like the window."

"Sure," she replied as she stood up and backed into the aisle, "if you don't mind,"

"No problem, we can switch later when you get bored," Brett said as he climbed in front of her in the aisle.

Just as Margo teased "Don't bet on it," the train crossed over a switch, doing a little wiggle, causing Brett to lose his balance and fall against Margo. The tall redhead had to reach out and catch Brett in a bear hug to keep him from falling onto the passengers across the aisle. Margo felt a thrill as she caught the scent of Brett's aftershave and the feel of his body pressed against hers.

Brett also felt the heat of the moment but tried to dismiss it. "Sorry," he said as he quickly regained his composure. "I gotta get used to walking on a moving train."

"Don't worry about it, no harm done," she said as she smiled and crawled into the window seat and sat down.

Brett sat down next to her and pulled out his book to read, but he couldn't get focused, as he was still reeling from his brush with Margo. *What if something went on between us?* he thought. Would he be able to handle it? He thought of the pros and cons of a serious relationship and decided—yes he could handle it: The train raced on as it made the Christmas journey toward Everett, where it would head east and over the Cascades.

Margo was also trying to figure out what had happened during that innocent mishap a few minutes back. She decided it was best to let her instincts do the talking, and if something worked out—so be it. The thought of a new romance thrilled her. She stared out the window as the city turned into suburbs and finally to more trees and less houses.

The light was beginning to fade as the conductor announced that the next station of Edmonds was approaching—any passengers departing were to gather their belongings and move toward the center of the coach. George, the car attendant, walked to the coach car, descended the stairs, stood in front of the stainless steel door and watched as the train pulled to a stop in front of the open platform. Once the motion ceased, he swung the door and latched it open. "OK, folks," he instructed, "watch your step. If you are stepping off for a quick smoke, you only have about three minutes, so don't move too far from the door. We *will* leave without you," he finished sternly.

The three minutes passed quickly as he had no passengers boarding his car. When the conductor called the "All aboard" he took a quick note of everyone standing around smoking and politely called, "OK, everyone back onboard."

After the eight passengers got aboard, he closed the door with a slam and opened the square window in the upper half of the door. He watched as the train began rolling onward into the early evening. *No sense leaving anyone behind,* he thought. *It is Christmas.*

More than once he stopped the train for a passenger who calculated wrong, strayed too far and ended up running after the train. Usually the engineer would stop—but not always. *It must be sobering,* he thought, *watching the train pull away leaving you stranded in a strange town, with no luggage, and possibly no money.*

After a couple of minutes George closed the window and returned to his business of attending Amtrak's passengers. He ascended the stairs and was starting down the aisle when a redheaded woman stopped him.

"Excuse me, can we just wander around the entire train, or must we stay in this car?" she inquired

"No ma'am, you are free to move from car to car. We have the diner car available for meals, and once we get to Spokane, the lower-level lounge is available for snacks and beverages. We will also be showing a movie in the lounge," he informed her. "If you listen to the announcements you'll hear the times for the movies."

She replied, "Thanks!" and returned to watching out the window.

The train was now following the Puget Sound coastline at water level. Brett startled and stopped reading when he heard Margo gasp, "Wow! Look at that sunset."

Outside of the window the sun was playing hide-and-seek behind the clouds just above the horizon so that what looked like the entire Sound had turned into a golden sheet of glass, only broken by the lonely fishing trawler cutting its way through the scene. The couple just sat and stared as the train wandered along the shore, providing an ever-changing perspective of the postcard view. Eventually the glow turned from golden yellow, to deep red, to pink, then purple, and finally a dull gray as night descended on the Empire Builder. Both Brett and Margo continued on in silence as they sat absorbing the view and beauty of their experience.

Once the sun went down the anticipation and waiting for the trip finally dissipated and the fatigue began to set in. Now the realization that they had finally made it on vacation, which combined with the sound and motion of the train, forced the couple to relax.

In a few minutes the train stopped at Everett, picked up several more passengers, left the sea-level grade and headed east and upward into the spires of the Cascade mountains.

Margo was starting to get sleepy and her head bobbed with the motion of the car. She caught herself and quickly said, "Let's go exploring; it's too early to take a nap," she invited Brett. "The attendant said we could cruise the entire train."

"I don't know. I'm right in a good part of my book," he responded.

"Come on, you got all night to read," she persisted. "Otherwise, I'll go myself."

Brett closed his book and got up from his seat conceding, "Alright, I need to stretch my legs. Let's check it out. Which way?"

Margo pointed toward the rear of the train. "That way."

Brett stepped back and allowed Margo to lead the way down the aisle toward the doors at the end of the coach. The train rocked and bounced in a continuous motion as it passed over the rails at 79 m.p.h. It took a few steps for the two to obtain their balance, gain the rhythm of the coach and negotiate the narrow corridor between the rows of seats. At any moment's notice, one had to be able to grab a handhold to keep from losing your balance. Yet it was an invigorating feeling to realize you were walking on a vehicle traveling across the land at more than a mile every minute. An even greater challenge than the aisle was the passage between two cars—where the rocking motion opposed itself between the two cars. Margo stopped briefly, studied the motion and then quickly crossed the walkway between the coaches. Brett followed closely behind.

The first coach the pair entered was the Superliner Sleeper which consisted of berths for the first-class passengers. Margo stepped ahead apprehensively, looked on both sides of the hallway at the closed curtains and wondered what was behind each barrier. Three rooms down, her curiosity was answered—the curtain was pulled back, revealing a small room with two seats under the window and a folded-up bunk near the ceiling.

Margo poked her head into the room to look around and exclaimed, "Dingleberry, we should have gotten one of these."

Brett replied, "Sure, and are you going to pay for it?"

"How much is one?" Margo inquired.

"I'm not sure, but I bet it's not cheap," he replied. "We could ask the porter, just for the hell of it."

"Let's," the redhead responded. "We'll be tired on the way home and we can at least sleep in these seats; it'll be dark with the curtain closed. Let's check out the downstairs. Didn't the porter say there was a lounge on the lower level?"

"OK," Brett said as he headed down the stairway. Once at the bottom of the stairs he stopped as he immediately realized this wasn't the lounge. "Just more rooms," he instructed as Margo almost piled into him from behind.

"Really?" she asked. "Let's look."

There was a hallway running the length of the car separated by the loading area in the center. One way down the hall there were three rooms like the ones upstairs—while on the very end was a closed door. Down the other hall were several small doors with an open doorway at that end. Margo started for the open door. Brett grabbed her sleeve and asked, "Where are you going?"

"I'm just going to check it out," she said, as she pulled away. "It won't hurt anything."

She quickly poked her head through the open door and exclaimed, "Now this is cool. This room is huge." Margo walked into the empty room and sat down in the booth-like seat next to the window. Above her head was the folded-up bunk, across the room the sink with towels, and in the far corner was an odd-shaped toilet.

Brett followed cautiously and stood in the center of the room looking around. "Come on," he said, "we're not supposed to be in here."

Margo just grabbed one of the magazines in the rack between the two seats and started paging through while exclaiming, "We're not hurting anything. There isn't anyone in here anyway."

"Margo, this is the handicap room. We don't belong in here. Now, come on, I'm leaving!" Brett reprimanded. Just as he was about to turn there was a faint growling sound followed by a *woosh.* Both of them flinched and jerked their heads toward the window; outside was a blur of hopper bottoms and wheels. It took a few seconds for Brett to figure out what was happening. "Holy shit!" he laughed. "We just met a freight train on the other track. It looks so different down this low."

"It did scare me," Margo giggled as she got up from the seat and stepped through the door ahead of Brett.

"Look these are showers," she said as she opened one of the small metal-trimmed blue doors. "They are so cute. Look at the way they really use space," she continued from inside the three-foot by four-foot room.

Brett figured this was legal so he wiggled his way in behind her. "Ya, this is pretty clever. Not really built for two people though," he said as he pressed himself against her side to inspect the shower stall.

It took a moment for the two to realize the intimacy of the situation. Brett blushed slightly and started to back away but Margo turned and put her arm around his waist to gently restrain him. "Kind of cozy, isn't it?" she said playfully.

Brett turned to face her and whispered, "Ya, kind of."

"You familiar with the Mile High Club? I wonder what they call it on a train?" Margo asked as she put both arms around his neck drawing herself closer.

"Don't know" was the response, cut short, as the two sets of lips pressed together in a kiss. Brett moved his left arm up and pulled Margo's warm body even closer while his right hand slipped beneath her shirt.

"Let's join it, whatever they call it," Margo whispered as she dropped her right hand, gently reached down the front of Brett's jeans and quickly found what she was looking for. Just as the two were entangled in love's grip the train crossed over another switch doing its little wiggle, causing the spring-loaded shower room door to open slightly and bang back shut.

Brett startled and whispered, "I'd better lock that."

The response was whispered back in a teasing voice, "You better, I hope you can reach it, because I'm not letting go of what I've got a hold of."

There was a click as the door locked.

George walked the length of the coach car and headed for the first-class sleeper. Passing between the cars he checked to see which room light had come on for service. After checking in with the occupants he headed down the stairs to get the extra pillow stored in the utility closet next to the handicap berth. As he walked past the second door his ears picked up the familiar sounds of the romantic interlude going on in the shower. He continued to the closet, grabbed the pillow and headed back toward the stairs to give the pillow to the requesting occupant. *What is it about the train?* he thought. George figured on noticing at least one shower love encounter per trip. *I hope these two don't leave things a mess in there when they're finished*, he continued thinking. No point in stopping them. It's their life he figured. It was just that, with all of his bodily fluid pathogen training, he almost hated cleaning up after that sort of event worse than when someone had motion sickness. George made a mental note to go back in an hour to check on things.

As he passed the entry door of the car George stopped and looked briefly out the window. Opening it he quickly poked his nose outside. Since the train had slowed as it ascended the mountain grade, the tall pine trees were not whizzing by the window as fast. The cool moist air, heavy with the smell of pine, overwhelmed his senses. Oh, he loved that smell. He took a big gulp of the cool mountain air and thought that in a few hours they would be out of the Cascades and he would miss the air. *That is one of the benefits of Seattle,* he thought, as he closed the window and continued on with his duties.

Meanwhile up past Skykomish, the winding snow sheds, and the long trestles over frozen creeks—the engines labored against the forces of gravity bearing the holiday travelers toward their destinations.

Several minutes after George returned to his duties the amorous couple emerged from the shower not noticing the outside air or the spectacular scenery. Margo kissed Brett's cheek softly as she straightened her sweatshirt and started back toward the center of the car. "Wait," she exclaimed as she turned and walked quickly back to the handicap room, grabbed the Empire Builder magazine, and headed back to where Brett had just finished tucking in his shirt. "There were two of them and I figured no one would miss one," she explained, as they turned and climbed up the stairs to the second level.

"Where to now, your highness?" Brett asked joking.

"Let's go back to our seats," Margo replied. "I need a rest." She smiled as she continued down the aisle. Once they were back to their seats Margo crawled in first to get the window seat as Brett followed. For almost a half an hour there was an awkward silence between them as no one wanted to ask the inevitable question. Finally Margo was the first to break the silence as she asked,"Are you sorry with what happened?"

Brett thought for a long few seconds before answering, "No, I'm not. I am glad it happened. How about you?"

"Oh no, trust me, if I hadn't wanted it to happen, it wouldn't have. I enjoyed every second," she said as she leaned over and planted a kiss on his cheek.

"Good," Brett continued, " to be quite honest, I've been thinking about it for a long while. I just never got up the nerve. Besides you have another boyfriend, don't you?"

"No, I was never really dating that guy. We just saw each other when it was convenient," she explained. "So I am looking forward to getting to know you better," she continued.

"Me too," Brett said. "You know we'll save some money if you cancel that room at the Schwitwzer ski lodge. I don't want to be involved with a woman who is not money-conscious you know," he laughed, "but seriously, I would love it if you canceled your room. You might lose something the first night, but I bet it would be cheaper and a lot more fun."

"Oh, you money-hungry old dog," Margo snickered, "I bet all you are thinking about is the money."

"Oh, you think so? Come on let's go check out that shower once more. I'll show you," Brett replied

"All right, calm down. I'll cancel my room. Do you have the number?" Margo asked as she reached into her pack and dug out her phone.

"Sure, it's right here in my Franklin," Brett said as he reached down and opened the page with the number. "Here, it's right here," he said handing her the book.

After a short conversation on the phone Margo closed the phone and said, "That's all taken care of."

The train was winding around the sides of the mountains and along the frozen streams originating in the snow field of the high Cascades. Margo stared out the window into the blackness looking for landmarks that would let her know where they were located. It was too dark to see anything; all she knew was that there were not any grade crossings, so they must be in the heart of the mountains. She glanced away from the window at Brett and saw that he had begun to read his book once again. She returned to the window but quickly grew restless. So she began talking not really caring whether Brett was listening or not.

"I've read some of the books my father had about this area of the railroad," she began. "We should be pretty close to where the one of the worst railroad disasters in this country took place. There was a town called Wellington somewhere along here. I think it was in 1910 or something like that. Anyway 96 people were buried when an avalanche wiped out a whole town along with a passenger train that was parked on the siding waiting for the storm to pass."

"Are you serious?" Brett interrupted, "or are you telling ghost stories?"

"No, I'm serious," Margo responded. "It was somewhere along here. They changed the name of the spot to Tye afterward. The tracks don't got through there any longer so you are safe. Besides, since then, they built the New Cascade Tunnel. We should be hitting the tunnel pretty quickly: you'll know it when we do. We'll probably be inside of it for ten to fifteen minutes. It's seven miles long." She continued, "That tunnel was opened in 1929 and when they first ran the steam engines through, it just about killed the engineers and even some of the passengers. The carbon monoxide and smoke would cause the engineer to pass out: the train would stop. Several times the passengers almost died. They ended up using electric locomotives to pull the trains through the tunnel until the diesel electric locomotives arrived."

Brett interrupted once again, "What the hell are you trying to do? I'm about ready to get off this death-trap right now."

"Oh, don't be silly," Margo chided. "We are perfectly safe. That was years ago. Anyway once the diesels arrived they found out that the smoke didn't kill people but that the engines acted like a plunger and pushed all the fresh air out ahead of the lead locomotive. The heat from the first locomotive would be sucked into the second locomotive causing it to overheat and shut down. Each consecutive locomotive would suffer the same fate. With only the lead locomotive still pulling, it too would overheat and the train would stall midway through the tunnel. Imagine a train stuck inside of a tunnel: pretty devastating to your schedules. That problem was solved by putting doors on the entrances to hold the air inside the tunnel and also now they have these, like 5000 horsepower, fans blowing fresh air in toward the advancing train. There haven't been any problems since, so that's how you'll know when we are in the tunnel."

"You really do know some stuff about trains," Brett said as he asked, "Did your father teach you all kinds of other neat stuff like that?"

At that moment the Superliner coach entered the 7-mile-long Cascade Tunnel. The noise inside the car changed from a distant hum into a more noticeable clack-clack and the exhaust from the locomotives added a bit of nostalgia to the experience. Margo piped up, "We're in the tunnel. Wow! I hope the fans don't break down or we're toast."

Brett looked at the fellow traveler with a visible look of shock. Margo cracked wide open in laughter. "I got you again, Dingleberry, Nothing is going to happen. Even if it did, we wouldn't be in trouble. It might smell a bit like burned diesel but we'd be fine. Don't be so gullible."

"Don't be such an asshole. When in the hell will I ever learn not to trust anything you say? I hope you are enjoying yourself," Brett said with only a half-hearted reprimand.

"I love teasing you. But you know it's only in fun. I think you are really smart: maybe a bit good looking too. I might become attached to you if you are not careful," she said with a smile

"Oh, you think so, do you? Well maybe I'll become attached to you first. Then what will you do?" Brett countered.

"Well I suppose I'll just have to love it," Margo replied as she leaned over and pointed to her lips. "Put one right here, smarty-pants."

Brett leaned over and the couple launched into a long and passionate kiss. After the two came back up for air, Brett said in a fair Bogart imitation, "This could be the beginning of a beautiful friendship."

Margo responded with her rendition of Ingrid Bergman, "We'll always have Paris." She continued, "You were asking about my father: I'm a Minnesotan from way back. My father worked for Pillsbury in the elevator until he retired, so he would spend all week unloading the grain cars and then weekends we'd chase trains all over Minnesota. It was kind of fun; we got to know Minnesota really well, and as a matter of fact we got to know the Midwest pretty well. I remember as a little kid, my dad packing a lunch, filling a gallon milk jug with water, throwing me in the car and heading off in some direction only he'd know. Eventually we'd come across a set of tracks where Dad would stop under a tree, turn on his scanner and we'd wait. While we were waiting he'd always read to me—sometimes railroad stories, sometimes the newspaper and sometimes a book that I'd bring along. Finally the scanner would start to crackle and we'd pick up the conversations of an approaching train. Dad would get so excited. We'd quickly gather up everything, even if it was right in the middle of eating. We'd jump in the car and head off to meet the train. He'd find the closest grade crossing and watch as the locomotives thundered by. Dad would describe the locomotives as they passed, "There goes an SD45" or "That's an SD40-2" or on the rare occasion, he'd say "Wow! There's an old F7." I got to know the locomotives fairly well just listening and watching. I really did enjoy those times. I know it doesn't sound like much fun, but most of the time it was just one-on-one time with me and my dad. Most kids don't get that." Margo paused as she stared at her reflection in the window. Brett waited for her to start once again as he didn't want to interrupt her train of thought.

She continued on, "As I grew older I started to get a little bored with the waiting. You know, there's friends or TV that you think would be more fun than spending time along a railroad track somewhere, waiting for a locomotive you've probably seen a dozen times before. But do you know? I went, more times than not, when Dad asked me. By this time I'd do homework or read some teen romance novel I'd bought. Dad would still read bits of whatever he was reading out loud to me. I picked up the habit and would read portions from what I was reading. I can't imagine he was interested in what some Nancy Drew-type character was doing, but he never complained."

There was a long pause once again. But Margo continued without looking away from the window. "I stopped going along about the time I became a freshman in high school. Wow, that's been ten years already." She stopped.

The train emerged from the tunnel with a noticeable decrease in noise. Brett watched her face as she turned away from the window. There was a tear trickling down over the freckles on her face. He reached over and gently took hold of her hand. Without saying anything, he conveyed his compassion so she continued.

"Last week Mom called and told me that Dad was going in for Alzheimer's testing. Mom thinks that Dad is forgetting things. He is only 66 years old," she said as she sniffled and wiped the tear on her sleeve. "Brett," she asked, "will you go back to Minneapolis with me this summer? We could take the train: Dad would just love to know that I rode the Empire Builder into St. Paul. Then I would like to take him and Mom on a small round-trip train ride, say up to Grand Forks or something, maybe over to Wisconsin and back. Even if Dad can't remember anything else, I'd be willing to bet, he'd know what each locomotive was that we passed along the way." Margo stopped and looked into Brett's eyes and now tears filled her eyes. "Will you do that? Even if things don't work out between us and we aren't romantically involved any more?"

Brett took his finger and wiped the tears from Margo's cheeks. "I'd love to go with you. So far, you are the best person to travel with that I've known. And besides by that time, I'll be dying to meet your parents and they'll want to meet me. When we get back let's pick a week and make the arrangements."

Margo squeezed her companion's hand and just said, "Thanks." She sniffled and continued, "Well now that that's over with, let's try to figure out where we are."

As she looked at her watch she said, "We must be getting close to Leavenworth, so pretty soon we'll be in Wenatchee. We are supposed to be there around quarter to nine."

Brett reached down and began fumbling around in his pack and came up with two aluminum foil-wrapped sandwiches. "You hungry?" he asked as he held out the package.

"Yeah, as a matter of fact. Thanks," she replied as she accepted the sandwich.

"I figured we'd be hungry, so I made them before I left," Brett said as he unwrapped the foil. "I hope you like it. It's lettuce, tomato, Swiss and humus."

Margo replied as she finished unwrapping the meal. "Boy, whole wheat bread too. How did you know I like this type of thing?"

"Oh, I've watched what you eat whenever we'd go on ski outings with the club. I knew you liked to eat healthy, so I tried it, and found out that I like it," Brett said as he took his first bite.

Margo turned a bit red and replied, "I'm embarrassed. I didn't know you were watching me."

"Oh don't be embarrassed," he replied. "You are quite noticeable in the fact that you are so beautiful. I mean I was just naturally attracted to you and watched whenever I could. It is a pleasant feeling looking at you."

"Now I'm really embarrassed," Margo said with a lot more red in her face than before. "What a wonderful thing to say, you're so sweet." She bent over and kissed Brett's cheek once again. "You know I could really get used to this: a man making me food and whispering compliments in my ear. God, what a doll."

Brett just smiled and took another bite. After chewing a bit he said, "You can get used to it; I'll be around for a while.

Outside the window the scenery was changing from the heavy snowfields of the western Cascades to the drier eastern slope of the mountains which support the vast fruit growing industry, of which

Wenatchee is the hub. The great Northern Railway developed the community and since then, the railroad has been hauling 15% of the nation's apples out of the city's warehouses. As the Empire Builder pulled into the station, the moon broke through the clouds to reveal the skeletal silhouettes of the apple trees lining the hillsides above, and turned the Columbia River into a silver ribbon flowing through the city.

George opened the door as the train pulled to a stop. He helped the five passengers gather their luggage and reminded each one to watch their step as they stepped off of the coach. The air here was cold but dry and the pine scent was replaced by the smell of dry grass and sage. Here the wind had a different bite: Not the dampness from the ocean, but the bite of air flowing down from the arctic with nothing in its path.

The "All aboard" came so George rounded up the smokers and herded them onto the car. Within four minutes the train was rolling out of the station, followed the river for a short spell and began to tackle the grade out of the valley. The porter stood looking out the window in spite of his longing for the comfort of his berth. With the moon aglow he looked forward to the surreal scene that was about to present itself. Once the train climbed out of the valley he would get a glimpse of the vast Columbia Basin. Here about 10 million years ago, massive lava flows oozed out across the region and covered some places with a mile-thick lake of molten rock. Since then the rock has decomposed and turned this into a fertile wheat-farming area. As the train reached the broad rolling plain the landscape opened up revealing expansive wheat fields that in the moonlight turned from their burned brown to a pale yellow white. Thin, dirt-streaked snow drifts were scattered across the landscape in willy-nilly patterns, adding stripes to the two-dimensional fields. The sparse trees in the gullies were just black skeletons reaching their arms upward as if reaching for the moon to pull it closer for more light. Occasionally an antelope would raise its head to watch the train pass by in the white light.

George never tired of the wide open spaces of the high northern plains. Growing up in Chicago, space was a premium. Although he knew he would miss all the conveniences of the city he thought he may find some solace in these wide open spaces.

After a few more minutes of watching the wheat fields pass by, he turned and headed back towards his berth. The passengers would be restless and getting ready to settle in for the night, so he'd better get to work. He climbed the stairs and looked into his passenger's needs.

Brett watched as Margo finished her sandwich in silence. He was becoming sleepy and thought it would be a good time to read for a bit and fall asleep. Margo had the same feeling, so she grabbed her headphones from around her neck, put them over her ears, and watched the scenery roll by in the moonlight. She too noticed the vast moonlit fields and wondered what the moon was doing to the fields of her native Minnesota. She soon was dreaming of those cloudless, cold, moonlit nights where the temperatures reached into the double digits below zero.

Brett read for a few minutes before looking and noticing that Margo's breathing had slowed to a melodic rising and falling symphony. He closed his eyes and fell asleep. The train snaked its way across the prairie following the valleys and avoiding the steep gullies The moon continued its low path across the southern sky. Christmas Eve was only 24 hours away.

Margo awoke briefly as the motion of the train stopped while passengers departed and boarded at Ephrata. She looked at Brett who did not appear to be awake, so she just settled into her music and fell back asleep. It would be another three hours before the train would make another regular station stop: tonight the schedule held true as all the freights pulled into the siding before Amtrak 8 arrived.

A few minutes after midnight the train approached the lights of Spokane, the gateway to the western Northern Rocky mountains. The train passed through the suburban communities as it wound its way to the downtown station. Here the crew changed and the section of the train coming from Portland was joined to the section from Seattle. Now the train was prepared before the long hard trip over the Rocky Mountains.

George walked through the car and whispered to any awake passengers that this stop would be 40 minutes and if they would like some fresh air or a smoke it would be a good time.

Margo was the first to awake from the commotion as several passengers walked down the aisle toward the stairs. She glanced over toward her partner as he shook off the sleep in his head. Margo whispered, "Do you want to go outside for some fresh air?"

"I think that might be just the cat's meow," Brett replied. "I feel like I've been crumpled up like a piece of scrap paper and my mouth feels like the entire Russian army has been walking over it in their stocking feet."

"Yeah, I know the feeling," Margo replied as she attempted to stand up. "Oh man, it's hell to get old," she complained.

Brett had managed to un-wrinkle his body and obtain an upright position as he stepped into the aisle. Margo led the way down the aisle, down the stairs and out the open door into the cool December air. Both stopped and shivered as the air penetrated their lungs. The security lights bathed the platform in an orange light as the passengers milled about talking, smoking or both. Margo looked toward the front of the train and saw that the locomotives were gone. Toward the rear of the train she noticed that they were adding several more cars.

"Let's take a walk toward the back of the train and see what's going on," she said as she started walking down the platform.

Brett started in, "The air feels good, but it's really cold and dry. Quite a change from Seattle."

"Shit," Margo replied, "this isn't anything. I'll bet it's only in the mid-twenties. Wait until you get to Minneapolis one of these days: There you'll find out what cold is. Twenty-five below zero with a thirty-mile-an-hour wind blowing. Now that'll show you what cold is," she continued as they walked the length of the train. "Yet, you know, you get used to it. There will be guys out ice fishing in that weather, or if there is enough snow, they'll be snowmobiling."

Brett looked at her in kind of disbelief. "Really people will be out in weather like that?"

"Sure," she responded. "What else is there to do? Like I said, you get used to it: you have to get outside sometime, or you'd go crazy. Kind of like the rain in Seattle. You dress for it and go about your business."

The couple reached the end of the platform so they turned around and started toward the other end, more to keep moving in the cold night air than for the exercise.

Margo continued, "It is a bitch on your car though. If ever anything is going to break, it'll be when it's that cold. Everything gets so stiff and brittle. It really is amazing they work at all. Imagine these trains with all the steel getting cold and brittle. You'd think something would have to give. Steel wheels on steel rails pounding along at 79 miles an hour."

"I never really thought about that." Brett replied, "I've never been in that kind of cold."

Margo stopped and turned toward Brett. "Maybe we should stay on the train and just go to Minnesota for Christmas."

Brett looked at the young redhead and affectionately replied, "I'd love to, but I don't think it would work. We don't have tickets and we do have the reservation at Switzer."

"I suppose you are right," Margo replied as she turned and continued walking. "I didn't make any sense. Let's go skiing and have a great time of it."

Bret looked at his watch and said, "In less than two hours we'll be at the mountain." He took her hand and the two walked to the open door of the coach where they were met by the group of smokers standing in front of the door. As they passed the porter they asked, "How long before we leave?"

George looked down at his watch and said, "About 10 minutes."

"Thanks," Brett replied as he turned to Margo. "Let's go get our seats. The next time we get out will be Sandpoint."

Margo stretched a bit before she stepped through the door and headed back up the stairs. As the pair reached their seats Margo noticed that a young blond college-aged man had taken the seat directly in front of hers. The man was leaning forward with his head in his hands and displayed the classic signals of distress.

Margo stopped and politely asked, "Are you OK?"

The young man startled and quickly raised his head and removing his hands from his face revealing his reddened eyes, said, "Yes, I'm OK, just a tough week. Thanks."

"OK, I hope things go better for you," Margo replied as she smiled, stepped past her seat, turned to Brett and said, "How about you sit next to the window? I've been kind of a hog."

"Thanks," was the reply as the tall man slipped his way from the aisle into the farthest seat. Margo followed him, picked his book off of the seat, handed it to him and sat down.

"OK, Mr. Dingleberry, now it's time to spill your guts. Since I've been going on and on all evening it's your turn," Margo said putting her hand on his arm.

Brett turned toward her and replied, "All right, where do you want me to start? The details of my life are quite inconsequential. My mother was a French whore named Cloie with webbed feet. My father was a boulangerie owner from Belgium. He was a womanizer and would make outrageous claims like he invented the question mark."

Margo punched him in the arm and said, "Enough of the Dr. Evil, get serious. Where'd you grow up?"

"I'm grew up in L.A.," Brett replied. "It is not something you admit in Seattle, so I keep it pretty quiet. When I was a senior in high school, my father died and things were pretty shaken up. I stuck around L.A. through college as a courtesy to my mother but as soon as I graduated, I moved north to Seattle. My only family is my mom and one sister, who is six years older. I was never close to her and since she lives in Phoenix with her three kids there was nothing holding me back. I needed a change of scenery and my mom had put her life back together selling the house and moving into an apartment. I realized that since she had put her life back together, it was time I did the same."

At that point the train lunged a bit as it accelerated out of the station. Brett paused and then began "Well here we go, next stop Sandpoint and skiing."

Margo pinched him lightly on the bicep and scolded, "Don't stop—keep going."

"So, three years ago, I packed up my things and headed north." Brett continued, "I really like Seattle and don't miss L.A. at all. I do get back to see my mom once a year but otherwise I don't miss anything about California. I went to school at the local tech school and got my associate's degree in advertising, so I slipped right into Northwest Printing. That's about all I have. I don't have the Midwestern protestant family background that you do. You know, I've never really thought about it, or missed it, until I just heard you talking about it." Brett paused. "Is it really idyllic like they make it sound?"

Margo thought for a full minute before responding, "I don't know that it was so different. There were good times as well as bad. I'm not so sure my parents were really happy together. They are stoic and grew up expecting to stay together no matter what happens. There was a lot of pressure on my dad to work 40 to 50 hours a week. My mom waited on him when he got home from work and made his meals. This was just what was expected. I never saw my parents be intimate, never even a small kiss. It just wasn't them. So is it all it's cracked up to be? I don't know. They were good to me: again that is what is expected." Margo paused once again, then continued thoughtfully, "I don't think I want to live that way. I mean the family value thing is OK, but I think both parties need freedom and individualism."

Brett interrupted, "That sounds very insightful. I don't think where I grew up was that much different. You know I don't think I could ever stifle anyone. I enjoy watching people do their thing and grow in themselves. I hate it when some guys get jealous of women, especially their wives. I don't care if my wife would make more money than I would. What's the big deal! I like to respect people for what they are."

The conversation waned as the couple looked into each other's eyes. Margo piped up, "You are a pretty cool guy, Dingleberry. Don't ask me why I didn't get together with you sooner. I could have missed getting to know you all together, if I'd waited too long."

Brett smiled. "Thanks for the compliment. I would have waited for a spell," he said and let the conversation stop.

The train rushed through the night as it wound its way along the lakes and valleys heading north into the upper panhandle of Idaho. The pine scent returned to the air and carried a chill as the downhill breeze brought the effects of the high-elevation snow pack down with it. Brett looked at his watch and realized in only 15 minutes the train would stop and what could turn out to be his most exciting vacation would begin. The thought of spending time and sharing a bed with Margo for five days excited him intensely. Just as he was thinking that the 15 minutes would drag by, he noticed the conductor walking down the aisle toward them. The man stopped and whispered that theirs was the next station stop and they should proceed as quietly as possible to not disturb the other passengers. He then said he would meet them downstairs by the door.

Margo stood up and stepped into the aisle following conductor. Brett reached and touched her arm whispering, "Do you have everything?"

Margo patted her fanny pack and looked around the seats. "I think so. I really didn't have much."

Brett also looked under and around the seats replying, "I don't see anything. Let's go."

The couple descended the stairs and stood in the vestibule where three other passengers joined them. George, the car attendant, was standing directly in front of the door with one hand on the latch watching out the window. He turned slightly toward Brett and said, "Are you ready for some cold? It's about 24 degrees out there."

"I guess so," Brett replied. "I'll have to be. We are going to spend the week skiing so I'd better get used to it."

George smiled and asked politely, "Are you from Sandpoint, and visiting family?"

"No," Brett replied, "just vacation and skiing."

"It seems as though everyone is going to visit family for the holidays. Just kind of unusual, but it will be a great time for skiing. I hear the mountain is pretty nice and they've gotten a lot of snow," the stately porter said looking once again out the window. "It'll be about five minutes yet the way it looks."

Margo spoke up and asked George, "Where are you from?"

George said, "Chicago," without turning away from the window. "I'll be home on Christmas to be with my family. I can't wait. I normally really like this trip, but today it just seems to drag. I guess it is the thought of being home for Christmas and spending the next six days in my own home with my wife and kids."

"That should be nice," Margo replied. "How old are your kids?"

"Let's see the oldest is thirteen, then nine and finally the youngest is eight I think," George said with a smile.

Margo returned the smile and said, "Oh, that's great ages for Christmas. It should be fun."

"Yeah, the kids are all pretty good in spite of me being gone so much. Their mother did a fine job." George continued, "The thirteen-year-old is a handful though. She wants a tattoo around her navel and a pierced nose for Christmas. I told my wife that she can do that when she's eighteen, but until then I'm in control of what she does with her body. No daughter of mine is running around looking like one of those tramps you see in the ads."

Margo interrupted, "Oh, I'll bet she'll use the excuse that all of her friends have them."

George was getting worked up now so Margo calmed him a bit. "She'll get over it when she thinks about it. I remember asking for some foolish things at that age. My parents thought I was nuts and I thought my parents were neolithic cave men for being so old fashioned. I never did get a tattoo, at least that anyone can see," she added as she winked at Brett.

The train started to slow and George asked the small group to step back as he opened the door. He looked at Margo and said, "I hope you're right. She has a good head on her. I do think that she'll think about it."

The cold air rushed through the open doorway along with the mixture of pine, diesel and brake smoke. Both Brett and Margo shivered as the air hit them. When the squeal of the brakes ceased, it announced the car was at a full stop and everyone in the group jostled in unison; but they regained their balance when the train momentum ceased. George stepped through the door, turned and asked each passenger to watch their step as they left the train.

Brett and Margo followed a family of three off of the train and were immediately jolted wide awake by the brisk winter air. Margo quickly zipped her Polartec up to her chin while Brett just shrugged and stuck his hands into his pockets.

"Wow! it is cold." He shivered. "Where are our skis?" he asked George.

"They'll be coming down from the luggage car in a minute," George said as he turned toward a group of three passengers stepping off of the car behind Brett and instructed, "Please do not wander far from the train, people. We are only here for four minutes. You'll have to hurry your smokes."

Brett looked toward the baggage car where two Amtrak personnel were unloading several bags and four pairs of skis out of the car onto a green four-wheeled cart pulled by a small Kubota tractor. Up and down the platform, in front of the red brick station, people were milling around greeting incoming families with hugs and handshakes. Departing groups were saying their goodbyes with similar hugs and handshakes. Mixed among the arrivals and departures were the passengers who had stepped off of the train for a quick cigarette and were standing hunched over and shivering with their backs to the wind.

Brett turned quickly in alarm, as the tinny sounding horn of the tractor approached warning passengers to step aside. He noticed his and Margo's skis and luggage amongst the pile on the wagon. Grabbing Margo's arm he said, "Come on, let's go inside to get our stuff and get a ride to the mountain."

Margo walked astride of Brett briefly but stopped and turned around as the conductor yelled the "All aboard."

Within a minute the smokers got aboard and the doors closed. With the hiss of air brakes and the roar of diesels Amtrak 8 pulled out of the station and headed into the dark night on its Christmas journey toward the home port in Chicago. Margo stood mesmerized until all that was left were the red taillights, and then they were gone: only the silence and memories of her first Amtrak ride remained. She turned, quickly caught up to Brett and together they walked into the station and into a long life together.

Chapter 2
Coming Out

Chas Connor leaned his head in his hands more in fatigue than desperation as he sat down in his coach-class seat of the Empire Builder. He just sat there not trying to dwell on the events of the past twenty-four hours. What he needed now was a plan—A serious plan.

The voice from the aisle broke his thought process—he turned to see who was asking the question. "Are you OK?" the voice asked politely.

Without a hesitation, or even a thought that maybe he wasn't OK, Chas responded, "Yes, I'm fine thank you. Just a rough day." The tall woman smiled, then moved on and sat down in the seat behind him.

A rough day, he thought, *that's an understatement.*

The twenty-one-year-old blond-haired man sighed deeply and sat back in his seat. Two days ago he was expecting a pleasant major life change. Now he was experiencing a major life change but of a completely different magnitude. He fought the gut-wrenching desperation as he thought of the change in direction that had come about in just two days.

He turned and stared out the window as the conductor issued the "All aboard." In a couple of minutes he'd be on his way back to Whitefish where his journey began.

The train began to creep ahead and slowly accelerated out of the Spokane Station on its journey east. The door slammed shut downstairs as a final reminder that Chas was locked in a machine moving him back to a life he really didn't want to embrace. The young man just stared out at the passing deserted streets and darkened houses. The brightly lit Christmas decorations did little to cheer him up. In fact they did quite the opposite. It made him realize that this could become the worst Christmas season he'd ever experienced.

As he laid his head against the window he hoped fatigue would overtake him, that he would fall asleep and wake up and the entire nightmare would be over. But as he closed his eyes his mind only reeled faster, keeping his thoughts racing as if on a fast track to hell. The more he tried to calm them the more they flailed at him. *What are you going to do now? What are you going to do when ski season ends? What now?* He had to stop the thoughts or he'd go crazy. He thought about getting drunk. *No that would only make things worse.* He still wouldn't have the answers when he sobered up. He needed sleep. The sleep deprivation only compounded the problem. Finally he regained control of his thought by progressing through the events of the last two days.

It started out as the morning dawned bright and sunny over Whitefish. Chas and Phillip woke up early in anticipation of their trip to Spokane. This was to be the big event as Phillip was to announce to his parents his engagement to Chas. Once they made their formal announcement the couple was to head up to Vancouver, British Columbia, where a justice was to marry them into an official Canadian partnership.

Chas thought back on his Canadian heritage. He grew up in, what he considered, an upper-middle-class family. His father is a professor of English at the Calgary Community College and his mother teaches high school physics. He didn't feel that he had experienced anything special in his upbringing. Chas remembered that he first had thoughts that he might be different when he was a freshman in high school. While all of his friends were beginning to become interested in girls and curious about sex and the female anatomy, Chas didn't have that much interest. His classmates were interested in becoming friends with the girls to see which ones would put out for them. Chas would become friends just to be friends, for the companionship, for the support or for in-depth conversation. He thought, and talked about sex just to fit in with the crowd. Finally after a while, he just faced the fact, he wasn't interested in an intimate relationship with a female. He never made a conscious decision, but he just began to feel that he would be more comfortable in a long-term relationship with a guy. He realized when he was fifteen that he was homosexual. *Yes*, he thought, *he is gay.*

Throughout his high school years he concealed his sexual orientation by playing along with the guys and even semi dating a couple of girls. He bet that he asked himself a thousand times "Why me? What did I do to deserve this?" During his school years, Chas considered it a scourge to be afflicted with this malady called homosexuality. It wasn't until after high school on a skiing trip to Whitefish that he met Phillip Betman. They were both 18 and enjoyed the same things, skiing, biking, fast cars, and the same music. He and Phillip became close friends during that week at Big Mountain in Whitefish. All of the emails and phone calls over the next six months convinced Chas that his relationship with Phillip was more than platonic. He recalled the warmth and nervousness realizing that this feeling must be that same feeling his friends felt, when they were in love with a woman. This is a natural, unconscious feeling, he thought.

Outside the window of the coach, the scenery was rolling by at over a mile a minute. The moon began darting in and out from behind the scattered clouds developing in anticipation of the upcoming storm. The light accumulation of snow left over from the last storm reflected the white light illuminating the backyard secrets of the houses along the tracks. The roads crossing the mainline were deserted and off in the distance the mountain peaks displayed the white caps of their silhouettes. Chas just stared beyond the occasional pine tree blurred by the speed as the Empire Builder passed. He reminisced of that first summer trip down to Hayden Lake to visit Phillip. It was his summer break; he was as excited as only a teenager can get when pursuing a romance, and embarking on his first solo road trip. During that week of summer bliss, he and Phillip had done two days of hiking in the Cabinet Range, then miles of mountain biking on trails so tough they thought they would surely end up in the hospital, but most memorable were the hours spent talking and revealing their inner-most secrets. It was surely a love affair in the mountains, but nothing was spoken about their sexuality and no advances were made, or accepted by either partner. This was not the time for such forwardness. Chas knew that he needed to be sure, and that he would not offend the one person he deemed so highly.

When it came time to head back to their homes, the couple said their cordial goodbyes and made plans for one more visit before fall would set in, come September.

Maybe it was the innocence of that first trip, the bright sunny weather or just the spectacular mountain scenery. In any case Chas could practically remember every second of the entire week.

Vacations like that come only once in a lifetime, he thought as the cold night rolled by outside the window.

In the distance the lights of Sandpoint appeared on the horizon and in a few minutes the couple seated behind Chas got up, moved toward the front of the car and headed down the stairs. As he watched them disappear, he thought how much easier it would be to be straight. No one looked and sneered in disgust as that couple walked together—Yet when he and Phillip would walk together, the looks would kill the faint of heart. As the train sat in the station Chas watched out the window as the passengers met family members, loved ones or just friends and he wondered how many of these people were gay. Some people say one in a hundred humans are homosexual, yet, so far he wasn't able to find more than one, in all the hundreds of people he'd met.

Either he wasn't looking very well or the experts were wrong, he thought

The car attendant, George, stood in the door and watched the Sandpoint platform disappear into the darkness. As he checked his watch he noticed the train was running about four minutes late. The extra passengers departing and boarding the train took their toll on the schedule. Hopefully they would make up the time and keep their schedule when they arrived in Libby. As the porter ascended the stairs and walked the aisle, he checked on his passengers and headed back to his berth in the Sleeper car. He had over an hour before the next station stop, so he would try to get some sleep. As he lay down on his bunk he thought of his wife back in Chicago. How he would enjoy her company, and would share their bed on Christmas night. She was the one who would give him the best Christmas present he would get, herself, her body and her soul. He closed his eyes and became aroused at the thought of the intimacy they would experience that night. He could see her eyes, taste her lips and could almost feel her warm body pressing against his with her breasts rubbing gently on his chest. He knew every move he would make in this act of fulfilling her needs. He would reach down and massage her curly pubic hair until he sensed the right time and found the right spot. As she grew ready for him, he would enter her so gently and they would begin the lovely rhythm that would bring them both to their highest senses, co-mingling their bodily fluids and their love for each other. George opened his eyes and thought about using his hand to tide himself over until tomorrow night, but decided against it. He would wait another 24 hours when the anticipation would make the act even more enjoyable. He let his mind relax and fell asleep. As the train began to move and the scenery changed, so did Chas's thoughts. His mind drifted back to the second vacation he spent with Phillip. They had decided to meet in Whitefish since it was part way for both of them. It was early September, just after Labor Day—the air had that smell of fall and the mountains were bursting at the seams as the aspens decked themselves out in their fabulous show of colors before retiring for the winter. The sky was the shade of blue you only get when you know that in a few weeks it will be harboring the first flakes of snow. Chas liked the Glacier Park area after the tourists were gone, the roadside money hounds had departed for warmer climates, the locals were more friendly and the roads not congested with motor homes from California.. He and Phillip decided to save money and share a hotel room in Columbia Falls. The small hotel offered a nice view of the mountains, but little else for amenities. Once again the couple filled the days with hiking the trails of Glacier Park, biking and even more talking, laughing and sharing each other's secrets, all while absorbing the sunlight and the fresh air of the crown jewel of the northern Rocky Mountains.

About the time Chas could distinguish the lights of Bonners Ferry through the coach window he was remembering the first night spent with Phillip as lovers. He smiled to himself. Even through his present gloom, he felt the warmth of his companion. The entire day came back to him as he played the video of his mind.

The pair awoke early with expectations to rent a car and drive the Going to the Sun Highway. It was Phillip who had decided that the day should be one of complete rest. Renting a car and driving the highway would be a wonderful distraction from his sore muscles and tired feet. Chas had agreed whole heartedly telling Phillip, "My legs are also on the verge of rebelling and if my back and butt go over one more bump on my bike, I'll go into a coma."

After picking up the white Ford in Kalispel, they headed back east on Highway 2 toward the park entrance. As they passed Columbia Falls, Phillip realized they had nothing for lunch and suggested that they should stop at the grocery for picnic supplies. Thirty-six dollars and twenty minutes later they were back on the road.

As the couple passed over the Middle Fork of the Flathead River and into the park the sun had burned off the morning fog and the fall colors nearly burned through their retinas. Up the road a few miles Lake McDonald, off to their left, was a virtual mirror, providing exquisite fall mountain views in stereo. It seemed that every mile he or Phillip would scream to stop the car, jump out and snap off a photo or two, exclaiming this was the most beautiful place on earth. Yet every turn of the highway presented a view seemingly more beautiful than the previous. After nearly a half an hour passed, they lost the lake views and started up the narrow winding incline toward Logan Pass. As they climbed the winding road, the views changed from looking up at the peaks to looking down into the valleys and the winding streams meandering through them among the trees. Chas was concentrating on driving the steep narrow road as Philip would gasp in awe at the exquisite vistas presenting themselves at every turn. He had felt disappointed that he could not enjoy the full impact of the scenery. He had to focus his full concentration on maneuvering the car around the many corners while avoiding the oncoming traffic as he ascended the side of the mountain. Once they reached Bird

Woman Falls Overlook, Chas decided he needed a break from the white-knuckle drive so he pulled off and parked the car in the turnout provided. The sun was bright in the thin atmosphere of this elevation, so the pair just sat on the edge of the overlook marveling at the views and admiring the engineering feat it took to glue the road to the side of the mountain. As the two sat in silence, the grandeur of the park overtook the pair. Above them the gray, barren peaks stood against the crystal blue sky, below the green pines highlighted the yellow poplars and golden larch trees. It was in this spectacular setting that Philip reached over and took Chas by the hand, looked him in the eyes and said quietly, "This will be a day to remember for the rest of our lives."

Chas recalled the moment as vividly as if it were only an hour ago. He could feel the touch of Philip's hand, the feelings rushing through his heart and his body. He could still feel the sunshine on his face, the cool breeze on his back, but most importantly he felt the realization that he was in love, and that his partner had the same feelings. As his mind continued on with the video of the day, Amtrak 8 continued on its journey along the Kootenai River and crossed the border into Montana, the third state on its seven-state trip.

Back that previous September, Chas and Philip sat in silence holding hands while two or three cars passed the overlook. Once the coast was clear, Philip turned toward Chas, bent over and embraced his partner in a warm hug that naturally evolved into a deep romantic kiss. There was no surprise here, no revulsion, no holding back. Things had evolved naturally and both partners just embraced the feelings and let things progress at a comfortable pace. As Chas heard a car approaching, he pulled away from Philip, nervously stood up and told Philip they better get going. He knew Philip understood that this was not the time nor the place for public affection; that luxury would come eventually. He continued to grasp Philip's hand as he helped him up off of the mossy slope but let go as they walked back to the car.

The trip from the overlook, past the Weeping Wall, and up to Logan Pass escaped Chas' memory, but once at the pass things came back vividly once more. He and Philip grabbed their groceries from the back seat, hiked a few hundred yards from the Logan Pass information center to find a more secluded spot. Sitting in the bright sunlight, out on the red-brown alpine, moss-covered slope, the two shared a bottle of wine, the best French bread Columbia Falls had to offer and Oscar Meyer bologna. For here it didn't matter that the lunch was only just adequate; they had each other and the knowing that they were embarking into uncharted territory with each other.

The afternoon flew by quickly with a lunch enjoyed while embracing and sharing each other's feelings verbally and physically.

Chas was the first to take note of the fading light and wisely thought it best that they pack up their things, get going and head back into town. Instead of completing the entire circle around the park, the couple decided go back the way they had come. In that fashion the trip would be shorter and therefore they would be back in Columbia Falls and the motel quicker. Once back in the car, the trip back down from the pass seemed to last forever. In spite of wanting to race down the road to reach the hotel, Chas had to heed his instincts of self-preservation and embrace caution as he wound the car through the twists and turns of the Going to the Sun Highway. The sun was extending the trees' shadows well out into the clearings before they reached the park entrance and headed out onto Highway 2. Within 30 minutes they were in the seclusion of their hotel room and just let things take their natural course.

George's alarm nudged him awake as the train approached its stop in Libby, Montana. The stout man quickly pulled on his shoes, straightened out his shirt and vest, and got back to his duties as car attendant. As he walked down the aisle, he checked the manifest and realized that two of his passengers would be departing. He spotted the couple already preparing to gather their belongings and head down the stairs. He sighed with relief as he always liked it when the passengers were prepared; it saved the time and effort of waking them up and prodding them along so there would be no delays. After all a schedule was a schedule.

George whispered to the couple, "Follow me down the stairs; we should be stopping in a few minutes."

As he got down to the vestibule he opened the window of the door and stuck his head out as usual into the cold night air. Instantly awakened by the rush of cold air he shivered and pulled his head back inside the car. Turning around to the middle-aged couple behind him he asked the usual question, "Where are you from?"

The man answered, "Everett. Our daughter moved over here as an environmental engineer. We are going to spend Christmas with her and her husband."

George glanced out the window and turned back to the man. "Libby is quite an environmental disaster, I hear. Is she involved in the asbestos cleanup?

"Yes," the woman entered into the conversation, "it's a shame what the mining companies did around that area. The hundreds of people getting sick, and dying, with little or no compensation. No one is having to take responsibility."

"Now, Bev," the man interrupted, "it is in the legal system, and they are trying to pin the mining company down right now. If everything were settled right now Marcia wouldn't have a job."

The woman responded with a sigh. "Oh, I know, but it still isn't right. Besides, then Marcia would be back in Seattle where it is closer to home."

George just listened and watched as the Libby station lights appeared toward the head of the train. He turned to the couple and said, "We'll be stopping in a minute. Please stand back while I open the door." As he reached up and unlatched the upper latch the squeal of the brakes became noticeable and as he unlatched the lower latch the train slowed to a halt with the usual sound of screeching brake shoes. George quickly grabbed the yellow step stool from where it hung on the grab bars inside the vestibule and set it outside the door saying, "Watch your step please. I see you have all your luggage. You folks have a great Christmas"

"Thanks, you too, we've had a great ride on Amtrak," the man replied as he picked up his second suitcase and followed his wife down the platform toward a short blond woman waving madly.

After the couple passed, George glanced up and down the semi-deserted platform at the other porters outside of their respective coach doors; some were taking deep drags off of their cigarettes while shivering in the cold night air. *Thank God I never took up that habit,* he thought as he watched porters and passengers inhaling as much smoke as possible to tide them over until the next stop. "What a shame" he whispered to himself, "as if there isn't enough ways to get cancer, they have to bring it on themselves."

He turned and looked back up toward the other edge of the platform to get a look at the mountains and sky beyond. He couldn't make out the skyline. The moon had disappeared, there were no stars poking through to shed any light on the night sky. The platform lights blinded him as he searched the horizon past the white station for a glimpse of the mountains to the north.

The conductor called the "All aboard" so George took stock of the platform, smiled with approval as everyone headed for the doors, picked up his yellow step stool and climbed into the warm belly of the Superliner coach. In a minute the diesels wound up their high-pitch whine and the train began to move. With the slam of the door, George completed his duties at Libby, Montana, and headed back to his room to await the sunrise and the next station stop at Whitefish.

Chas watched the interaction of the people leaving the train and those greeting arriving friends and family. He couldn't help thinking of the times he and Philip would greet each other after being apart for weeks or even months. They would embrace formally in public, but quickly retire to private quarters, where they could more naturally embrace, kiss and as quickly as possible become entangled in their sexual fantasies. Chas thought they were just natural lovers, knowing each other's wants and needs, never having to ask what the other partner wanted, just knowing and doing what came naturally.

After the first winter and spring were spent in a long distance romance, Chas came across an ad on the Whitefish web site, looking for ski area help. He mentioned it to Philip, who embraced the idea of hiring on at Big Mountain and sharing an apartment in Whitefish, with open arms. As soon as they could arrange a meeting, the couple met in Whitefish, where Chas was immediately hired as a bartender at the Great Northern Bar and Grill and where Philip got a job as a bartender up on the ski hill. Within two weeks both packed up their belongings and moved away from home for the first time. Finding an apartment was easy, so the rest of the summer and that winter were heaven for the couple, sharing an apartment, meeting countless new friends and making good money living in Montana's paradise. Chas figured no one could ask for more. He and Philip knew they had to stay on for the summer and they looked forward to the slow time of year between the skiers and the summer tourists. It was during that slow time that they could get out and explore some more of the Flathead Valley. It was on one of those exploratory drives down to Polson that Chas hatched the plan for he and Philip to head back to Canada, where in Vancouver they could get married and enjoy the full benefits of married life. Philip grasped the idea with fervor, and the couple spent countless hours discussing the wedding, who they would invite, where they would honeymoon and what they would do afterward. The plan was for Philip to get his Canadian citizenship and the two would stay in Vancouver where one of them could go to the university while the other supported them both. Afterward they would reverse the roles. Since they would both have degrees, the couple were sure they would be able to move wherever they liked.

As Chas looked back in retrospect, he realized maybe these plans were a bit unrealistic, but they were certainly worth a shot. His parents had taught him to aim high—this was certainly high enough. He thought that a vision was never out of reach until now. Things were going along well until last week when Philip decided to tell his parents his plans. It was at that point Chas saw the clouds form over the sunshine of his plans.

Amtrak 8 followed the Kootenai for a short way out of Libby but diverged quickly from the original road bed and headed southeast along Fisher Creek and then back northeast along Wolf Creek. The original Great Northern Railway mainline ran north past the Libby Dam where, in the late 1960s, the Army Corps of Engineers dammed the river to provide hydroelectric power to western Montana and eastern Washington, flooding the original mainline. The ensuing lake forced the most ambitious railroad mainline relocation in U.S. history. Not only were the tracks moved, but it forced the boring of the eight-mile-long Flathead Tunnel. President Lyndon Johnson himself pushed the plunger in Washington DC to detonate the final blast to hole-through the project. What an achievement for a country on the move. Massive amounts of electricity to power the great northwest, a new modernized section of mainline furnished by the American people, and flood control to allow the population of the river valleys by a society on the move. But time keeps marching on. In two years the Great Northern ceased to exist; the merger of five railroads established the Burlington Northern Railroad; passenger rail as known up to that time would cease to exist shortly afterward and Amtrak would become the nationalized system it is today. As the train headed north to its closest proximity to Canada, Chas' mind came back to the details of the past two days. He and Philip made the five-hour trip down to Spokane without any memory-jarring incidents. The couple was as excited as any about-to-be-engaged couple would expect to be. The weather had been mild and the sun just heightened the excitement between Chas and Philip. In hindsight, Chas now realized that, as they were driving through the suburbs and winding their way to his parents' house, Philip's mood was beginning to change. Nothing noticeable at the time, but the subtle differences were now visible in Chas' mind's eye.

Once they were at Philip's parents' house, greetings were friendly and heartwarming for the season. Chas had become good friends with Philip's parents, but always in the context of friend or roommate. The same manner college roommates get to know each other's parents and family.

The couple had decided to let Philip make this most important announcement at his own pace and to use his own sense of timing. After all, it was his family. The first night of the visit was relaxed as the entire family shared a delightful supper followed by a few beers and lots of laughs and conversation. With things going so well Chas figured that this would have been the time for such an announcement, but he wasn't one to second guess Philip's judgment. After the rest of the family retired, Chas and Philip stayed up well into the wee hours of the morning talking about the day's events, future plans and recapping the previous conversations about the family. Chas remembered asking Philip, "When do think the timing might be right?"

Philip just replied, "You'll be the second one to know. I'll make it on the fly."

He then assured Chas, "Don't worry so much. It will be fine; just think about Canada. I'll decide when it's right for my family."

Afterward he grew a bit sullen, feigned sleepiness and headed off to his childhood bedroom leaving Chas to the couch. Not thinking too much about it, Chas just made up the couch with the bedding and blankets provided and fell into a fitful sleep.

The next morning Chas woke up with a sore neck but still in an excited mood. Today had to be the day. He still trusted Philip's judgment. The sun rose with a red glow and as it climbed higher into the sky it became more muted behind the haze of the high level clouds. For a while there was a rainbow—like halo surrounding the yellow orb as it crawled across he southern sky. By late afternoon the sun had completely disappeared—the day and mood had become noticeably darker. Around noon Chas helped Philip's mother, Janice, put together a lunch of sandwiches and a salad. They chatted pleasantly about the weather, Christmas traditions and Whitefish gossip. Philip poked his nose in once in a while and gave a discrete smile so Chas knew what the plan was.

After Chas, Janice, Philip and Philip's father, Vince, sat down and ate most of the meal, Philip commandeered the conversation and began, "Chas and I have had a lot of really great times, we've experienced a lot together, and it's almost spooky how we think alike."

Then with the skill of a news commentator he segued right into the fact that he and Chas were in fact more than just friends—they were partners and were indeed gay.

"Mom, Dad, Chas and I are more than just friends. We are lovers and would like to enter into a civil union. We both would appreciate your understanding of this matter and give us your consent and approval," Philip asked.

Even as Chas was admiring the skill with which Philip broke the news to the family, the entire conversation was quickly spiraling out of control. In fact the entire situation, the afternoon and, as Chas figured it, his entire life was spiraling out of control.

As Chas was recounting the conversations that ensued, the Flathead Tunnel swallowed the train. Chas did not miss the irony of the situation. How appropriate could it be that as he was recounting some of the most despairing moments of his life, he was plunged into total blackness while the earth swallowed both him and the train. He only hoped he could emerge from his emotional tunnel with the same speed and dignity as the Empire Builder emerging from its track beneath the mountain.

As Philip expressed the fact that he and Chas were partners, Janice, who was sitting across from Chas, dropped her fork and almost literally spit out the mouthful of salad she had been chewing.

"What?" she said in a completely astounded voice.

Philip repeated in a resolute tone, "Chas and I are partners. We are gay and are in love with each other. We would like to be married."

Janice regained a bit of composure and asked, "Philip, how can you say such things? Do you know what you are saying?"

Philip just repeated, "Chas and I are partners. We are gay. I know what I am saying. What more is there to say? We love each other."

Vince just sat in silence looking at Philip, and then just cast a quick glance at Chas. Janice, on the other hand, was a bit more volatile. As her face was beginning to turn red and her hands began to tremble she asked, "Chas, is this true? Did you put Philip up to this?"

"No ma'am," Chas responded in his most polite tone. "Philip and I have spent a lot of time together and have developed a relationship that is consensual. We love each other."

Chas recalled the conversation and wondered if anything he could have said would have affected the outcome. But nothing came to mind.

Janice, who was now standing, looked at her husband and said curtly, "Vince, how can you just sit there when your son is telling you he is living a life of sin and shame?"

Turning back toward Philip she said, "Do you know what this means to your father and me? We raised you in a proper Christian home, providing you with the best education, taught you the teachings of the Bible and then you slap us in the face by telling us you have decided to be a homosexual. How can you do that to your father and me?"

"Mom, I didn't decide to be gay," Philip said in a slightly elevated tone of voice. "Don't you read anything? Homosexuality is not something we choose. It just happens; it's in our genes or something. They are finding medical evidence."

Now Janice elevated the volume of the conversation. "Oh, don't give me that medical shit. The Bible specifically forbids sodomy and that's what it is. You know that it's a sin; we taught you that if something is a sin then you shouldn't do it. So don't give me any excuses for giving in to Satan's temptations."

"Mom," Philip interjected, "I am not giving in to the devil's temptations. Don't you understand? I don't feel the same way you do about the opposite sex. When I look at a woman I feel the same way that you feel about a woman. I can't fall in love with a woman any more than you can."

Janice had reached the point where her emotions were not allowing her to hear the conversation. "Don't you be telling me who or what I am feeling. You know damn well that what you are doing is not natural. I will not have my son rebelling against my religious beliefs by choosing to be a homosexual. I have nurtured you, fed you, cared for you, and yes, I prayed for you since the day you were born. Now you pull this shit." She began weeping. "What have I done to make you hate me so much? Oh dear God, what have I done to deserve this?"

Philip now stood up and walked directly in front of his mother. In a loud half scream he said, "You haven't heard a word I've said, have you? I am gay, not rebellious. I am not choosing to disgrace you. Why don't you listen? Do you know what I think? I think it's all about you. You don't want to face your church-going bigots. You don't know how you are going to tell them that your son is in love with another man. Well you know what I am going to do? I am going to walk down to that building you call a church tomorrow morning, and as all those so-called Christians walk out that door, I am going to announce that Janice Betman's son is a homosexual."

Vince, who had remained quiet and seated, now quickly stood up and stepped between Janice and Philip. "That's enough, son," he roared. "Philip, you don't talk to your mother that way. You go up to your room right now and wait for me to come up there. Janice, just calm down. Take a deep breath and sit down," he said as he lowered his voice while gently putting his hand on her trembling shoulder and guiding her down into the chair.

"As for you, Chas, I think you've caused enough trouble in this family. You had better gather your things and get the hell out of this house. I own this place, and if you are not gone in one hour, I'll call the police and have you forcibly removed," Vince said to Chas.

Then turning toward Philip said, "Get your ass up to your room before I do something drastic. Your queer friend here will be just fine; he can get a taxi to the train station and take the train back to wherever he came from."

Philip looked back at Chas with a hopeless look as his father turned and gave him a forcible kick in the rear end and said, "Get the hell going; I'll be up later to straighten this out."

Turning back to Chas he hissed "One hour" and knelt down to comfort his wife.

Outside Amtrak 8 the night air was growing thick with humidity and a light fog had developed as the fully loaded train did a 180 degree turn and began heading back south down the Tobacco Valley. Only 20 miles from Canada, the old Great Northern rail line crossed from the Kootenai Valley over into the Tobacco Valley and began the final leg of its journey into Whitefish. The mainline would then cross over the ridge to skim the western edge of Whitefish Lake before turning west again to reach the town of Whitefish and its station stop.

Chas stared out the window and looked for the peaks of Glacier park to the east. He was familiar with this stretch of the valley since the highway he traveled back and forth to Canada also ran through here. His thoughts quickly drifted back to the taxi ride to the station and the indeterminate amount of time spent waiting for the train. He just could not believe the whole scene, Janice screaming, not even listening to her son, who obviously was pained to tell her his most complicated feelings, Vince breaking in like a scrappy pit bull in a dog-fight arena. And that kick he gave Philip, totally appalling.

Chas remembered that, thankfully, he was so dumbfounded by the entire situation he couldn't react. If he had, he probably would have come unglued and gotten himself into some real trouble. As he replayed his mind's video once more, he was once again glad he was so dumbstruck. As he sat in the dark he tried to imagine what happened after he left the Betman house.

What happened to Philip? Why didn't he stand up to his father? What did Vince mean when he said he would straighten things out later? Is Philip OK? he thought. *Maybe Vince is some nut-case and he beat the shit out of Philip.*

Until now, Chas had not entertained thoughts of what was happening to Philip. He was so worked up about himself, he had not even imagined the consequences Philip had to face. His heart skipped a beat as a burst of adrenalin pushed through his veins. *How selfish,* he thought, *not even a single thought of his partner's well being for the last four hours. Some compassionate soul you are, Chas.*

There was a faint sound of the horn as the train charged over a highway grade crossing. George looked at his alarm clock and jumped quickly into action. He had not heard the alarm, and as he double checked the clock to his wristwatch, he understood that he had only 10 minutes before the train was supposed to pull into Whitefish and the station stop there. He quickly ran his duty list through his head as he pulled on his shoes. Check the manifest to see who was leaving, check to be sure they were ready and had all their belongings, then check the vestibule so no one would open the door prematurely and get themselves hurt or worse.

As he looked down the hallway of his car, he was relieved to notice that generally the passengers were prepared and ready to leave the car. *I guess the Christmas season has its benefits,* he thought. *Everyone is so excited to be where they are going they are more prepared than I am.*

George checked the manifest and used his canned speech to remind each departing passenger to check for all belongings and meet him downstairs. The other passengers he informed of the twenty-minute stopover and to not leave the station or platform as the train would depart without them. He then proceeded down the stairs and took up his usual position in front of the door. As he looked out the window on the opposite side of the train he could see Whitefish Lake; he played the sequence he had seen so many times in his career. Once the train passed the lake and rounded the curve they would whistle as they crossed the grade crossing, stop at the light and request permission to enter the yard. They would then proceed across the bridge at a reduced speed into the yard, crawl past the old roundhouse and idling freight engines, pass beneath the highway overpass and only then gently come to a stop in front of the historic old station.

Within five minutes the scene played out exactly as planned. George pulled open the door as soon as the motion ceased. The cold, but not frigid, air greeted him as he stepped outside the car. As the passengers departed, he automatically cautioned everyone to watch their step. He looked up and took notice of the thick cloud cover, turned his head toward the east, and the peaks of Glacier Park, to see that the sky had descended to within a thousand feet of the valley floor. "Someone is going to have a white Christmas," he commented to no one in particular.

Two passengers, having a smoke next to him, turned and asked, alarmed, "If it snows in those mountains, will we be able to get through?"

George turned back toward them and replied with a smile, "Oh, I think we'll be just fine. It would take several days of snow before we'd have trouble. I don't believe it's been snowing up there. Besides the freights have been getting through. The railroad won't let a little snow stop them from making money."

The passengers looked relieved and turned away from the wind to finish their cigarettes. George stepped back into the car to collect the garbage and set it out for the station personnel. All he could think of was that in fifteen minutes they'd be back on their way and that he'd be that much closer to his family.

Chas looked at his watch. Only 10 minutes until they were to reach Whitefish. All this time he was worried about what he would do when he reached the station. Now he had a plan. He needed to find out how Philip was faring with his psychotic family. Chas had come to the realization that he had a place to stay at his apartment, he had money, he had a job for a while. He was set. What was not set was Philip. He had to know if the person he loved might be in danger.

His mood changed with these thoughts from one of depression to one of anxiety. The adrenalin again began to rush through his veins and instantly awakened his half-sleeping brain. With his mind reeling he calculated every step he would take and every word he would say when he called the Betman home.

The first thing he decided was that he would need to be firm, yet peaceful. There would be no point in escalating the already explosive situation. His main concern was that Janice or Vince would hang up immediately upon hearing his voice. Plan "B" would then take effect—He would rent a car and drive back to Spokane. Christmas or no Christmas, he had to do what he had to do. During the four-hour drive he'd call into work and fake sickness. That would buy him at least one day to work out the next phase of his mission.

As the locomotive whistled announcing its entrance into the Whitefish yard, Chas was nervously rehashing his plan for the third time. He had to make sure the details were covered. When the brakes finally stopped squealing and the car came to a stop at the platform he was primed for action and ready to roll.

Chas looked around the car and felt somewhat crushed, it seemed everyone else in the car was just as determined to get out as he was. He shifted his weight from one leg to the other in anticipation as he waited for the line in front of him to make toward the front of the car and down the stairs. "What the fuck is the holdup?" he muttered as he poked his head to the left of the person in front of him.

Sure as hell, he thought, *I've got to be behind some SOB that doesn't have their shit together.* He stretched farther only to see a young woman picking up her sleeping toddler and struggling to gather her belongings. "Why doesn't someone help her?" he said aloud to no one as the woman finally shouldered her purse and started off the train.

The line then moved quickly and in less than a minute Chas bounded off the train and headed for the massive doors of the Whitefish station. Pushing himself around several skiers he squeezed through the door while a man and a pregnant girl where waiting to come out. With the tunnel vision of a man on a mission, he headed toward the doors on the far side of the waiting area, where he could descend the stairs to access the street and walk/run the six blocks to the apartment.

About three steps from the double doors at the south entrance to the station, Chas felt a firm grip tear at his arm and twist him around with such force that his feet tangled and he collapsed in a lump on the floor. "What the fuck?" he yelled as he untwisted his body to look up at what had just bowled him over. "Jesus H. Christ," he gasped. "What the fuck are you doing here and what the hell are you trying to do to me?"

Chas then planted his feet beneath himself and jumped up into the arms of Philip. Oblivious of the crowd that had gathered around the scene, they embraced each other in a passionate bear hug.

"Jesus, is it good to see you," Chas said as he released his grip and stood back to get a good look at Philip, and to make sure he wasn't dreaming. Picking up his scattered bags he stepped out of the crowded doorway and asked astonished, "How did you get here and what happened?"

"Come on," Philip countered as he grabbed Chas's bag, "I'll fill you in as we head for home. Geez, I damn near didn't catch you as you headed across the station. What the hell were you doing?"

Chas smiled as he replied, "I was coming to rescue you."

"Why do you think I would need rescuing?" Philip asked. "I had things under control the whole time."

"Bullshit, it didn't look that way to me," Chas interjected. "What happened after I got kicked out?"

"I told you I would tell you all about it on the way home. Do you want to get some coffee?" Philip asked. "I'm dying and need something to perk me up."

"No," Chas answered, "I want to find out what happened."

"OK, but I do need some coffee. I'll start, but we have to stop at the coffee shop or I'll never make it to the end," Philip said.

"Fine, let's get going," Chas said as he started down the sidewalk at a brisk pace.

"Well, after you caught the cab, I sat up in my room thinking up all sorts of scenarios of how things were going to go down. After an hour I finally figured there was no use stooping to their hypocritical level and make this into an us versus them situation. I called my mom and dad to my room and told them in no uncertain terms that no one was leaving that room until a resolution was reached," Philip said as they walked.

"Wow," Chas gasped. "You really did that? With the state of mind they were in before I left, I would not have figured it possible."

"Yeah, I guess during that hour before I called the meeting they had pretty well calmed down and talked to each other." Philip continued as he stopped in front of a storefront, "Hey, here's the coffee shop. You sure you don't want anything?"

"Naw, I'm too wired now," Chas replied. "If I have anything right now I won't sleep for a week."

"OK," Philip said as he entered the room where the aroma of fresh-brewed coffee overwhelmed his brain. Reaching the counter he asked, "What is the special this morning?

"Hi, Philip," the orange-haired girl behind the countered greeted. "We have your favorite dark roast, Montana Special, this morning. You want a tall?

"Ya, Jen, I think that will be just what the doctor ordered." Philip responded, "You working up on he hill tomorrow?

"I gotta," the counter girl replied, "five to close," she finished as she poured the paper cup full of the steaming life blood.

"Three twenty-five," she said as Philip handed her the five-dollar bill. "As she counted the change she said, "I'll see you tomorrow night."

Philip turned as he took a brief sip from the cup. "Yeah, I'll see you tomorrow, Jen."

Chas took the lead through the door and once both were on the sidewalk he prodded nervously, "Well, let's hear the rest of the story."

"Well, I asked them what it was like for them to be in love. They explained all the usual things and that it was nothing to take lightly. So I asked them if they would recommend going through life without ever experiencing love. Of course they agreed that it would be terrible and they could not imagine what that would be like." Philip stopped, took a sip of his coffee and shivered in the cool morning air of the Flathead Valley.

"So I set them up and dropped the bomb shell. I asked them if I should ignore my feelings of love and go through life without ever experiencing the very thing they so adamantly recommended just because their society dictates who you can and cannot feel love for. Should I live an unfulfilled life and pretend just for their sake?"

Again a sip of coffee and then further narration, "My mother still isn't sure she understands, but my father thought it best that they let me go through my phase, as they put it."

"Oh, spare me," Chas interrupted.

Philip took another sip, stopped and turned directly toward Chas. "Don't ridicule them. Do you know how hard it is for them to just come this far? Their whole life is turned upside down. Anyway, my dad made me promise that we wouldn't get married for one year."

Chas looked back at Philip and shook his head slightly. "That's OK with me. I am glad that you worked things out. I can wait, if it means that both of our lives will be happier."

"Thanks," Philip said turning back up the sidewalk. "I asked them if they couldn't figure out what was going on the whole time. Dad said he knew but didn't want to admit it to himself, and Mom didn't have a clue. I think she was completely blinded by her religious beliefs."

Chas followed a half step behind. "And that's it?"

"Sure," Philip responded. He took another sip and yelled as he sprinted up the sidewalk toward the apartment, "Last one home is a wimpy queer."

"Cheater," Chas yelled as he quickly took up the chase a full ten yards behind Philip.

Off in the distance there were two short blasts of the horn as the Empire Builder signaled the "all aboard."

Chapter 3
Cycles and Circles

Bill Pershkin awoke feeling particularly spry considering he'd only been off for eight hours. Last night he brought Train 7 in from Shelby, two hours late, and this morning he expected the eastbound Empire Builder, Train 8, to be running about the same. With Christmas only a day away it seemed everyone was traveling to get together with family or friends. Anyway he thought, *I'll be in Havre in plenty of time to have a relaxing Christmas with Diane.* He thought of Diane, his wife of 34 years, probably still tucked warm in bed at home. "Oh well," he muttered to no one in particular. "She'll pay the price when she gets to work at seven this morning and has to work with all those crazies."

After a quick shower, Bill got dressed and started his eight-block walk to the Whitefish train station. It wasn't particularly cold for December 24th, so he enjoyed the cool early morning air. He looked around at the sleeping town and took note of the deep railroad history that brought Whitefish from Stumptown to the present day tourist destination it enjoyed. He walked past the Great Northern Bar with the famous Great Northern mountain goat, Rocky, as its mascot. He looked across the street at the Great Northern Brewery which was related to the railroad in name only. Ahead was the most prominent building in town, the Whitefish Railroad Station, a chalet-style building, built by the railroad in the twenties with the sole purpose of drawing tourists to the mountain areas of western Montana and Glacier National Park. Still preserved as a station and historical museum, Bill thought the building must still be as impressive as when it was built. With its steep gabled roof, stucco siding and exposed timbers, he supposed this is what European buildings would look like.

About the time he reached the civic center, a block from the station, the familiar smell of diesel fumes and the high-pitched whine of the locomotives brought him to the reality of what the railroad really is, steel and oil, tracks and ties, but most of all the blood, guts and muscle of men, real working men. From the pioneers who built the original right of way, to the maintenance of way workers of today, these are the guys that keep the machinery rolling.

Bill crossed the parking lot and walked up onto the platform in front of the station. He noticed the beehive of activity off to the west in the roundhouse. Otherwise not much was moving, so Bill just stood and looked at the silhouettes of the Glacier Park peaks to the east, Big Mountain loomed across the yard to the north with its lighted ski trails and condos, and the vast areas of pine forests surrounded this tip of the Flathead Valley to the north. Behind him the fertile agricultural land lay to the south. Bill thought the pioneers must have thought they reached heaven when they settled this spot.

Well, better get inside and get to work, Bill thought as he turned and entered the station. As he passed through the heavy wooden doors he immediately spotted Clarence, the station agent, behind the counter to the right. He glanced around the massive waiting area and noticed what looked like two families were already waiting on the long wooden benches.

"Morning, Clarence," Bill bellowed in the most chipper voice he could imagine.

He knew this would have the same effect as scratching a blackboard with his fingernails. As he crossed in front of the blackboard with the train status, the thought of doing the actual act crossed his mind. *But it is Christmas,* he thought. He liked Clarence and loved ribbing him at every chance. Bill especially liked the professionalism Clarance brought to Amtrak. Not too many irate passengers could rattle him even at this early 5:30 hour.

"How's eight running?" Bill asked

"She's running 15 minutes late and as long as BNSF 6342 with its grain empties can get out of its way at Radnor, she may make up a couple," remarked Clarance without even looking up from his passenger list. "Looks like you could hit some snow up on the hill," added the station agent.

Bill had not even paid any attention to the weather this morning. "As long as they keep the freights in the sidings I'll be fine," replied Bill as he dug through his paperwork and began reading the reports.

After a few minutes, Bill glanced around the waiting area as he took a break from his orders. *Boy, that woman is really pregnant,* he thought as his eyes settled on the petite, good-looking Native American woman sitting uncomfortably on the hard 70-year-old wooden benches. *I wonder how many other women in her condition have sat on these benches waiting for the Empire Builder.* He guessed, *Hundreds? Maybe thousands? Naw! Too many.* He got back too work.

Marie Lightfeather thought, *This damn kid better be worth all this discomfort.* But then her maternal instinct kicked in and she smiled as the thoughts of her own child curled sleeping in her arms came to mind. *Oh ya, it'll be all worth it. My kid'll be the smartest one in the class, get a scholarship, get off of that fucking reservation, get out of Browning and go to school in Chicago, New York, or even one of the Ivy League colleges. Then he'll get me out of this hell hole. I'll flip off those BIA bastards, and go get a real job in the real world.* Marie thought back on the past year and all of the events that brought her here. She smiled as she thought of the day she graduated from high school as valedictorian with the scholarship to go to the University of Montana in Missoula. Then the excitement and waiting to leave Browning for the wonderful world off of the reservation. Marie also recalled the loneliness of those first weeks of college and then the realization that she could and was making it after all. Her heart swelled with the pride that comes with the sense of accomplishment.

She remembered how the first semester flew by, how Christmas vacation seemed to drag on, due to the fact that she had gotten used to the freedom of the campus. Marie thought that it must have been the long winter that drew her to Max. He wasn't tall or especially handsome but he was exciting and fun to be around. It's too bad he turned out to be such a shithead.

Marie was jolted back to reality by Clarence announcing that the Empire Builder would be arriving in about 10 minutes. He also added the reminder for all passengers to stay back from the yellow line on the platform.

Bill grabbed his duffel bag and briefcase and headed toward the far door leading out to the platform. He then made a quick check for the pregnant girl. Spotting her, he made a beeline toward her and asked, "Can I help you with anything?"

Marie was startled with the question. "Pardon?" she blurted.

"Can I help you with anything?" Bill repeated.

"If you don't mind, you could take this damn suitcase while I try and find my ticket," Marie said with a smile between winces of pain as she stood up. "Could you please tell me where car 0338 will be in the train?"

Bill replied, "Oh that will be the third car from the engine."

"Oh, of course, I'll have to walk a fucking mile before I can get on the damn train," cussed Marie.

"Here," Bill said, "I'll take your bag and you take my arm. I'll walk you up to your car. I'm going up there anyway." Bill grabbed his luggage and hers in his right hand and held out his left for Marie to hold on to.

"At least the platform is clear of snow and ice this morning. Unusual for this time of year," Bill said, trying to make conversation

Bill held the heavy wooden door as Marie passed through, and as he followed, a twenty-something blond man bolted through the door, almost bowling both of them over.

Without hesitation Marie snapped, "Hey, asshole, watch it." Marie looked at Bill with a bit of red in her cheeks and uttered, "Sorry."

Bill and Marie could see the headlights of the locomotive as it entered the yard from the west and passed under the highway bridge. First a short blast of the air horn as the train entered the yard, then the surge of heated air from the engines as they passed and finally the whine and screech from the brake pads pressing on the steel wheels as the Empire Builder came to a stop on its journey from Seattle to Chicago.

After the noise of the train ceased Bill asked, "What's your name and what brings you to Whitefish?"

Marie replied "Oh sorry, I should have introduced myself. Marie, and I am on my way back to Browning after a doctor's appointment in Kalispel. The idiots at the state won't pay for any more doctor appointments in Great Falls. I gotta come over here because it's their provider. Morons don't realize it's a two-day trip by Amtrak. I gotta find a place to stay overnight. Then the assholes in Washington want to take Amtrak away. I ought to make them ride the stinking bus over the mountains. They'd change their minds. When will they realize that this is the only means of transportation some of us have? Pisses me off." She paused. "Sorry for the language but it gets me so mad. I guess I'm preaching to the choir, ha."

Bill just nodded. He'd heard he story so often he'd become immune. What happens, happens. He can always go to BNSF.

The skiers were almost finished departing the train when Bill and Marie reached car 0338. The porter took Marie's arm as she stepped up into the Superliner car. She turned as Bill walked toward the head end.

"Hey," Marie hollered. "Thanks, and what is you name? You're a pretty cool engineer to help a fat pregnant girl like me."

Bill turned and waved. "No problem. It's Bill. I'll make sure you have a smooth trip home."

Svigrud Andersen gazed out the window as the hoards of college kids with skis bounded off the train with energy that was only a memory of 70 years ago. He'd boarded the train in Spokane and was on his way to Wolf Point where his granddaughter was living. He always thought his granddaughter had inherited the best of both sides of the family. Each time he looked at her, he could see his wife Gertie, and at the same time she had the disposition of her father. Thank God, she didn't inherit the bitterness from her mother. Maybe it was just that grandchildren look at their grandfathers different than children look at their parents. In any case he was looking forward to the visit.

He was pleasantly surprised when the young, nice-looking, pregnant woman came up and asked if the seat next to him was taken.

"Dat hoodlum skier got off and I don't know if anyone else is gonna sit there," he replied.

Marie interjected, "My assigned seat is next to some fat pig that has his shit all over. I couldn't sit there if I wanted. I hope you don't mind. I'm not the picture of skinnyness myself but I promise I won't have my baby right here in the seat, at least, I hope," she ended with a smile.

Svigrud was dazzled with the beauty and spunk of the girl. "My name is Svigrud Andersen but ya mide as well call me Sig. It's a pleasure ta have someone of yur beauty and spunk sitting next to me. I live in an old fart's home they like ta call a retirement community. Ders a bunch'a old clucks dat are all trying ta win my favor by bakin and cookin. I'm lucky I ain't as big around as you." After he made the remark he caught himself and quickly added, "I don't mean no disrespect, miss. You're actually quite beautiful and glow like so many expecting girls. I remember my wife Gertie before she had our Denise, just like you."

He trailed off in the thought of his wife who had passed away in 1949 after an infected tooth worsened and spread into the bone in her mouth. Penicillin wasn't as available then as it is now. Shame she could not have waited a couple of years.

Marie saw the faraway look in his eyes and figured he was thinking about someone far away or long ago. "My name's Marie. I'm on my way back to Browning. How far are you going?"

"Oh I'm on my way ta my granddaughter's in Wolf Point. Supposed ta spend two weeks dere," Sig replied.

Just then there were two blasts of the horn signaling the all clear to leave the station. The conversation paused as the train began to ease from its stop and head out of the yard. Marie remembered what Bill had said about the smooth ride and wondered if he'd do it.

Bill was in his seat on the right side of the locomotive before Marie began her conversation with Sig. After doing a review of his orders and checking everything out, he settled into his routine. Basically, it was a preflight check for a means of transportation that carried twice as many lives as an airplane, yet relied on metal rails to hold it off the ground instead of wings and air pressure. After he had gone through his air brake check, Bill waited until he heard he conductor yell the "All aboard."

A few minutes later the radio crackled, "Highball Amtrak"

Bill replied, "Roger Highball."

The engineer pushed the horn button twice and moved the throttle to notch one and eased off the air brake lever. In a few seconds the train started to move. Time to notch up to two he thought. Not too fast or the passengers will be all over the floor if they are standing. It was about three miles before he got out of the yard so he had to keep the 9000 horses under 25 mph until the yard limit sign passed. The signals were all lined green so the distance passed in a couple of minutes. Bill gradually moved the throttle to run eight, unleashing the energy of the sun stored in the fossil fuel millions of years ago.

"Keep it smooth," he said aloud to no one.

"I promised that nice Indian girl with the foul mouth I'd keep her comfortable. I sure hope she cleans up her mouth before the kid learns to talk. I'd hate to hear what comes out of its mouth." He mused thinking of a small girl talking back and forth to her mother with the foul language Marie used. Things are sure different now days. He remembered the days of having his mouth washed out with soap with not too much affection.

Watching the telephone poles whiz by at 79 mph brought Sig back to the days of working on the Hi-Line division. Sig started speaking, knowing Marie would listen even if she did not particularly care to. She was inquisitive, as he could tell from her eyes as he spoke.

"I been ridin da Empire Builder going on 75 years now. Used to work fur da Great Northern. Started doin track work up on da pass. Back-bustin work in dem days." He nodded his head slowly as if agreeing with himself. "Hired on in 1928 when I was 15. Lied about my age. Had an Italian foreman, Batista was his name. Boy, he sure could work da skin off yur bones. When Saturday'd come he'd hightail it down here ta Whitefish and sure raise hell. After a lotta wine and hell raisin, he'd end up over at Maggie's Whore House where we'd have to pick him up bout four o'clock on Sunday afternoon. He was always praying on da job but I never once seen him set foot inside a church. I guess he got his church goin at Maggie's. Don't mean ta get too detailed fur ya but I figure ya know all out da birds and bees looking at da condition yer in."

Marie just smiled so Sig continued on. "In '32 I moved over to Wenatchee to work repairing da apple stubs. Figured I'd at least be livin in da same house fur a spell. Nice job, hard, but not as hard working fur dat Italian. Dats where I met my Gertie. We was married dat very summer." Marie just listened.

Sig interrupted himself as they passed into a tunnel and quickly out again. "Dat was tunnel 5. I worked rebuilding the track here after a string of log gondolas got away on a hogger one summer day. What a mess, track and logs everywhere."

Sig continued telling stories about his railroad days and every point of interest in practically a mile by mile sequence. It seemed to Marie he had something to say about every railroad structure and tie all the way to Wolf Point. But he was interesting, even if a bit windy.

Bill eased the train into West Glacier; there were three people waiting on the platform. *Kind of unusual,* he thought but this is Christmas Eve after all. After the conductor gave the "Highball Amtrak" announcement over the radio, Bill confirmed the order and notched the throttle forward. Glancing up toward the peaks he could see the clouds were descending and it would only be a matter of time before he would be in the snow. No worries—the freight traffic and those slow grain trains will all be holed up in the sidings.

Just then the conductor broke the moment with the "four off, three on, 16 and 19." This was the number of passengers getting off at West Glacier and the number getting on. The time is when the train stopped and then started once more from the station. Bill got the consist of passenger cars up to track speed and relaxed a bit.

This was his favorite part of the trip. He was following along the Middle Fork of the Flathead River and diving in and out of the tunnels. The *woosh* as the engines entered the tunnel and the glow of the rock walls in the headlight just a few feet on either side of the locomotive always gave him the same rush as the first time he experienced it years ago. As he burst from tunnel three he could see the snowflakes beginning to fall and he noticed that above and to the right Highway 2 was unusually desolate. He figured the snow up in the mountains slowed things down and the fact that it was Christmas Eve compounded the situation.

The Middle Fork of the Flathead River flowed green with its white rapids to the left. The quiet pools were frozen and covered with snow which gave the river a surreal image in the falling snowflakes. On the opposite shore, five elk grazed on the exposed vegetation at the water's edge. The white snow, red rocks, green water and brown elk blended into what could be a perfectly painted picture through the forthcoming snowstorm.

Some people admire scenes like this on their Christmas cards, reflected Bill. *I've got the real thing. Gosh, I love this job.*

As Bill passed into another tunnel he thought out loud,"I hope the guys at Essex have the platform clean so we don't have to wait while all those people struggle with their luggage."

Sig had been staring out the window in one of his brief moments of silence when suddenly he popped up, "Say I been doing all da talking here and I never once asked what your story is."

Marie didn't really mind telling her story and besides maybe she could bore the old man to sleep or something.

So she began, "Nothing too exciting to talk about here. Last fall I went down to Missoula to go to school, met some guy from one of the frat houses, was stupid, and bingo here I am living back at home with a kid on the way."

"Oh, come on there's more to it than that. What do your parents think?" Sig asked

"Well," Marie continued, "they were disappointed I'm sure, but have been very supportive, I guess, or they wouldn't have invited me to come back and live at home. My parents own the Amoco gas station in town so they don't have a lot of money. But they have done OK. They always encouraged me to keep up my grades and to stay away from the alcohol and drugs that seem to consume everybody's life in Browning. So I got a scholarship to Missoula.

"And now everything is all fucked up," Marie added with her eyes starting to well with tears

Marie paused and then just let it out. "Do you wanna really know what happened?" Marie hissed. "The fucker raped me. Yah, that son of a bitch fucking raped me. We were on a date alright, but I said no! I didn't want to have sex. That fucker actually held me down and forced himself on me.

Marie continued with heavy anger in her voice, "But who's going to believe an Indian girl from the reservation when she accuses Missoula's most prominent Realtor's son of date rape. When I reported it, they treated *me* like the criminal, like I was the on who instigated it. They never even questioned the son of a bitch."

Marie quivered, then continued, "They said it was all my fault, the way I dressed, the way I acted, the way I looked." Marie stopped then declared, "What a bunch of racist bastards. Now I'm sitting here with a kid on the way and no way to get out of this mess. And the rich son of a bitch is running around like nothing happened. He's probably raped more girls by now."

Everything that happened in the last year seemed like such a blur right now. Things were really coming to a head so she just swore, "What a fucking mess. I've really fucked my life up."

"No you have not," Sig interjected. "This may be a setback but yur not down and out. You have lotsa options. First you have yur baby. It'll be a boy, I know dat, den you take care of him while you check the options to get back down to Missoula. I'll bet dere is a lotta jealous people on da reservation who are snickering bout dat snot-nosed, smarty-pants Indian girl going off ta da college and den coming back all knocked up. Marie, prove dem wrong. Show 'em dat you are more dan some stereotypical Indian coming back ta fall into da pits of dat reservation, drinking and living in squaller on da federal government. You can do what you wanted from da beginning. In fact now ya got more reason than before. Break the despair cycle, Marie. Dere will be a way, I know it. Trust me."

Marie wasn't so sure right now, but didn't say so. Instead she kind of whimpered, "Thanks for the support I hope you're right."

She paused in reflection and just stayed there, as she was relaxing now and thought she needed a nap.

Sig beat her to the punch and said softly, "I tink I take a nap for a while. If I snore shove a pillow in my mouth."

Marie asked politely, "Can I get a blanket or anything for you?"

Sig replied softly, "No tanks, I'm plenty warm."

In a couple minutes his eyes were closed and his breathing was shallow. Marie thought, *Must be nice, I'll probably have to wiggle around for a half an hour just to get comfortable, and then some SOB will come and disturb me.* But it didn't take long for her to fall asleep either.

Marie found herself waking up to the screech of the brakes and the movement as the train slowed down. The first thing she noticed was that Sig was awake and watching intently out the window.

He looked over and said, "Essex. I used to stay in dat hotel when it was crew quarters. Now dey tell me dese people pay over a hundred dollars to stay dere. Was nothing but a flop house in dem days. Wonder what it's like inside now."

Marie looked out and saw the snow was falling quite heavily but she could still make out the Izaak Walton Inn, with its chalet-style peaked roof and stucco siding. As the train glided past she noticed there were four people on the steps waving a friendly greeting.

"Cool," she said aloud. She felt a bit foolish but did wave back without even realizing she was doing it. Then noticed most of the people in the car were doing the same. As the train came to a stop Marie was disappointed in the fact that she could not see anything more than a few hundred feet from the train. She did notice the lighted walk bridge over the tracks leading somewhere off to the right.

Sig piped in, "Seen a lot worse snow dan dis up here on the hill. Hell with all dis equipment dey got nowadays dis won't even slow us down. I used ta have ta shovel a lotta snow up here. We used ta shovel da drifts down so dat da rotaries could get through without getting buried. You'd get avalanches across da tracks, den we'd have to dig all the stones and trees out before you'd get da rotaries going.

Sometimes you'd get a big old boulder stuck in da damn blade and oh the foreman would cuss." Sig continued even though he though Marie might be dozing off again, "All we could do was back er up and get the bars to pry dat rock out. We'd all hold our breath nothing was busted. Bend a shaft or something and we'd haffta go back to da shop and we wouldn't get paid the rest of the day. Or else we'd haffta shovel da track clear. Boy dem was hard days..." he trailed off as he noticed Marie had her eyes closed.

He assumed she was asleep. *Good for her,* he thought. *She's a nice kid. I hope she makes it good. Gonna be tough.* He checked the weather outside the window and dozed off himself.

Bill moved the train slowly out of the siding and eased through the switch onto main track two heading up to Marias Pass. The snow was thick now, but there wasn't enough to impede his progress. Only about two inches had fallen so far. In a couple of minutes he passed into the first snow shed, followed the curve around the mountain and then back out into the snow. *No avalanches to worry about this time of year,* he thought. *Wait till spring when all this snow falling right now starts to soften and comes rolling down the chute. It's amazing these old concrete sheds take that abuse after the 70 plus years of sun, rain, frost and snow.* The next shed appeared out of the blinding white. The noise of the engines roared inside the enclosure and the smell of diesel exhaust infiltrated the cab. Out again into the snow. Twenty more miles to the summit, then downhill from there and into the sunshine that was most likely bathing the plains in the cold arctic air. Amtrak 8 crossed over the Java East highway bridge and was making its way up the steep mountain grade as it passed over the Java East detector. The automated voice came over the radio and announced "BNSF detector mile post 1162.1, one defect, repeat one defect. Hot axle, axle 24, temperature 26 degrees BNSF detector out."

"Doggoneit, what's wrong now?" Bill sputtered as he eased the throttle back and applied the air brakes.

At the same time he pushed the radio button and called, " Amtrak 8, one defect, repeat one defect."

He brought the train to a halt as quickly as possible without jamming everything. The automated detector had sensed a dragging brake on the train. Bill was disappointed but at the same time relieved. These detectors served their purpose in preventing catastrophic accidents.

Floyd, the conductor came on the radio and said, "Amtrak portable to the head end."

"Go ahead portable," quipped Bill

"I'll walk the train and see what's going on." Floyd moaned, "Probably that brake rod hanging up again with all this snow. Portable out."

"Roger out," responded Bill.

Marie and Sig both woke as the train shuddered to a stop. Marie rubbed the sleep from her eyes and glanced at Sig.

He just smiled and said, "Ya know I been tinking. You got a nice life ahead a ya wit da kid an all. I seen a lotta girls who wudda been all bent otta sorts being in your spot. I like you; I ain't got long ta be around anyhow so how bout I give you dis watch I got when I retired from da Great Northern. I vant you ta give it ta yur son when he is big enough, as a remembrance of his first ride on da Empire Builder. My granddaughter has plenty'a stuff ta remember me by so dis old watch don't mean nuttin."

He handed the watch to Marie.

"I can't take this," Marie retorted and flushed, thinking, *I don't need any help. Is this guy some sort of racist, sexist pig or what?*

"No please do, I am an old man and I vant ta help in some way." Sig continued, "I only had one son and he died in da war. Now I have no one ta give dis to. When I die my daughter and granddaughter won't vant it so it'll just go ta da Goodwill or be trone in da junk. At least this way you can give it to your son and remember da ride on Christmas Eve and the stories of an old man who worked on the Great Northern many years ago. Please take it and no disrespect intended."

Marie held out her hand and accepted the watch. She slipped it over her wrist where it hung loosely but still felt warm.

"Thanks, I'll be sure to tell my son all about you and your family. You said your name is Sig Andersen, right? I will be sure to mail you when I have my baby."

Sig smiled and rested his head back in his seat. He felt warm inside and really genuinely comfortable. "Ain't it something how the circle of life keeps going round. I am ready ta leave da circle and you're bringing in a newcomer. I tink I lived my life da best dat I could because I've always tried ta be fair and honest. Never was much of a church-going man, but always respected everything fur what it is. You teach yur son ta respect everything, no matter how small or how large. Whether it's the smallest insect, da ugliest human or da entire universe, you gotta respect um. Then you'll get respect back. And work hard. Teach him ta work hard. Nuttng comes fur free. I know ya vant him ta have a better life than you but teaching him ta work pays off. It's hard sometime but teach him that. Will ya? Give him da watch and teach him dat." Sig paused with a puzzled look on his face. "You know what? I don't tink I'm feeling so good. I'm gonna miss her. I'll ruin her Christmas," he said as he sighed his last breath.

Marie didn't realize what had transpired as she thought the old man had fallen off to sleep. After about a half an hour passed she noticed that something wasn't exactly right. Upon a closer look she realized the old man was not breathing. Her eyes grew wide as she realized that Sig was dead. *Oh my God,* she thought, *what the hell do I do now?* She took a second look at Sig to see if she could see his breathing. Nothing! *Oh shit, is this really happening?* She sat back to compose her thoughts, took a deep breath and closed her eyes for a moment. She could still hear Sig's voice in her head and the line about respect. *OK, I know what I've got to do,* she thought as she raised herself out of her seat. No one else seemed to be notice that anything was wrong.

Marie walked to the back of the coach and looked around for the car attendant. Not seeing one, she pushed the call button and in a couple of minutes the same attendant who helped her get on the train appeared.

"May I help you?" he inquired

"Ya. Can we get somewhere a bit more private?" Marie petitioned impatiently

"Sure," the porter replied as they stepped closer to the back of the car.

Marie began, "I believe the old gentleman in the seat next to me has passed away. I don't want to make a scene and most of all I want him to be respected." All of a sudden she felt the tears well up in her eyes. "He is so nice," she sobbed. "His name is Sig Andersen and is on his way to visit his granddaughter in Wolf Point."

"Sorry this had to happen to you, miss," apologized the porter. "I can take care of this from here on out. Which seat were you sitting in?"

Marie replied, "I'll show you."

The porter objected, "No. Just tell me so I can go and check without raising a bunch of commotion."

"OK, it's, let's see, one, two, three, four, five, six rows up on the left," Marie counted. "The old guy next to the window."

"Stay here till I get back," instructed the porter.

Just then the train started to move and Marie had to grab the hand rail to steady herself as she watched as the porter moved down the aisle and sat down next to Sig. The porter seemed to be talking to the man but Marie noticed there was no answer. She then watched as he picked up Sig's limp hand and discretely felt for a pulse.

In a couple of moments the porter stood up and headed back to Marie. "I am afraid you are right. I can move you to the next car for the remainder of the trip. I apologize for your inconvenience."

"No," Marie responded, "I would like to sit next to him until you do whatever it is you are going to do."

"Are you sure?" the porter gasped in disbelief.

"Yes," Marie stated authoritatively, even as it was in disbelief of herself.

The porter just replied, "Alright, let me see what the chief wants to do. You can go and sit down if you want. I sure wouldn't. It creeps me out."

Marie just gave the man her fiercest glare and headed back up the aisle. *He wouldn't understand anyway,* she thought.

She sat down next to Sig and gently touched his hand and said, "Thanks for the watch and advice."

She then gently put his hand on his lap and began sobbing softly. "Nice old guy didn't get to see his granddaughter for Christmas. It's going to be a rough holiday for them."

The radio in the locomotive cab squawked, "Amtrak portable to the head end. Bill?"

"Go ahead portable," Bill replied.

It was Floyd with an update on the problem with the train. "It's the brake rod on the 2386 sleeper. I think if I knock some of the snow off I'll be able to get it back where it belongs."

"Roger, Floyd, let me know how you make out and I'll call ahead to Shelby so they can check it," Bill responded

"Roger, give me a couple of minutes. Portable out," Floyd signed off.

"Amtrak out," signed off Bill.

Then there was silence except for the whine of the turbochargers on the diesels behind the back wall of the cab.

Once again a voice came over the radio, "Glacier East dispatcher to Amtrak 8." This time it was the local dispatcher wondering how things were going so he could keep things moving on this important mainline.

"Go ahead, dispatcher," cut in Bill.

"How are things going up there?" asked the dispatcher.

"Looks like a stuck brake rod.. We should have it fixed up in a bit," Bill reported.

"Roger, let me know so I can get the helpers over the top to get behind BNSF 6583," instructed the dispatcher so Bill knew what the plans were when things got rolling again.

"Roger, dispatcher. Amtrak 8 out," Bill signed off once again.

"Dispatcher out," signed off the dispatcher.

Quiet again, then more radio traffic. This time not for Bill. The dispatcher was letting the helper units stationed at Essex know what their next assignment was.

"Glacier East Dispatcher to the helper 4483," signed on the dispatcher.

"Go ahead, dispatcher," replied locomotive number 4483, which is the helper consist.

"When Amtrak gets clear, you can follow him over the top to get behind the stack train 6583," instructed the dispatcher.

"Roger, dispatcher, follow Amtrak over the pass to get behind 6583," repeated the helper engineer. This repetition is required by federal law so no one is confused with instructions. The helper crew was going to go east over the pass and down to the East Glacier siding to help priority freight number 6583. It is the helper's job to couple onto the rear of heavy freight trains to push them up to the top of the pass and then, more importantly, to provide additional braking power on the steep downhill slopes to keep the train under control.

"Roger, dispatcher out," signed off the dispatcher.

"4483 out," signed off the helper engineer

"Amtrak portable to the head end," called Floyd

"Go ahead portable," replied Bill

"I got the rod back where it belongs. Can you release the air for a bit so I can check it?" requested Floyd

"Roger, Floyd," replied Bill.

Bill set the engine brake and then released the air to the train. The couplers strained a bit under the weight of the train but the engine held fast.

"Looks good, Bill," was the report from the back of the train where Floyd was watching to make sure the frozen rod moved freely.

"Roger Floyd," responded Bill with a sigh of relief. At least he could get moving again and maybe make up some time.

"I'll start walking back and check the rest of the train. Amtrak portable out," replied the conductor as he started trudging his way back toward the front of the train. It is the conductor's job to take care of any mechanical problems with the train while the engineer can sit in the cab and delegate authority. So it was that Floyd was outside slogging through six inches of snow while Bill was in the heated cab doing paperwork.

"Roger head end out," signed off Bill

Bill started organizing his things so he could get going as soon as Floyd gave the highball.

It wasn't even five minutes before Floyd came back on, "Amtrak portable to the head end."

"Go ahead, portable," responded Bill from the cab.

"Looks good to go, " Floyd said, "highball Amtrak."

"Roger highball," Bill signed off.

Bill called the dispatcher, "Amtrak 8 to the Glacier East dispatcher."

"Go ahead, Amtrak," the dispatcher responded.

"We are ready to go here. We got the brake rod freed back up, but we better have Shelby take a look at it," instructed Bill, so the dispatcher could make the arrangements for the maintenance department to check the troublesome car.

"Roger, Amtrak, you have permission to proceed at track speed. I'll have the helpers follow you over to East Glacier," replied the dispatcher giving his instructions.

"Roger, permission to proceed at track speed. Amtrak out," repeated Bill as he signed off.

"Glacier East dispatcher out," signed off the dispatcher

Bill opened the throttle a couple of notches and let the engine strain a bit before releasing the brakes. A bit of sand on the tracks and the 24 drive wheels of the locomotives gripped enough steel to get the train rolling. More throttle and the train picked up speed until the speedometer showed 50 mph. Then back off enough to keep things at a steady pace. The train pounded through three more snow sheds before reaching the Blacktail detector. "BNSF detector milepost 1157.2—no defects, repeat no defects, total axles 56, temperature 22 degrees. Detector out."

Bill breathed a sigh of release and radioed Floyd, "Amtrak, no defects, out."

We're on our way, thought Bill when the radio cut in once again.

"Amtrak portable to the head end. Bill?" Floyd called to his engineer.

"Go ahead, portable," Bill responded thinking, *Now what?*

"Bill, we got a medical emergency back here. Seems we have an elderly passenger who is deceased. No one is in a panic yet, the fellow passenger was discrete about reporting to us, but I think there is some suspicion. We probably can't get an ambulance up here in this weather. So what do you think? We head down to East Glacier and hope the weather is clear enough for the ambulance from Browning?"

Bill thought for a second and replied "Roger, I guess that's the best we got. I'll let dispatch know to get an ambulance in front of the station."

"Roger, I'll keep things as quiet as possible back here. Amtrak portable out," signed off Floyd.

"Thanks, Amtrak head end out," Bill responded

Bill called the dispatcher and relayed his previous conversation so they could get an ambulance to meet the train.

Marie sat in the aisle seat next to Sig and gazed out the window on the far side of the train. She couldn't bring herself to gaze past her lifeless friend. She wanted to remember Sig as the way he was prior to their arrival at Essex. As she already felt lonely and missed his constant chatter about his exploits on the railway.

At first she couldn't make out much outside of the coach window, because of the snow. Only pine trees close to the tracks and occasionally the rock outcropping blasted away to make room for the railroad right of way. Soon the snow was diminished enough to watch the automobiles on Highway 2 below them as they plowed their way through the six inches covering the road. Just as they reached the broad saddle that formed Marias Pass the landscape opened up. Marie could see the monument dedicated to Robert Stevens who discovered the pass while working for the Great Northern Railway. Mr. Stevens had been soliciting help from her ancestors, who had known such a pass existed long before the arrival of the white men. It is this pass, which is the lowest crossing of the Rocky Mountains, that enabled the Great Northern Railway to establish itself as one of the great transcontinental railroads.

The train rounded a sweeping curve and Marie could see her hometown of Browning, some 30 miles away, nestled down on the open plains. She kind of looked forward to getting home after this tumultuous trip, so she could relax with her family. She just continued on her way gazing out the window without really seeing anything.

Bill eased the train over Marias Pass as the snow started to let up and by the time they reached the Bison detector the snow had stopped completely, but the wind was picking up. After holding the train back as he eased down the east side of the divide, he let the Empire Builder glide through the curves and out onto the high plains. Crossing the Midvale Creek bridge he slowed the train to a stop just west of the East Glacier station platform. The locomotives of the 6583 train were stopped directly in front of the platform, and its mile-long string of containers stretched out like a multicolored ribbon out onto the high prairie. This priority freight, which until this point, waited for nothing except Amtrak, was going to have to wait until the helpers could get around the freight and head west, and those helpers were not going to arrive until an old Great Northern veteran got off of the train in front of them. Though the 70-year-old log station was boarded up for the season, there was activity on the platform this morning. Bill could see Floyd meeting the ambulance crew and leading them to the first coach. Nothing to do now but wait.

Inside the coach, Floyd announced to the passengers that there was a medical problem with one of the passengers and there would be a slight delay. He led the EMT's to the seat next to Marie and asked if she could wait outside the coach. They then carefully checked for signs of life, found none, and placed Sig on the stretcher. The whole process took less than five minutes. After rolling the stretcher down the aisle and out the door, they had to carry Sig across the mainline in front of the idling freight. Marie watched with tears in her eyes but saw the irony as they carried Sig in front of that train. For once the railroad had to wait for him. Instead of Sig making way for the trains all those years, the railroad finally stepped aside for Sigrud Andersen

"Congratulations, Sig," she said aloud.

Floyd came alongside and touched her arm. "Miss, we will need to ask you a few questions. Are you related to him?"

"No, I just met him on the train. We kind of hit it off I guess," Marie commented.

"Do you know his name?" Floyd asked.

Marie replied, "Svigrud Andersen, he was on his way to visit his granddaughter in Wolf Point. I didn't get her name though. He did mention he was living in a retirement home in Spokane."

"OK," Floyd said, "I guess you can answer the rest of the questions as we go. Please get aboard."

As Floyd helped her aboard Marie asked, "Where are they taking him?"

"The ambulance is from Browning, so I imagine they'll bring him to the hospital there," Floyd answered.

Marie was silent for a second and then asked, "Can I ride with them? I'm from Browning and the hospital is closer to my house than the train station anyway."

Floyd looked shocked at the odd request but replied, "I'll go ask. Get your things quickly, so when I signal you can get off."

Floyd quickly crossed the main line and talked to the ambulance crew, then crossed back to the open door just as Marie came back with her bags. "Ya, come on, I'll help you across the tracks," he instructed.

He helped her down from the coach and across the tracks in front of the patiently waiting freight. Floyd made sure she was OK and quickly got aboard the Empire Builder, shut the door, grabbed his radio and signaled, "Highball Amtrak"

Bill got the signal and eased the throttle forward to get the train back in motion. But kept the speed down as he crossed the Two Medicine bridge. He glanced down to see the containers still lying at the bottom of the canyon where the wind had blown the double stack off the bridge earlier. It was windy today but nothing like that day—no sense chancing it. Once across the bridge it was a flat out run to Browning, Cut Bank, and then Shelby. Hopefully there would be no more slow downs. He glanced at his watch and thought, *If the guys in*

Shelby take their time checking that brake hose we'll lose more time. But that wouldn't be his problem. *Well let's see how it goes,* he thought as he let the horses run across the flat prairie.

Marie stood bracing herself against the cold arctic wind as she stood on the desolate platform waiting for the crew to make room for her in the ambulance.

"Here you go, Marie," said Josh Blackbear, whom she had known since she was a child at the gas station, as he helped her into the van and showed her the seatbelt.

"You know this guy?" Josh inquired.

Marie answered, "I met him on the train and he was really nice. We kind of took to each other."

Josh started in, "Marie, you really should go into some sort of healthcare field. You really care about people. I know the doctors and directors at the medical center so I can put in a word for you. I'll bet they can work something out while you are taking care of your child and I'd bet your mom and dad will help out too. In fact your dad is excited about a grandchild in the house. Your mom would jump at the chance to help babysit."

Marie sat silently.

Josh continued, "Break the cycle, Marie. Get out of this place. You can do it."

Marie burst into an uncontrollable sob. In her mind she could still hear Sig telling her about the cycle.

"Why is everybody being so nice? I've failed. It's so impossible now. What the hell am I going to do? The cycle this, the cycle that," she sobbed. "Sig said I was part of the cycle of life. That he was leaving, and I'm adding. Then there is the cycle of despair that I need to break. Fucking cycles. Break one add to one. How the fuck am I supposed to know what to do?" she screamed, as she put her face in her hands and cried. Just cried and cried, until she thought her heart and spirit would break.

Nine months of fear, uncertainty and now kindness, just welled up and flowed out with her tears in this ambulance ride with an old man she hardly new.

Josh waited until her crying slowed to a controlled pace. "Marie, things will be fine. You watch, it'll all work out for the best. I'll help you get into the center. You'll get the education you deserve and your child will be everything you imagine, and more. Come on now. It's Christmas, cheer up and enjoy the season. Things will work out, you watch."

Marie paused and mumbled a muted "Thanks" and just sat in reflection for the rest of the trip.

Josh just looked at the attractive girl and wished his daughter had Marie's ambition.

As the ambulance turned at the stoplight, off Highway 2, and into Browning, Josh asked, "You want us to drop you off at your house? This guy won't mind the detour."

Marie wiped her eyes with her sleeve and mumbled, "I'm a mess, ya, I guess, if you don't mind?"

It was just before noon when the ambulance stopped in front of the small, purple, ranch-style house on the gravel path that served as a street. Marie got out, thanked Josh for everything and briskly walked to the front door. Her mother, a stout dark-skinned woman with thick black hair, opened the door and asked, "What happened? Why did the ambulance drop you off? Your father is waiting for a call to pick you up at the station. What's wrong? You're crying."

Marie broke down once again, stepped inside and hugged her mother crying, "Oh, Mom, I've got to grow up. I'm so confused. I've got cycles to break, cycles to add to. I don't know what to do. Oh, Mom." She just hugged and cried.

Jenny, her mother, patted her daughter's back and asked gently, "Are you and the baby all right?"

"Yes, it was just a tough ride. That's all." Marie sniffled as she relaxed her hug and stepped back.

"Sorry, Mom, I didn't mean to scare you," Marie apologized. "I'll tell you about it, but I am hungry and tired."

"Come on into the kitchen and sit down," her mother comforted. "I better call Dad or he'll have a heart attack when he sees the train and you didn't call."

Marie sat down at the old steel table while her mother called the gas station, talked briefly and hung up.

Jenny walked over and put her hand on Marie's shoulder. "OK, tell me what happened. I'll make something while you talk."

Marie told the story of Bill, Sig and Josh as the two of them heated and ate some canned ravioli. It didn't taste good, but it was comfort food. After she finished her story, Marie asked her mother what was going to happen to Sig and how to get in touch with his granddaughter. Together they decided to go talk to someone down at the sheriff's department, who they imagined would be in charge of notifying the next of kin. Marie decided she had better go right away since it was Christmas Eve and there wouldn't be anybody there as evening approached so she put on her coat and headed back out into the cruel world.

Marie fought the fierce north wind as she walked the four blocks to the County Justice Building. Once inside she told her story to the dispatcher on duty and conned her into giving up the address of Sig's daughter who lived in Wolf Point.

Later on that Christmas Eve Marie sat down and penned the following letter:

Dear Denise,
You don't know me, but I knew your father for his last few hours on earth. I just want you to know what a wonderful man he was. He only had a few passions in this world. The first was you. Even though he could never figure you out, he still tried. And he still loved you. The second passion was your daughter. I never learned her name, but she definitely was the apple of his eye. His last words were that he'll miss her and he's sorry for ruining her Christmas. I thought you would like her to know. The third passion was his Great Northern Railway. He told me stories of his railroad career and I sensed the pride in his work as we rode over the rails and ties he helped lay those many years ago. They gave him his feeling of accomplishment and pride. The final passion

was helping people. This is where I come into the picture. Your father gave me his retirement watch and asked that I give it to the baby that I am expecting in a couple of weeks. You can have the watch if you would like it. I know it rightfully belongs to you. But more importantly he gave me advice and a feeling of my self-worth. He said that he was leaving the cycle of life and that my baby would be filling the spot he left. I hope I can teach my child to be the person your father was. He left a very large vacancy and I don't know if anyone will be able to fill it.

You have my condolences during this sad time and I want you to know your father touched my life and I will never forget him. Please let me know if you would like me to send you the watch. If not, it will be a reminder of what my job is in raising a child to fill the position your father left in that circle.

She signed the letter and mailed it that same afternoon.

Marie had a nine pound, six ounce baby on January 6th. The strapping, dark-haired boy was named James Svigrud Lightfeather. Marie picked the names in honor of that memorable train ride on Christmas Eve. James for James J. Hill the Empire Builder whose namesake train Sig so proudly rode on that final day of his life and Svigrud for the man who inspired her to keep up the fight for a better life.

Marie is currently working at the Browning Medical Center and is attending the local reservation college. She is planning to head back to Missoula when she gets enough credits to get into the social work program. The watch is hanging on a hook alongside the mirror in her room. Marie looks at it each morning and plans the day so she can help James follow in the footsteps of the giant who filled that watch band, and yet had the nimble fingers to twist the knob to wind it every day.

Chapter 4

The Cowboy and the Women

The cold wind blew wisps of snow across the Cut Bank platform as Bill eased the silver and blue locomotives to the far end of the station. The idling diesels seemed to whisper their relief at the rest stop as Bill filled out his paperwork while the passengers boarded. The engineer waited for the "Highball" as he looked out at the vast prairie with its sparse snow covering. The few clouds in the sky were casting shadows that seemed to race across the fields competing with the snow drifting and piling up on the leeward side of the scarce trees and in the washouts outside of town. The radio crackled and Bill recognized Floyd as he gave him the highball.

Just as the conductor yelled the "all aboard" and radioed the "highball Amtrak" to the engineer, an old bowlegged man stepped out onto the platform and waved to Floyd the conductor on the Empire Builder. Floyd quickly grabbed the microphone button on his radio and yelled to the engineer, "Hold on, Amtrak. We got one more coming."

"Roger," responded the radio from the cab of the lead locomotive.

Floyd swung open the door on the last coach as the train ground back to a stop. "Lyle, you almost missed it this time."

The old man walked toward the train with a brisk stride but his gate showed the definite signs of many miles and countless hours of work. "Sorry, Floyd, the darn old cab was late and I had to chew some ass just to get here," Lyle said as he threw his duffel bag onto the train, and stepped up through the doorway without waiting for the conductor and the step stool.

"Lyle, dang you, you know you're supposed to wait until I put that step out there. Do you want me to lose my job?" Floyd reprimanded the old man.

"Oh hush yourself and highball this train; I don't want no engineer writing in his report that he lost minutes because of some old geezer not getting to the station on time. Besides what do I care if you get your ass fired? You are making too much money anyway."

Floyd just laughed, pushed the microphone and gave the highball. Amtrak 8 quickly burst alive and with the smooth hand of the engineer, picked up speed and headed out of town.

"Lyle, do you have your ticket or do I have to get one for you?" the conductor asked politely.

Lyle responded, "I got my ticket right here. I'm going a lot farther than Havre today," as he pulled the white and blue ticket envelope from his breast pocket.

Removing the ticket packet from the envelope the old man handed the tickets to the conductor who whistled and remarked, "Holy cow, you're heading all the way to Grand Forks? What's the occasion?"

"I'm going to my grand niece's wedding. I haven't seen my sister in two years and now her granddaughter is getting married," Lyle answered as he stuffed the tickets back into the envelope and shoved it into his breast pocket.

The train lurched as it crossed a switch causing the bowlegged old man to grab the handrail. Floyd grabbed Lyle's free arm to assist and stabilize the old cowboy.

"You know, Lyle, you had better get upstairs to your seat before you give me a heart attack. You don't want me kicking the bucket before you even get to Grand Forks, do you?" the conductor kidded as he helped steer Lyle toward the stairs.

"By the way what's your grand niece's name," Floyd asked half testing the old man's memory.

"Jennifer Hanson, she's marrying some guy name Scott," he replied with a snicker knowing full well what Floyd was up to.

"You old son of a gun," Floyd replied, "I hope my memory is half as good as yours when I'm 96."

"I hope so too." He smiled. "I'm 97."

Outside the right side of the coach windows the Bearpaw Mountains were visible in the distance. Lucia and Megan Hartlage were deep into their novels with only an occasional glance out the window to view the passing scenery. The mother and daughter had boarded the train in Seattle and were now more than settled into their seats as they still had another twenty hours to go before reaching their home in Minnesota. Coming back from visiting family in the Emerald City, they were both looking forward to getting home and enjoying Christmas night in their own beds. Neither Megan nor her mother Lucia even glanced up from their books as the old man sat down across the aisle from them. In the twenty-four hours that they had been on the train, the ebb and flow of passengers didn't arouse curiosity any longer.

Megan was in fact a bit startled when Lyle asked politely,"Miss, would you mind if I stowed my bag above your seat? The area above my seat is full and I noticed that you had some room."

"Sure," Megan replied quickly. "Here, let me help you with that," she added standing up and taking the bag from the man and placing it above her seat.

With her height, blond hair and commanding poise, the 16-year-old Megan presented a startling contrast to the rest of the sitting passengers.

"Thanks. Boy, you are a tall one. How tall are you?" the old man inquired.

Flushing red, Megan replied, "I'm six two."

"Good for you. Have you been on the train for a while? You look like you are pretty well settled in," Lyle continued.

"Yes, my mother and I got on in Seattle. We are on our way home to Minnesota. Where are you getting off?" Megan asked more politely than nosy.

"I'm on my way to Grand Forks for my sister's granddaughter's wedding. I haven't seen my sister in two years and I don't think I've seen her granddaughter since she was in grade school," the old man said settling into his seat.

Bored with her book and seeking some adult conversation, Megan kept up the conversation with the guy, just to find out some of the experiences from other parts of the world. "Are you from around here?"

"Yes and no. I spent most of my adult life around western Montana, but I was born and raised in St. Cloud, Minnesota. I've kind of drifted around a bit before getting this old and wrinkled body settled down here in Cut Bank," the old man answered as he broke into a big smile. The smile was in part from the satisfaction that this pretty young woman was striking up a conversation with him and also the satisfaction of having a younger adult to talk to.

"Oh, I'm Megan and this is my mother Lucia," Megan interjected almost as an afterthought. She didn't want to appear rude and also thought her mother needed to pull her nose out of her book and meet some of the interesting folks on the train.

"Nice to meet you, Megan, and nice to meet you too, Lucia. My name is Lyle Crookston," Lyle said as he bowed his head slightly in a respectful gesture. "I can sure see the resemblance in you two. You both have such bright eyes," the old man commented.

"Oh gosh," Megan giggled, "I always think we look so different. I guess it's hard for me to tell. Thanks though. You know us kids never want to be associated with our parents."

By this time Lucia had closed her book and was beginning to get intrigued by the conversation. She pulled her legs up underneath her and turned sideways in the seat to face the passenger across the aisle. Meanwhile, Lyle took off his long jacket and folded it neatly stowing it gently on the back of his seat. "Sure is warm on the train today. I've ridden this thing when I could have frozen a steer for next week's supper."

Megan noticed immediately how stylish and well kept the old man was dressed and how appropriate and dignified he carried himself. His thin gray hair was perfectly styled and cut, his hands, though worn and wrinkled with age, were perfectly manicured and though his suit was a not the latest trend, it was classically styled and immaculately cleaned and pressed. Though she thought of complimenting Lyle, she felt maybe it best to wait until she got to know him a little better.

Lyle turned back toward the women and asked politely, "What, may I ask, were you doing in Seattle? It's not the place to visit this time of year."

Megan replied, "We were visiting family and just taking some time off to do some vacationing."

Lyle brought Lucia into the conversation by asking, "Lucia, what do you think of the vacation so far? I'll bet you are the one paying for it so we need to let your opinion be known to Megan here."

The mid forties mother pushed her red-blond hair back from her face, thought for a second and then responded, "I think I enjoyed most, visiting my sister-in-law and the horseback riding in the mountains. It has been a good vacation."

It was as if a curtain had been lifted from Lyle's face. His face relaxed, his eyes brightened and a broad smile stretched across his face. "You really like horseback riding? Do you do much?"

Lucia replied as she squirmed more in her seat to face the kindly old gentleman, "Yes, I do like riding, but I don't get to do much of it. Two years ago I went to a horseback riding camp where I learned how to ride well and to take care of the horses. Last year my husband and I went to Wyoming where we rode for a week at a ranch in the mountains. But with the kids and everything going on for school, I don't get a chance to do a lot with horses."

"Well, I was a cowboy for close to 65 years. Just about all I did was ride horses and chase after cows. Heck some of those years I would stay out on the range for three months at a time. I would sleep under the stars and never set foot in a building for months at a time. My best and darn near only friend was my horse. But you probably aren't interested in a bunch of stories about an old man. You young people are more interested in music and video games. Beside I've got to go visit the restroom," Lyle said as he started getting up from his seat, grabbing the back of the seat in front of him as he got up.

Megan quickly piped in, "We would love to hear your stories when you get back if you don't mind, right, Mom?"

"Yes, I think it would be very fascinating, better than my book," Lucia agreed

"OK, when I get back I'll tell you some of the old stories," the old man said as he worked his way down the aisle toward the end of the car.

Outside the coach window the late morning sunlight bleached the colors from the brown and gray grasses of the expanses. The only highlight was the sunshine turning the small patches of windblown snow into specked jewels hidden among the fence rows along the tracks. Out in the fields the fallow strips alternated with the planted winter wheat. It was only these alternating strips of color that broke the monotony of the high plains as the railroad wound its way around the rises and depressions on its journey to the Great Lakes.

After his ordeal with the dead body, George was happy to be on the move once more. He quickly settled back into his routine. He walked the aisle reminding passengers to make dinner reservations early. He checked the pop and water supplies and just generally made sure his stable of passengers was well attended. *Twenty-four hours to go*, he thought. Twenty-four hours and home with the wife and kids. Pleasure and relaxation pulsed through his body just thinking about it. He would have to wait. *It will come*, he thought

As the car attendant continued on with his rounds, Lyle made his way back to his seat across from the two anxiously awaiting Minnesotans. "I hope you didn't mind waiting," he said as he wiggled back into his seat. "Bladder ain't what it used to be. Maybe all those years of riding and sleeping on the ground have taken their toll."

Lucia smiled and said, "Tell me about it, I know the feeling." Megan rolled her eyes and blushed lightly at her mother's frankness.

Lyle ran his hand across his cleanly shaved face in thought and asked himself out loud, "Where should I begin? How about the beginning? Megan, if you get bored just tell me to move on and get to something interesting. I told you I was from St. Cloud, Minnesota, but my parents were very poor and couldn't afford to keep me. There were a series of dry years and there wasn't enough money or food to feed me and my sisters. So when I was about 12 years old they sent me out to my uncle who had a dry goods store in Great Falls. At least there I could work for my room and board. On the farm it didn't matter how much you worked; the crops just wouldn't grow. My aunt and uncle didn't have any children so I was welcomed into their home and treated me like their child. I really liked my new parents, worked hard to please them and I worked a lot of hours in the store. I know they had great ambitions for me and would have liked for me to take over the business some day. I just couldn't seem to suppress the wanderlust inside of me. Maybe I was still scared of being abandoned or not having enough to eat again. I wanted to control my own destiny and if I was going to be hungry it would be my own doing. Finally I made the decision to disappoint my aunt and uncle. I took a job at a ranch down in Harlowton where I first became a cowboy. At first it was a young restless boy's dream. I got to wear the traditional hat, boots and chaps, ride horses and listen to the stories of the real first-generation cowboys at the ranch. The first summer I spent with the cattle up in the high ranges just watching the herd and moving around from the different grazing and watering spots. It was like a dream, sleeping out under the crystal-clear skies, spending the days riding the high country, checking the cattle and just relaxing following the herd. I was the rookie and the old guys did the work. Sure did take a lot of ribbing though. I learned all about the jackalopes, abominable snowmen, haunted valleys and evil witches.

"Then winter came to Montana. We moved the cattle down to the winter ranges closer to the ranch and I had to do some real work. Feeding stored hay, rescuing stranded calves and living in the ranch bunk with a bunch of smelly old cowboys. Things were not so glamorous now, but I was still new to the business of cattle husbandry, so I stuck with the job, awaiting for the next summer season."

The overhead speaker broke into the story announcing the coming arrival to the Shelby station. With the interruption Megan took the opportunity to break in and excuse herself to visit the restroom.

The train came to a stop and the sound of the opening doors passed through each coach. Passengers flooded out of each door and once again the dance of greeting and departing loved ones was played out. Each in its own ritualistic way. Handshakes, hugs, kisses, and even tears were the common ground when saying hello or goodbye. The Empire Builder was the catalyst bringing people together or moving them apart. The same scenario since its inaugural run in 1929.

After the train came to a rest, Bill opened the door for the oncoming crew. As he finished the paperwork he looked in the mirror and saw Gene Fallow walking down the platform toward the locomotive. *Good,* he thought, *Gene will take care of these people and will make up some time along the way.*

Gene Fallow had been an engineer for Amtrak for 11 years which followed a six-year career with the Soo Line in North Dakota. As he climbed up the ladder into the cab of the idling locomotive he said to Bill, "Kind of a strange ride today."

"Yah, strange is an understatement," Bill replied as he got up from the seat and gathered up his papers to shove them into his briefcase. He picked up his coat, duffel bag and briefcase and moved to the side so Gene could sit down and take over the control of the train. After briefing him on the details of the trip and the condition of the train, Bill set his things next to the door, backed out, and climbed down the ladder to the pavement below. As he grabbed his things he halfheartedly saluted Gene and wished him a good trip. He turned to face the biting wind and walked down to the station where he could get his truck and head for home. It would be a nice Christmas with his wife.

Floyd exchanged his details of the Whitefish-to-Shelby trip with Ken Grebshaw, the oncoming conductor. Floyd explained the old man dying and some of the other things to watch out for on the upcoming ride. He then left Ken in charge and departed the train. He too headed for home and a welcomed Christmas Eve night.

Ken checked the platform and quickly yelled the "All aboard." As soon as the platform was clear he radioed Gene the highball and the Empire Builder headed out into the Christmas Eve afternoon, heading for Havre, Malta, Glasgow and Wolf Point, Montana, before crossing into North Dakota.

Gene looked at his watch and notched the locomotive up. If he pushed things a bit, he would make up as much time as possible before reaching Minot. He knew that once he got back into the more populated areas he didn't stand a chance to gain time.

Floyd, the conductor had radioed ahead to have the Shelby repair crew look at the sticking brake rod. When the train stopped at the station two members of the crew blue flagged the train while another crawled under the suspect coach to inspect the brake rod. Upon emerging from under the car, the crew member radioed Floyd the good news that nothing was wrong and a chunk of ice had been removed to allow the brake rod to move freely.

After Bill climbed down from the cab and handed the train over to the new crew, the blue flags were removed and Gene notched up the throttle. The diesels came to life and turned the generators faster to provide the electricity to power the 500 horsepower motors on the axles. The steel wheels gripped the rails, brought the train back into motion and carried the passengers back out onto the prairie.

Lyle turned and looked out the window as the smoker passengers stood out in the wind cupping their hands around their lighters trying to get their cigarettes lit. Prancing around and clapping their hands together, the passengers struggled to stay warm for the few minutes boarding passengers crossed paths with the departing people.

Lyle turned and asked Lucia, "You don't smoke, do you?"

Lucia wrinkled her nose and replied in disgust, "No, that's a disgusting habit."

"Good," Lyle replied. "Look at all those fools out there freezing their butts off just to drive a another nail in their coffin." He was quiet as he stared out the window. The slight jar of the coach as the train started moving seemed to break his trance. He looked at Lucia, gave her a quick smile and returned to the window as the small collection of city buildings passed by.

Megan came back down the aisle grasping each row of seats to stabilize herself as the coach swayed from side to side as it crossed the switches leading out of the yard in Shelby, Montana. The tall blonde carried in her free hand three bags of Tostidos and a couple of bottles of water. Handing the items to her mother she said, "I thought you might like a snack."

"Thanks," Lucia said politely to her daughter.

Megan turned to Lyle and offered him one of the bags. "Would you like these?"

"Sure, thanks," the old man replied as he took the bag of chips. "This is one of my downfalls. I love the salty snacks."

Megan sat down and said, “Sorry to disturb your story. It is very interesting; I hope you will continue.”

As the cowboy turned back toward the aisle he continued, “I guess I proved too good of a farmhand during that winter because I became part of the farmhand crew planting crops, and harvesting the hay for the following winter. It wasn’t all bad. I had good meals, slept in a comfortable bed and had weekends off to visit town and its vices. For the next two years I was a farmer, planting and harvesting, not really following my heart as a cowboy. After the third winter I decided I needed to get back out onto the range. That first year proved to be an irresistible attraction and beside I didn’t like what the weekends of drinking and visiting the brothels was doing to me. So I took on as cowhand on a ranch near Helena. I got my wish and spent the summer in the high country watching the herd. Much like last time, the summer was glorious and the job everything ever dreamed up by young aspiring cowboys. Again winter set in. Instead of moving to the ranch, this herd was moved to winter pastures 30 miles from the ranch house. I spent that first winter sleeping in a ramshackle cabin just trying to keep myself and two older guys from freezing to death. It was a full-time job staying warm and even harder to keep the cattle alive. As hard as the job was, it was one of those experiences that allows you to prove to yourself that you are self-sufficient and can withstand anything mother nature can throw at you. I remember those days, getting up around 4:00 am, stoking the stove to get some water hot, checking out the door of the cabin, and just seeing what the weather was going to bring that day. Once you had enough water heated, all three of us would clean up using the same pan of water. Then we would take turns making breakfast of pan-fried beef and biscuits. As the sun came up we’d head out to chop a hole in the ice to provide a watering hole for the cattle. Some of those cold mornings it would take a couple of hours to make sure the ice stayed clear for all the cattle to drink. We didn’t have a thermometer so we never knew what the temperature was, but once it was below zero we knew it. You couldn’t keep the pond open for more than a few minutes at a time, the more miserable the weather the harder we had to work. The cattle could find their own grass under the snow but we had to make sure they had water to drink every day. By the time the sun went down we were ready for supper and bed. Supper was once again fried beef, but at night we'd eat beans or rice. Even though it was the same every day, we never tired of it. I guess we were so hungry we really didn't care. We were generally so exhausted we just ate and went to bed. Once spring arrived and we headed back up to the summer range, I had matured and found that living out in the open was where I was master of my own fate."

Lyle paused as he munched on the chips Megan had provided. He held up the bag and said, "Thanks again, I appreciate the snack."

"You are welcome. It's not pan-fried beef and beans," Megan replied with a giggle.

The old gentleman smiled and replied, "No, better."

Lucia asked a question to the old man, "What did you do for groceries and supplies?"

"We would travel into town about once a month with the wagon to pick up food and supplies. We would pick up the beans, rice and flour and we'd butcher a cow for beef. With the cold weather the beef would stay frozen or at least cold enough to keep from spoiling. We always had beef, but things could get a bit dicey when beans and rice ran out. We survived all right, it's certainly not for the faint of heart or the weak, but we had some fun and got to know each other really well. In fact we played a never-ending game of cribbage that we only totaled up when we moved out of the cabin in May. The score was 3658 to 3602 to 3564. I still remember the numbers because I was the loser and I had to pay a penny a point for the difference. That was the winter of 1929–1930. People thought the stock market crashed that December, imagine having to pay half your winter pay in a cribbage tournament. Now that's a market crash! I learned a lesson and I never gambled for money again."

The roar, and following whoosh, startled both the story teller and the audience as a passing freight turned the sunlight shining through the window into a flashing strobe as the loaded grain cars passed by on their way to Seattle. There was no communication as the commotion outside would have drowned every word. The passing freight continued past for a full three minutes. Finally the noise stopped and the bright sunlight regained its constant status, bringing its physical and psychological warmth with it, into the car. Lyle was the first to speak asking, "Didn't you just come from Seattle?"

"Sure," Megan replied, "why?"

"Well, those grain cars are probably going to Seattle to be unloaded. I just thought you might find it interesting."

"Yes, that is interesting, even on Christmas?" Megan replied

"Oh, yes, the railroad doesn't really shut down for holidays. These grain cars might not move tomorrow but the railroad is not shut down. Anyway, the bladder is telling me to take a break once again. Please excuse me. I'll be back in a few minutes," the aging cowboy said as he hoisted his body out of the seat and agilely maneuvered his body down the aisle toward the stairs and the restroom.

Gene checked his watch to calculate his arrival time in Havre. They would be almost an hour late, and as long as no one ran through a grade crossing and he hit them, or a freight derailed in front of him he'd be home in a few hours. He checked his speed and watched the green lights of the signal masts pass. As these rails glistened in the sunlight he just hoped to keep things in order and to make his passengers as happy as possible by delivering their Christmas wish of being with friends and family.

Lyle came back down the aisle and settled into his seat before he began his narration once again. This time it was obvious he had been thinking of his story, didn't have to fumble for the beginning and jumped right in. "After that first winter in that God-forbidden cabin, I was determined to make the next winter more comfortable. I got permission from the ranch owner, so that on the few days I could break away from the summer range, I would ride back to the cabin and patch the holes, clean it up and generally make it fit to live in. I even went to town and bought a new wood-fired cooking stove. Top of the line too. A Monarch, with a built in hot water heater and a thermometer built right into the door. That store owner couldn't figure out what a young cowboy would want with such a stove. By the time fall rolled around, I was set, and could hardly wait for winter to arrive. Well guess what. It did arrive, and with a fury that I'll never forget. We started out with a blizzard the second week of October, followed by three weeks of bone-chilling arctic winds driving snow and cold right through my fixed-up cabin. I sure learned that no matter what your plans, Mother Nature can out think and out play you, hands down. Following the three-week cold snap it warmed up into the sixties for a couple of days. I should have known better but, being young and stupid, I relaxed. On the third afternoon about three o-clock, the wind shifted, the clouds rolled in, and there let loose the most hell-raising snowstorm I've ever been through. I was scared through to my bones as I truthfully thought that the cabin was going to blow away. Those old timbers were creaking and groaning in that wind, so I thought they were going to break. The whole world turned white in a few seconds.

"Jim, one of the two other cowboys spending the winter, was down by the pond clearing ice for the cattle when it let loose. It was my turn for supper that night so I was in the cabin getting the fire going. When the wind started howling it darn near sucked the flames right out of the stove; I remember that I had the darndest time keeping that fire lit.. As I got things settled, I looked out the window and I couldn't even see five feet from the cabin. I opened the door and hollered for Jim but I am sure the wind carried my voice away. Herm, the other cowboy, was behind the cabin chopping wood for the stove so he just hung on to the cabin and followed it around to the door.

"Just as he struggled through the door I grabbed a rope we had lying around and I tied it around my waist. I told Herm to play out the line while I try to find Jim down by the pond. I ventured out into that storm but I might as well have had my eyes shut. I couldn't see my hand in front of my face, the wind was blowing the snow that hard. You couldn't open your eyes more than a slit or they would sting so bad. You wouldn't open your mouth either because the wind would just suck the breath right out of your body. I fell down and tried crawling to the pond as it was only a couple of hundred feet. There was no way I could find that water. I called and called to Jim but to no avail. Finally with my hands and feet freezing and the skin on my face peeling from the wind-blown snow, I crawled back to the cabin following the rope. Herm dragged me the last ten feet and I just collapsed on the floor inside that cabin. I just couldn't fathom giving up on Jim. I tried to get up but couldn't manage the strength, and besides Herm held me down. Being older and wiser, he realized that by this time there was no hope. The cold and wind had taken their toll. It was far better for the two of us to be alive than risk it for a lost cause. We would need each other in the next few days.

"After that initial afternoon, the snow decreased in intensity, but the wind picked up the bite of the arctic air. With the wind still howling and blowing the foot of snow that had fallen, going outside was still treacherous at best. Since we were not prepared, we had no wood stored inside the cabin and no water. We roped each other up and grappled our way around the cabin to the wood pile and managed to bring in a couple of days' worth of wood. However the price for ill preparedness was frost bite on all of my fingers. Herm frostbit three toes. At least with the wood safely indoors we could melt snow for water. We were safe for the time being but had abandoned the cattle until we deemed it safe to go outdoors. Finally after three grueling days of howling wind and blowing snow the storm broke. Although the temperature was still well below zero, at least the wind calmed. We reluctantly ventured out in search of Jim. He as nowhere to be found. In fact, we never did find his body, the poor man. It was a terrible time; we lost Jim, 65 cattle and five horses in that storm. But we also learned a valuable lesson. Never trust the Montana winter weather and more important always be prepared for the worst. It could have been me down at the pond that day. If had not have been my turn for supper that day I would not be telling this story.

"Well the rest of that winter was a walk in the park compared to that November and I continued on at the ranch in spite of losing a cowhand and those cattle. Every summer I fixed up some more of the cabin and eventually it felt like home. That rancher figured I had so much time and money invested in that place that he gave it and 600 acres to me. Nice fellow that rancher. I'll never forget him."

Lucia broke into the conversation and asked, "What about while you were the range cowboy? What was that like? It seems like it would be such a wonderful carefree life. Riding and being in the outdoors and away from all the pressures of everything. Was it enjoyable?"

The old man smiled and replied in a reflective manner, "Oh it was nice enough and some of it is like you say, carefree. But you have to remember we were not dude ranch cowboys showing a bunch of green horns how things are done. We were out there on the open range taking care of several hundred head of cattle. Now grant it, cattle don't need a lot of attention but the rancher is in business to make money. So the more attention paid to those cattle the more money he made."

The train began slowing down as the paging system announced the approach of Havre, Montana. Lyle paused so he would not have to compete with the overhead system.

Once the announcement was finished the tale began once more. "We had to keep track of these cattle. You wanted them to stay near any source of water, keep any wolves and even bears away and keep the animals in green pasture. During calving season you would watch the cows to make sure you were around for any calving trouble. We didn't ride horses just for fun; it was from this vantage point you could recognize trouble. There were more than one night spent astride your horse watching for problems. Lucia, did you ever spend a whole night riding a horse?"

"No," the woman replied, "I don't know if I would care for that."

"It's certainly not something you do on a dude ranch," the cowboy continued. "On a dark moonless night riding a horse among several hundred head of sleeping cattle, you can begin to imagine you hear things that will make your skin crawl. But it is this intuition that will save you and your cattle. You recognize the sounds of cattle breathing normally, a cow in labor or an animal that is being preyed upon. It is also on these types of night that you can get yourself in real trouble. Have you ever been out on the prairie when it is too dark to see your feet in the stirrups of your saddle?"

"No," Lucia replied. "It really gets that dark?"

"Sure. Back then there wasn't the light pollution we have today." Lyle said, "When it was cloudy it could be so dark that, like I said, you couldn't see your feet in the stirrups. You'd be riding around on rough terrain with prairie dog holes, rocks and gullies. It was on one of these nights that I had another one of those hair-raising experiences."

The train ground to a halt in the railroad town of Havre, Montana. The car attendants had announced that this was to be a longer station stop and passengers would be invited to get off the train to get some exercise, fresh air or have a smoke break.

Megan looked at her mother and suggested, "Mom, let's get off and move around a bit. I'm getting so cramped in here and beside it looks pretty nice outside."

Lucia agreed with her daughter and asked Lyle, "Are you getting off for some air?"

"No,"replied the old man, "I think I'll stay here and maybe hit the restroom again while things are stable."

"Sure," Lucia replied. "Can I get you anything?"

"No thanks, I should be good for a while," Lyle responded.

The two women proceeded to the stairs and headed out the door, where the cold, Montana air gripped their senses and the bright sun burned their eyes. Walking toward the front of the train the pair stopped and read the wooden sign explaining the origin of the Havre name. Not knowing to believe it, Megan asked her mother if it might be true. "Do you really think they could have named a town because some guy didn't want a woman and said you have'r?"

Lucia replied with a shrug of her shoulders. "You never know. A lot of very strange things happened during those times. Places were named for a lot of more bazaar reasons."

As Lucia looked around she took note of the old station, the menagerie of railroad equipment and junk lying about, and the old brick building still with the old Great Northern Railway sign painted on the brick. She realized that there was indeed a lot of railway history here. What else would make a town like this grow in the middle of the Montana prairie? She turned to her daughter, touched her long arm and said, "We probably should head back aboard."

Megan nodded in agreement as a shiver ran through her body. "I'm getting cold."

Back aboard the train they quickly ascended the stairs and reached their seats. This time Megan crawled in first and let Lucia sit in the aisle seat. Across the way Lyle was smiling and said, "How is it outside?"

Lucia replied, "Nice but cold. Air feels good."

"Good," the old man said. "You mind if I continue before I forget where I was?"

"Go ahead, you were talking about a time on the open range," Lucia reminded.

"Yes, it was during calving time. We'd watch the cows, during the day, to see which ones were going to calf shortly. It is in the cow's nature to go off, by itself, away from the herd to have her calf. This is to try and fool any predators and keep the calf safe. It also makes our job tough when the cow has problems like a breached birth or some other problem. Every calf is income for the rancher, as that is where he makes his money, so we had to try and maximize the number of calves that lived for the year.

"One day I was watching this cow who was going to calf any minute. When night fell I watched that old cow head off up a draw into a brushy spot. I followed the best I could until it got so dark I couldn't see anymore, figuring I'd wait to listen for the bellowing of this cow in labor. In about an hour it started to thunder and shortly thereafter the lightning got pretty hairy. Now since I was down in this draw, I couldn't see the sky so the storm kind of snuck up on me. Before I knew it I was right in the middle of a tornado. I jumped off my horse, wrestled it to the ground behind an outcropping, covered its eyes and hoped for the best. The wind howled, over my head, dirt, rocks and sticks were flying, my horse fought to get up, so I was fighting my horse, the wind and the rain. Suddenly my horse went still and stopped fighting. I thought, good, at least that's one less thing to fight.

"After a couple of pretty long minutes the wind let up. Then the rain and hail came down in buckets. I actually had to lay halfway under my horse to keep from getting seriously hurt. Those hailstones were the size of baseballs. When one hit you, it was mind numbing.

"Finally the hail quit but the rain and lightning continued. I knew I'd better get out of that draw before the flash flood came roaring down the gully. As I stood up and pulled on the horse I saw in the lightning flash that a tree branch the size of a fence post had speared him right through the hind quarter and he was a goner. Now I was in a bit of a tight spot. The rain was driving down, I had no horse and I had better get my ass out of that draw and fast.. I am sure you know Lucia that riding boots aren't much good for climbing, especially in the mud.

"Anyway I crawled and slithered through the mud and rain to get myself up that canyon and out onto the flat, just in time to hear those flood waters come on down. I just sat there shivering in those muddy wet cloths for the rest of the night. I wasn't about to venture out looking for camp in the dark.

"I was never so glad to see that morning sun. I looked around and surveyed the sight, not much on the grassland showed what had taken place, but in the valleys any tress and brush were gone or tangled into a rat's nest. I found my horse and the cow dead, about a half mile down where the draw fanned out. I rescued my saddle and walked back to camp. There was no reason to lament. I was alive and I still had my saddle. I selected a new horse from the herd and went back to work. That's the way it is out there. It's a balance of nature. Some survive and others don't. It may not be your choice; sometimes you are just in the wrong place at the wrong time."

The dining car attendant walked through the car announcing dinner reservations were being taken for the dining car. Since the train was full he recommended everyone get their reservations early. Lyle turned to Megan and Lucia and asked, "You two young ladies care to join an old man for dinner in the dining car?"

"Sure we'd love to. I think it would be fun. Beside I am starving, all this sitting makes me hungry." Lucia giggled.

As the attendant stopped and wrote each of their reservation in his book, Lucia asked that they all be seated together. The man said he would see what he could do, but couldn't guarantee it.

Lyle turned to the two women and asked politely, "Do you two mind if I take a break? My throat is a bit dry and I have to think of some more stories for you."

"Not at all," Megan said. "In fact I'm going to use the restroom. Can I get you a bottle of water or something?"

"If you don't mind, I would like some water," the old man replied.

As Megan stood up, Lucia stood also and said, "I'll go with you; I need to stretch and move."

The two stepped out into the aisle and proceeded to the center of the car and down the stairs.

The Empire Builder headed east closing in on the line where the sun disappeared below the horizon. Right now the sun was still bright enough to produce sparkles on the light dusting of snow covering the fields and pastures of north central Montana. The farther east they traveled the more snow appeared to be on the ground. With no trees to block the fierce arctic winds the snow made miniature drifts behind the tufts of grass and the small brush of the open fields. In the ditches the drifts had piled up to several inches deep. Not enough snow to cause any problems but enough to show what is in store when the next storm blows through.

The engineer looked out the cab window and in this light the world looked cold and desolate. And indeed many settlers in the last part of the 19th century found out that to be the case. Now as the electric lights appeared in the homes and the automatic yard lights came on to break the darkness, the world had become a smaller more hospitable place in northern Montana. Winter was no longer that dangerous time of year but now it was a time for celebration. Christmas Eve night was unfolding in its winter glory around Havre. The early Russian immigrants named the town after the town of their origin. The railroad had promised a cornucopia of bountiful harvests. But these never materialized. Instead the life proved hard and even with unending hours of back breaking work the earth sometimes just proved too much for the settlers and sucked the life out from their bodies. Still many stuck it out and eventually the small community survived and even flourished under the auspices of the Great Northern Railway. So as the sun began to set from the endless Montana sky, Christmas Eve would be celebrated as it has been for over 120 years.

Soon Malta station approached and the train slowed to a stop. Again the mix of passengers departing and boarding.

When Megan and Lucia came back to their seats, they handed the water to Lyle and picked up their books. "We'll just read until dinner so you can rest," Megan told the old man in a kindly voice.

The pair were soon lost in their novels and the train glided on toward Glasgow on those tracks first laid nearly 150 years ago by immigrants hungry for work, looking for a new life and prosperity.

Lyle snoozed and the two Minnesotans continued reading. In their eyes the landscape was boring. After growing up among trees, hills and green lawns, this was desolate.

Up in the cab of the lead locomotive, Gene the engineer looked at his watch as he wrote the arrival time down. He had made up ten minutes but they were still running almost forty-five minutes behind schedule. It was going to be a long evening. By the looks of things they would usher in Christmas somewhere between Devils Lake and Grand Forks, North Dakota. It wouldn't be on his shift, but he wouldn't be home in his own bed either. He'd have to bring train 7 back to Shelby, his hometown, tomorrow. Someone had to do it, and he would still be able to celebrate with his family the next day.

The "highball" came over the radio so Gene reached for the T-handled throttle and shoved it forward a notch. The engines revved slightly but the train didn't respond for a few seconds. Just as the wheels began to grip the rails the radio cracked to life.

"BNSF dispatcher to Amtrak 8."

Gene responded, "Amtrak 8 to the BNSF dispatcher—go ahead."

"Are you still at the station in Malta?" the dispatcher inquired.

"Yes, I've just received the highball and we are moving out," Gene replied.

"OK" the dispatcher responded, "I'm going to have you wait there while I let 5762 pass."

Gene quickly backed off the throttle and applied a small amount of air to the brakes. "OK, dispatcher, Amtrak 8 will wait at the station until 5762 passes."

"That's right, Amtrak 8 wait at Malta station until z train 5762 passes. BNSF dispatcher out," the dispatcher signed off.

Gene signed off, "Amtrak 8 out."

Gene sighed and pulled out his notebook once again and began filling in the report. It seemed to him that there were always endless volumes of papers to be filled out. But that's what kept the railroad safe, so he was all for it.

After only a couple of minutes Gene spotted the headlight of the approaching freight. Within a minute the light flew past and the roar of the diesels drowned out the purr of his own engines. As a trained engineer his eyes automatically glued to the passing freight looking for potential problems with the loads, wheels or axles. As the last container flew past, Gene pressed the microphone button and called to the passing freight.

"Amtrak 8 to BNSF 5762, you are looking good on the roll-by."

The radio responded, "Thanks, Amtrak 8, BNSF 5762 out."

Gene responded quickly responded, "Amtrak 8 out."

Soon the dispatcher cut in and gave the all clear for Amtrak 8 to continue on its journey to North Dakota. Gene wasted no time throttling up the locomotive and getting the train in motion. He had lost more than the time he gained since leaving Havre. It was going to be tough out there tonight.

The next fifty minutes passed quickly, there were no more red flags or slow downs for Gene, the young women remained embedded in their novels and the old cowboy dreamed about his life on the prairie and his past years of his life.

The calm was broken by the announcement that Glasgow, Montana, the next station stop, was approaching and they would be there in 5 minutes. George got two passengers ready to depart, Gene throttled his locomotives back, and Ken the conductor checked his manifest to see who would depart and who would board. The crew had an understanding that, when they were late, every minute counted. It was their duty to the engineer to give him as much room for improvement on the time as possible. So when the train stopped, everything clicked, passengers were escorted off and new passengers brought aboard with as much haste as deemed appropriate. In three minutes from stop, the highball was dispatched over the radio. The locomotives revved up once again and out onto the open tracts the Empire Builder charged.

As the train pulled away from the station the intercom announced that the diner was open and that Megan's, Lucia's and Lyle's seats were available. Lucia stood up, gently touched the old man's shoulder to wake him, then offered her hand in assistance, more out of courtesy than pity. Lyle accepted the help with the dignity of a gentleman bowing his head and saying, "Thank you."

Megan led the way down the aisle, followed by her mother, then the aging cowboy brought up the rear. At the diner Lyle stepped in front of the women as the waiter escorted the trio to their table. When the waiter stopped and pointed to the correct table, Lyle quickly and effortlessly pulled the farthest chair out from under the table and said pleasantly, "Here you go, Madam Megan."

Megan, not being aware of the situation, just stood still for a few seconds until her mother touched her arm and whispered for her to sit down. Once sitting Lyle, assisted the pretty teenager by pushing in her chair. Megan quietly squeaked a thanks and promptly turned bright red.

Lyle then grabbed the outer chair pulled it out and motioned with his hand saying, "Madam Lucia."

Lucia also turned a bit red but smiled gratefully as the old gentleman pushed her chair up to the table. As Lyle crossed to the opposite side and sat down the two women reached for their menus, more out of nervousness than hunger. "I'll tell you what," the old man said authoritatively, "I'm buying this for you. Anyone who can put up with these stories deserves at least a meal and a glass of wine." Reaching for the menu Lyle asked, "What type of wine would you ladies like tonight?"

Lucia interrupted, "You don't have to buy us dinner for listening to your stories. I really enjoy listening and learning about your experiences. If anything we should be paying you to learn from your knowledge."

"Nonsense," replied the cowboy, "I would very much enjoy treating two very beautiful young ladies to a fine dinner. This is not something I get a chance to do very often and I would consider it a pleasure if you would allow me this opportunity. I have the financial means so you will not be depriving someone on a fixed income. "

Megan sat fumbling with the menu not really knowing what to say. Her inexperience in such social situations proved a disadvantage while her mother was able to handle the situation gracefully. "Thank you. If I had known we were invited to such a lavish party, I would have taken more time to dress and apply my makeup," Lucia replied giggling half joking and half serious.

This seemed to lighten the situation. At the same time the waiter ushered another woman passenger to sit at the table. "Since seating is limited," the attendant explained, "we ask that you accept the full table of four."

"Sure," the trio replied almost in unison. After all introductions, Lyle continued where he left off. "You two are just fine the way you are. After all, we are aboard the twenty-first century Empire Builder, not the twentieth-century version with parlor and observation cars. And besides, both of you are a fine sight for these old eyes," Lyle said.

Megan blushed and figured the old man's flirting was harmless, and besides, as a teenager, no one talked to her like that. She figured she would embrace the situation and might as well enjoy the charms of this elderly man. She decided to play the part and responded, "Why thank you. I am not used to such compliments Were I not so young, I might perceive such flattery as an invitation to get to know a certain distinguished gentleman a bit better." When she finished she glanced at her mother, who's jaw was noticeably hanging open, and winked with a smile. A slight nudge with her elbow brought Lucia out of the trance so she once again began fumbling with the menu.

Turning visibly toward Megan, Lucia asked, "What kind of wine would you like? I'm having the Charaz. I think you might like it also."

"Sure, I'll have the Charaz," Megan replied. "What are you going to have to eat? The salmon looks good. I think I'll try it."

Lucia picked up the menu and looked briefly down the right side of the brightly colored page. Yes, I'll have the salmon also."

"Mom," Megan questioned, "aren't you supposed to have white wine with fish?

"Oh, it doesn't matter anymore. People drink whatever kind of wine they like," Lucia responded.

As the waiter approached, Lyle instructed that they would like a bottle of Charaz. Unfortunately the train only carries the tiny one-serving bottles of wine. So everyone agreed it would have to do.

Waiting for the wine and for the server to take their order, there was just small talk about the upcoming wedding, Christmas wishes and the weather differences between Montana and Minnesota, and a bit from the fourth, visibly uncomfortable seated guest.

The waiter quickly opened the small bottles and dispensed each into the pedestal wine glasses on the table.

Lyle was the first to reach for a glass, Tasting it and nodding politely to the waiter he placed the glass back down on the table. When the two women had their glasses in front of them, Lyle raised a toast. "A toast to a very merry Christmas, and to the deepest and most sincere wishes bestowed upon two of the most lovely and polite ladies that I have become friends with."

When he finished they all raised their glasses to the center of the table, said "Cheers," clinked them together and took a sip.

Megan held her glass up a little longer and replied to the toast, "Thank you, Mr. Corman. Here is to a fine gentleman who is right now making a middle-aged woman and a teenager feel like the first lady of Montana. Cheers and may all go well for you on your trip and wedding."

All three took sips as the waiter approached to take their order. After they ordered there was more small talk until the food arrived.

As each member of the group took stock of their plates and

assessed how they were going to eat the meal as elegantly as possible, Lyle began to relinquish more stories from the past.

"After about three years of cowboying and living out with the cattle, the boss asked me if I'd like to try my hand at traveling with the stock on the railroad. I didn't know much about traveling, but I did know how to take care of cattle. With a little persuading, I accepted the task.

"The first batch of steers I had to move were going over to Butte to feed the miners. We had to drive about 50 head into Harlowtown, where we loaded the cattle onto the Milwaukee Road stock cars. This was September so the weather wasn't too hot or too cold. At that time a lot of railroads had what they called Drover cars. These were just cabooses, or converted boxcars, where the cowboys attending the traveling stock would sleep while the train was moving. It was the rancher's responsibility to feed and water the stock. On this first trip there was a bunch of us local ranchers bringing steers over to Butte so it was pretty easy. We all knew each other, the trip was short and the weather was perfect. We only had to stop and feed and water the cattle once, so it was mostly sitting around shooting the bull and playing cards."

With each bite of his food Lyle would pause long enough to chew. He would quickly resume his tale between bites without a loss of momentum. He continued, "Well I thought that was just the life. When I got back I told the boss that I'd be happy to babysit those cattle anytime he needed.

"I'm sure you've heard of the dust bowl of 1935 and 1936. Out on our ranch we had a good source of water, coming down from the mountains, so we really never suffered. But it did have a large impact on beef prices in the east. We started shipping cattle to St. Paul, Milwaukee and Chicago. Now that is when things got interesting. It started in January that year. I volunteered to take two loads to market in St. Paul. I thought it would be neat to go and visit my birthplace on the way home. For some reason we had to ship these poor cows all the way up to Malta on the Great Northern mainline just to ship them to St. Paul. When I got the steers loaded I went looking for the Drover car. Well this train didn't have one. I guess they were all busy or something. I was told I'd have to bunk in the caboose with the train crew. When I stepped into that caboose I was greeted by the meanest bunch of SOB's I ever encountered. Instantly they began calling me names and that I smelled like cattle dung. They made it clear, in no uncertain terms, that I was not bunking in their caboose. I asked politely what I was supposed to do. They held the door open and said I could walk behind the train or I could bunk with the cattle in the cars. They really didn't care."

Lucia interrupted, "Why would they do something like that? Isn't that what the caboose was for?"

"Well," Lyle replied, "you had to know what the railroad was like in those days. These were bull-headed, independent men who spent most of their lives out on the railroad and worked for very little pay. They just wanted their way, and no one was going to stop them. In any case, there was no point arguing, so I just headed back toward the cattle car. I had only been in this car once and I couldn't believe they would want me to sleep with a bunch of wild cattle in a moving train car. The steers would surely trample me each time they lost their balance on a curve or at a stop.

"Thank goodness, I met another drover as I was walking toward my cattle cars. He explained that it was not unusual to find train crews reluctant to share their quarters with cattlemen. He explained how to build a bunk across the end of the car by finding old lumber laying around the yard. You just stuck the planks between the side boards of the car and you had a cozy place to stay. You remember, we had to feed our cows on their journey to market so we would have hay at each stop. We grabbed a bunch, threw it on our bunk and crawled in. There were regulations that said every 26 hours we had to rest 8 hours or so. During that time we fed and watered the animals. It was in our best interest to keep the cattle healthy and fat so we would get the best price at market. The drover showed me how to bunk in the hay and actually survive fairly comfortably. Now, this was January and the temperature was around zero so it was no Holiday Inn or anything. The heat from the cattle provided a little warmth and combined with the insulation of hay I survived. We would stop frequently so I could get off and head into the local beanry for warm food and coffee. At the 26-hour mark I would let the cattle out of the cars into railroad holding pens so they could get feed and water. It was freezing cold carrying water and hay to those cows; it didn't matter if it was 1:00 o'clock in the morning or in the afternoon. You had to unload, feed and then reload the cattle."

The old cowboy's narration stopped as the train went over a particularly rough switch. Outside the window the sky had darkened so the millions of stars began to dot the Montana skies. The cold arctic wind had driven all moisture from the air leaving the stars an unobstructed opportunity to poke through, to dazzle all eyes that gazed upward. Eventually the moon would rise and steal the show with all of its overpowering brightness. But meanwhile the stars ruled the night as Amtrak 8 plowed through the evening and toward the North Dakota night.

Lucia finished her meal first and waited politely as Lyle continued his yarn. "This was not the same trip I took in the fall. Eventually, we reached St. Paul where I was abandoned down at the stock yards. Not thinking about bringing along a good set of clothes I pretty much had to clean up and sleep the best I could at a local fourth rate motel next to the stockyards. There were drunken cowboys singing all night, whores knocking on your door and every type of criminal lurking behind each bush and card table. I quickly abandoned the idea of looking up my relatives and hopped aboard the first passenger train back to Montana. I was never so happy to see my little cabin and the big skies of Montana."

Everyone had finished eating and the waiter returned to collect the dishes. Lucia offered once again, "You don't have to buy our supper. We should be paying for yours since you are sharing such wonderful stories with us."

"No," Lyle replied sternly, "this one is on me. I told you before I don't get many chances to buy supper for two beautiful young ladies."

Megan thanked Lyle saying, "Thanks so much. We both appreciate it very much. Are you sure there is nothing we can do to repay you?

"There is nothing. You have been more than kind just listening and providing intelligent conversation. It is not something I run across every day in these parts of the world," the old man replied. "And now I must succumb to the forces of nature and visit the restroom. I will meet you fine women back at the seat."

When Megan and Lucia got to their seat and settled in, Megan turned toward her mother and scolded, "Mom, this guy is hitting on you. And you are flirting back. It's kind of sick; this guy is 40 years older than you."

Lucia turned and said seriously, "Megan, sometimes you need to make people feel good. He wants to think he is impressing two young women. It makes him feel young, something he lost many years ago. I know there is nothing between us and I am pretty sure he knows it too. I am not flirting."

"It's just kind of gross—your mom acting like a teenager with an old man." Megan retorted, " I guess I'll understand when I'm old like you." She smiled.

Lucia reached over gave her daughter a hug and began tickling her ribs saying, "I'm going to abandon you and Dad for this guy. When you wake up in the morning I'll be sitting over there locked in a huge kiss."

"You're sick, Mom," the teenager replied laughing out loud. "Stop tickling me or I'll pee in my pants."

George, the car attendant, looked down the aisle at the passengers: some were sleeping, some reading, some talking, others visiting and a few just staring out the window. It was those last few that made George wonder, *What are these people thinking? What makes them so pensive on this the eve of one of the most celebrated and family-oriented holidays in the U.S.?* As he walked down the aisle he paid particular attention to these passengers. He would make a stop and ask them if they needed any of the amenities. It seemed the response was always the same. "Thanks but they were fine."

None of them ever seemed to want the extra attention. As an experienced car attendant, George had seen thousands of these passengers and could never quite figure them out. He would imagine some story behind each one ranging from lonely to psychopath. It was just something he did while attending to his duties.

When he approached the mother and daughter from Minnesota, he was greeted by the opposite type of personality, bubbly, friendly and very much appreciative of kindness. When he offered the pillow or blanket they accepted and were articulate as they expressed their gratitude. These were George's favorite. This is what made him love his job. Helping people and being appreciated for it.

As George moved down the aisle, he stepped aside for an old cowboy he'd seen before on other trips. As he passed the man he asked, "Lyle, you old cow dog, how the heck are you doing?"

Lyle smiled from ear to ear. "I'm doing as well as can be expected considering the company I keep."

George gave the old man a very slight punch on the arm and, with a smile, said, "Come on now, I'm not that bad, am I? Now don't you answer that, because I'll make the rest of your trip mighty miserable if I don't like what I hear."

"Oh, I know that," the old man answered, "I've seen that you can be mighty mean when you want."

"Come on now, I've never given you anything but the best service Amtrak has to offer," George replied with a wink.

"Oh, I know," Lyle remarked. "I'm just keeping you on your toes. Now get on with your work; I gotta go and finish my story as two beautiful young ladies are waiting for me."

George turned to face Lucia and Megan. Winking, he said to Lyle, "You old dog. Now don't you be harassing my passengers. These two are the nicest ones in the coach and I don't want you chasing them away on me."

Lyle turned and sat down in his seat. As the old man was sitting down, George bent down and whispered to Megan, "This old guy is full of stories and I think I believe all of them. He's been around a long time. Only thing is you have to be careful or he'll bend your ear all night. He is harmless. I've known him for a few years. He's a regular."

Megan smiled up at the attendant saying, "I figured so. I love listening to him; it won't be a bother."

George whispered in reply, "If it is let me know."

"Thanks," replied Megan

Just as George turned and headed back down the aisle the overhead announced that the train would be arriving in Wolf Point in a few minutes.

Megan turned toward Lyle and said, "You were telling us about your train trips with the cattle."

"Oh ya, that second trip was a bust all right. Well when I got back to the ranch I told the boss all about it and he just smiled and told me I must have done something right. He then told me that he had just gotten the best price ever for his beef. At that point he proceeded to give me that cabin I'd been fixing up and 600 acres around it. Now that may seem like a lot, but in those days 600 acres wasn't worth but 600 dollars and that old cabin was worth a few thousand dollars.. But it was something all the same. I appreciated it.

"The next month we had 35 more head to send to St. Paul. Again we were to use the GN up here in Malta. So we trucked the cattle up there and this time, when I got them loaded, one of the crew came and directed me to the drover car. There were six of us bunked in the car from all over Montana. As soon as we got moving they started drinking, playing cards and just carrying on. I wanted nothing to do with drinking and gambling with a bunch of strangers so I just hung back and took the ridicule from the rest. I tried to catch some sleep, but with them carrying on so, I couldn't really get much rest. These guys just kept it up. I took it upon myself to mind the cattle and ventured out to feed and water the cows each time the train stopped. They were still going at it when we had the 26-hour rest stop. I was alone and had to take care of all six cars of cattle. That meant I had to feed and water close to 200 head. It was no easy chore, so by the time I finished I was pretty steamed. It was not the cattle's fault that their drovers were a worthless bunch of hooligans. I kept trying to think of something to do to make these drunks pay for what they were doing.

About the time I finished carrying the hay and water to the animals it was about time for us to load back up. Thank goodness the crews of that train felt sorry and helped me out. I'd probably still be out there trying to get those beef up into those cars. The conductor even invited me to bunk in the caboose. I accepted without hesitation and collapsed once I got in the door and warmed up. After twelve hours of sleep I finally woke up with the conductor standing over me with a cup of hot coffee and a plate of eggs cooked on the stove right there in the caboose.

After a hearty meal we talked for a while and came up with a plan for the drover car. There was a car of hogs on the train right behind the cattle and the conductor had keys to all the padlocks on the cars. At the next stop, it just so happened that a nice boar the size of a small horse escaped from its car and somehow ended up in the drover car. By this time these guys were so drunk and passed out they didn't even hear the door open and that boar come through the door. Even more amazing is that somehow the door got locked from the outside so these guys couldn't even get out.

That train got going again and didn't stop again for about an hour. By this time we had plenty of time for laughs. As soon as the train stopped, we walked back to their drover car and you should have heard the commotion. Those poor bastards were about half out of their wits by the time we got that door open. Once we got that door open that old pig shot out and darn near knocked us down, but even funnier was the five of them drovers falling over each other to get out, all of them in their skivies. I thought I was going to die from laughter. The inside of that car looked like a war had been going on—there was shit everywhere. I still don't know if it was from the guys or the pig. We never did let on just how the old boar got in that car, but I suspect they knew. I spent the rest of the trip in the caboose. But I was never alone feeding those cattle."

Lyle looked at his watch during the pause. "Looks to me like we should be in North Dakota pretty quick. I didn't notice the train stopping so I'd bet we'll be in Williston soon."

Lucia pulled out here schedule card and reached for her purse to find her glasses. Just then the overhead announced that soon they would be arriving in Williston, North Dakota, and that the train had just passed into the central time zone. Spontaneously everyone in the car looked at their watches. At the blink of an eye everyone had lost an hour of their life. Unless they returned back over the time zone that hour was gone forever.

As the train passed by Fort Union on the Missouri River, the moon began to dart in and out of the clouds. Its bright light showed a coating of two to three inches of fresh snow on the ground.

Gene slowed the locomotives as he looked out at the landscape and thought that this was what Christmas was supposed to look like. Fresh snow, cold, clear air and everything looking so peaceful. As he passed the grain elevators on the outskirts of town, he applied the brakes and slowed to a crawl. At the station Ken radioed, "Two more, Amtrak. One more, Amtrak. That'll do, Amtrak," as he guided the engineer with the number of car lengths for when to stop.

Soon the twelve passengers departed and eight more got on. Ken radioed the highball and off they went once more. Gene checked his watch. He'd made up 16 minutes with the help of the crew. If they got to Minot without delay there was a possibility they could cut down the time by another ten minutes. He was feeling good. He would be off the train before Christmas arrived in North Dakota.

Outside, the wide open North Dakota fields were bathed in white moonlight broken by the shadows of clouds darting up and down the hillsides. Off to the south, the Missouri and Yellowstone Rivers co-mingled their waters to begin their arduous journey halfway across the continent down to St. Louis. It was at this point that the steam boat captains had to abandon their ships on the way up the mighty Missouri. Many a fur trader passed through this confluence bringing his load of furs to be traded for life's necessities. But tonight the river was quiet, no steamboats or even a canoe plied the waters on this Christmas Eve night. The river had been replaced as the transportation medium, surpassed once by the railroad and once more by the automobile and the concrete highway. Now only the shadows of the clouds danced across its waters, climbing the banks from side to side, up the rock-strewn bluffs, and down the ravines and draws. The light glistening off the snow faded and brightened as the shadows moved. The river was as peaceful as it had been two hundred years earlier.

Back on the mainline, the steel wheels of the cars sang in rhythm to the dancing shadows passing miles of desolate fields and pastures. Up on the hillsides occasional oil wells raised and lowered their heads following the rhythm. These were the rhythms that men dreamed about. First was the gurgle of the river and its transportation system, then the singing of the steel wheel on the rail and its more efficient and faster mode of transportation, now the oil well providing the fuel for the personal mode of transportation with all of its benefits and short comings, the automobile.

Yet on this Christmas Eve hardly a person aboard the Empire Builder even thought about those oil wells, the river or even the rest of the rail transportation system. They were on their way to see loved ones and the celebrations and enjoyment that accompanied such occasions.

George finished his rounds as the last of his passengers returned from the diner. He was relieved that everything had gone smoothly since East Glacier; he really would like to get some rest tonight and be in a good mood when he got home tomorrow. As he reached the end of the car he turned and looked back at his passengers, thinking what a nice mix of people he'd run across on this trip. Maybe it was the holiday spirit in them, or maybe it was the holiday spirit in him; it didn't matter. They were behaving themselves and that was all that mattered. The car attendant then descended the stairs and checked on the rest of the coach before retiring to his bunk for a cat nap.

Lyle watched silently as Fort Union passed by in the moonlight. After the train stopped in Williston, he turned to Megan and Lucia and said, "I am going to make another trip to the restroom. I'd be happy to get you something while I'm up."

"No thanks," Lucia said. "Do you want something Megan?"

"No, I'm fine thanks," the teenager replied.

Lyle got up and repeated his trip to the bathroom downstairs in the coach. The young woman opened their novels and began reading once again. After several minutes passed the old man made his way down the aisle and returned to his seat.

Lucia turned toward the old gentleman saying, "You seem to know this route pretty well. Do you take it often?"

"Yes, my wife was from Four Buttes up near the Canadian border. We would take the train this far to visit her family," the old man replied.

"Is she still living," Megan inquired making a face at her mother, still not understanding the relationship between her mother and this old cowboy.

"No," he replied, "Verna died about twelve years ago now. But I still go to visit her family about twice a year. Her nephew owns a spread up there so we sit around and swap cattle stories."

Megan cut in, " Sorry about your loss. It's nice you still visit with her family. How long were you married?"

Lyle responded, "Thirty-eight years. I didn't get married until I settled down and had a ranch of my own."

"Still," Lucia commented, "that is a long time."

"Yes, I guess so," the old man responded. "It just seems like such a short time. It is only about a third of my life. That means I've lived two thirds of life without the companionship of my soul mate."

Lucia looked wide eyed and remarked, "You know, I never would have thought of it like that. That's amazing and a bit depressing. How are you doing with that?"

"Oh, I get up every day, miss her and then go about my business." Lyle replied, "It never really gets easier. All my friends told me I would get over it and that it would get easier with time. That is just not the case. Everything I see, hear or feel, I want to tell her, and I do. But she can never tell me anything back."

Lucia reached across the aisle and put her hand on the old man's arm. "It's tough, but just keep talking to her. I'm sure she's listening and perhaps she's talking back through different means, like you going to this wedding. I am sure those young people will have plenty to say; the circle of life continues."

"Yes, you are right," Lyle whispered. "I actually can hear her saying the same thing right now. It's amazing. I just need to listen."

"Yes, I believe we all just need to listen. Our loved ones and ancestors talk to us every day We need to take the time to listen to them and discover what they are trying to say," Lucia replied.

"Let me tell you how we met," Lyle said as he tried to brighten the mood. "It was June of 1946 and I was coming home from one of the cattle selling expeditions in Chicago. I took the Empire Builder because I had to meet my boss in Minot, North Dakota, to help pick up a new tractor for the ranch. I got to Minot and had to wait for my boss to pick me up so I sat outside the station on one of those benches. I noticed a good-looking redhead walking down the platform carrying a large carpet bag. All of a sudden her heel caught in a crack right in front of me. I heard a snap and I watched as she crumpled like a rag doll, screaming in pain. I flew off of that bench to help but the pain continued and she let me know it. As a cowboy I knew how to take care of broken legs but never one as petite as this one. I helped relieve the pain as best I could, by laying her on her back. I could see she had a nasty break so I got the station agent to call a doctor. By this time a small crowd had gathered, so I dug through my bags to get the blanket I always carried with me. I apologized to the woman for the crude blanket, but she accepted it with a smile. Once the doctor arrived, he diagnosed the severe fracture and immediately prepared to transport the woman to the local hospital. As they put her on the stretcher, the poor lady grasped my hand and asked if I would go along. I agreed and told the station agent to let my boss know where I was and that I'd be back as soon as possible.

"After the doctor set her leg, I remained in her room where we talked for over an hour about her life. I learned that her husband had just been killed in the war, that she really had nowhere to go and that she had no money to pay the hospital bill. She had pulled up roots and was on her way to an aunt's in Fargo to make a fresh start.

"I told her I'd pick up the hospital bill and that I'd be back to visit in the morning. First I had to get to work with my boss and that tractor. She held my hand, said she understood and then made me promise I'd be back. She really was not someone you could ever break a promise to—so the next morning I was there. We talked for hours and I helped so she could take care of herself. I had asked my boss for the rest of the week off. He realized the importance of this mission, so he gladly approved.

"I spent the next few days at her side until the doctor released her. I wanted to continue helping but I couldn't hardly have her come back to my cabin. I called my boss and persuaded him to hire her on as a maid and secretary.

"From there we dated for a year and were married once the war was over. She continued on as secretary until my boss sold me the ranch. In fact she was the ranch's secretary until she died."

Lyle let the conversation trail off and neither one of the women could think of anything to say. The old man just smiled to himself, sat back in his seat and closed his eyes. In a few minutes he was dreaming of the open plains and the big sky of Montana. He didn't even wake up for the station stop at Stanley, where the train took on several new passengers before resuming its journey.

Lucia and Megan continued with their novels until sleep overtook both.

Up front in the cab, Gene applied the brakes as he crossed over the highway bridge coming into Stanley, North Dakota. The small wooden station was a remnant of the old Great Northern days and was completely dark. Apparently there was a problem with the electrical system at the station so the platform lighting remained dark. As the boarding passengers emerged out of the darkness the open doorway of the train appeared as a beacon calling its passengers home. Once the highball was given and the doors slammed shut all was dark and quiet at the Stanley station. Hardly anyone in town even noticed the train as it slid in and out in the darkness. The moon slid behind a cloud for the last time as the train began catching up on the Alberta Clipper weather system, which had pushed its way from Western Canada into the Midwest, bringing its light dusting of snow along for its proof of existence.

Gene looked down at his speed indicator on his computer screen and noted with satisfaction that he was holding it right at 79 mile per hour. On this relatively flat stretch, he could allow the locomotives to hold their own. In about an hour and a half he'd pull his train into Minot and hand the reins over to the next crew. He'd made up several minutes in spite of the delay with the freight. If he held the speed real close and had no more delays he'd make up a few more minutes. He loved BNSF railway, whose tracks he was using, when they allowed him the room to move. In the meantime a few flakes of snow glistened in his headlights. He was going to catch up to that weather front after all. No big deal, a little snow on Christmas Eve would be a welcome sight.

The track side detector broke the spell and brought Gene's mind back to the present.

"BNSF detector milepost 923.6—No defects—Repeat—No defects. Temperature—minus 18 degrees. Think safety—BNSF detector out."

Gene radioed the confirmation to the dispatcher and kept the speed right at track limit.

Lyle woke as the train slowed down as it crossed the Gassman Coulee bridge. Looking out the window he saw the city lights reflecting off the blanket of fresh snow on the ground. *Now this is Christmas,* he thought. The few flakes still falling really presented a postcard scene of every childhood memory. He glanced over at the women and noticed Lucia was awake and reading. Whispering he pointed to the window, "Take a look; it's beautiful."

Lucia put her book down and leaned over he daughter to get a closer look out the window. "Wow," she whispered back, "that is really gorgeous. It looks like a Currier and Ives painting."

"Yes, there is something so peaceful about newly fallen snow. It reminds me of the first Christmas Verna and I had together. We had been married for four months and were living with my boss at the main ranch house. We decided to spend Christmas at my cabin. I was fixing it up and wanted to show it off to my new bride. I had things pretty well tidied up by this time and it was comfortable and not just a bit romantic. Early Christmas Eve morning we took two horses and rode down to the cabin. On the way down I chopped down a small fir tree and dragged it into the house. The afternoon sky threatened with occasional flakes of snow so fearing the worst, and remembering the blizzards of past, I quickly went about chopping a week's supply of wood and brought in enough water to last three days.

As I was working, Verna made popcorn and decorated the tree with popcorn and homemade cookies she'd brought along. I recall kidding her that if we got snowed in we could at least eat the tree.

About the time I finished my chores the snow came down in earnest. Not the howling, white out, of a blizzard snow, but the gentle soft type of everyone's dreams. We just watched out the window for a while and just before dark we decided to take a walk. There is still nothing quite as memorable in my life as that walk in the falling snow holding hands with the first and last woman I would ever dream of doing such a thing with. We walked in that silence for over an hour, neither of us really talking. We just enjoyed each other and the serenity of the world that night. About midnight we regretfully had to return to the cabin. It was wet and we were cold so we couldn't stay out all night.

We returned to the warmth of the cabin, stripped off our wet cloths and made love in that cabin for the first time. We held each other for hours, realizing that things would never be the same again. The timing was right, the weather was perfect and the location was a dream. Only once in a lifetime do the stars come together for a night like that. You know that Verna and I never took a walk like that again. It seems like we always had something going on, so when we did walk, we always discussed something. Never did we just walk and enjoy each other's peace. In any case nine months later our son was born."

Lyle paused, as the train stopped for the crew change in Minot. "I can finish this later," he said. "Let's go outside and get some of this fresh air."

Lucia nodded in agreement. "Megan, wake up. Let's go outside for some fresh air."

Megan whimpered, "No, I'm tired."

The mother prodded the teenager and said, "Come on you need to get some fresh air and exercise. You can come back and sleep in a little bit."

"Oh alright, alright, where's my jacket?" the teenager moaned stretching her long arms over her head, which revealed her midriff.

Lucia quickly tickled Megan's bare belly giggling, "Come on, pumpkin, don't be so lazy."

In a few minutes the train rolled ahead to the platform where the doors opened to allow the passengers to stroll the platform and gaze in awe at the retired Great Northern Steam locomotive parked next to the station. The arctic air bit hard at the exposed skin of anyone venturing out on the platform. The two women shivered and clapped their mitten-covered hands together to combat the shivers. "Wow, it is really cold out here," Megan said turning toward Lyle so he could hear above the noise of the other passengers. "It has to be twenty below zero."

Lyle smiled and replied, "Close, the thermometer over on the station says about fifteen below. But isn't it pretty with all the snow glistening? You know, snow only looks like this when it is so cold. Once it gets warm it seems to lose so much of it's sparkle."

Lucia looked around at the streets and alleys that were untouched by tire tracks. The street lights provided circles of light glistening on the fresh snow. In a few seconds she responded, "I've never really noticed that before. But you are right. The snow seems so much fresher in this cold air."

Megan just jumped up and down with her hands covering her ears to prevent frostbite.

Lucia said to the old man, "Will you excuse me? I've got to take care of my daughter here before she freezes to death." Turning to her daughter she yelled, "I'll race you to the end of the train, you rag a muffin."

Megan looked at her mother like she had just escaped from the psychiatric unit.

So Lucia picked up a handful of the fluffy powder, threw it at Megan and took off running down the platform. Megan quickly gave chase. With the head start, Lucia reached the end of the platform first where she grabbed another handful of snow and threw it at her approaching daughter. Laughing loudly she yelled, "Merry Christmas, pumpkin."

In the cold winter air the snow did not pack but just turned to powder as it sailed through the night air. Brushing the glistening snow from her hair the taller Megan grabbed her mother in a bear hug, reached down and stuffed a handful of fresh snow in her mother's face. The pair wrestled playfully giggling the entire time. Using their feet and hands the pair created their own blizzard on that platform in the middle of North Dakota, a few hours before Christmas arrived on the prairie.

Many of the passengers stood amazed at the cheerfulness of the pair and more than a few even created their own snow fight. Soon the entire platform was embroiled in a snow free-for-all. Running back to the door of the coach, the two women wished everyone a Merry Christmas. Even the conductor smiled at the sight, disregarded the safety regulations and allowed the fun to continue. Surely someone could slip and fall in the snow, but this was just too much enjoyment to break up. In a few minutes the cold and wet brought the joy to its own end. With smiles reminiscent of childhood, the passengers talked, joked and even hugged each other as the crew members began herding the passengers into their respective cars.

Lyle stood on the edge of the platform watching and even twice kicked a bit of snow at passing revelers. It was this joy that made his life still worth living.

Soon Lucia and Megan were back at his side panting from the exercise. The melted snow quickly refroze in their hair, providing a crystal-like sparkle to the women. Lyle smiled and put his hand on Lucia's shoulder saying, "You are a terrific mother and a very beautiful woman. If I were not so old and you so happily married, I might try to win your fancy. But this is not to be, so we had better get inside before you and your daughter catch cold." With a smile he held out both of his arms and asked politely, "May I escort you two women to the train?"

Without hesitation Lucia replied, "Well of course," and then she quickly looked at Megan, giving her that look of approval, and took the old man's arm. Megan took the other and on that cold winter night the 97-year-old man escorted two much younger women on to the Empire Builder.

George paused from his duties at the station to watch in amazement as the group of passengers braved the sub-zero cold to engage in a snow fight. First he thought that they must be crazy, then he realized that he really wanted to join them and, finally, came the feeling of longing for his wife and kids. If the Clipper weather system hit Chicago after he got home, he would engage his kids in the same kind of snow fight. As the old man with a woman on each arm entered the train, George smiled and wished each a merry Christmas. He also winked at Lyle as he passed by thinking, *I wonder how he does it: that old cowboy has a woman on each arm.* He then finished cleaning up the vestibule.

George heard the "All aboard" so he quickly stepped outside the door to make sure everyone got into the car safely. After the platform was clear, he stepped aboard and slammed the door shut. Shivering, he removed his jacket and hung it in the closet beside the luggage racks. In a minute the motion began and the train began the click-clack as it crossed the switches in the yard. With each switch came the sway and screech of steel wheels as they crossed the frog. Finally the yard was behind them and they were cleared for the mainline to Grand Forks.

George checked with everyone to make sure they were back in their seats and then retired to his room and bunk. Sleep came quickly and with it the dreams of Christmas Eve present and past.

When the Minnesota women and the Montana man reached their seats, they removed the heavy coats and sat back relaxing in the warmth. Lyle turned to Lucia after a minute and asked, "Do you mind if I finish my story?"

Lucia replied, "Of course not, please do."

"Thanks," the old man responded, "I like to tell about it. Well after my son was born, my boss offered to sell me the ranch. He would build a house a mile down the road so Verna and I could have the ranch homestead. I quickly accepted and went to work on my own ranch. My cowboy days were over and the train trips took on a different meaning. With a lot of good luck, and much hard work, we did pretty well on that ranch. Each Christmas, without fail, Verna and I would visit the cabin where we spent that first Christmas Eve. Never again was it as perfect as that first time, but we always had the memory. My son is grown now and has the ranch. In fact, he is ready to turn it over to his son. I put in the contract for the ranch, that as long as it is in my family, that cabin is to be cared for, like the way I took care of it. It is my wish that some young couple will visit that cabin and experience the same feeling that Verna and I experienced those years ago. When I get to Grand Forks I will give instructions to Jennifer and Scott that next Christmas Eve I will provide an all-expense-paid trip to that cabin. One of these years things will come together like they did for Verna and me."

The old man stopped and reached into his breast pocket, pulled out his wallet and found a business card which he handed to Lucia instructing, "Here is my son's card. If you or anyone in your family needs a break, call my son, explain how you came upon this card and you may use that cabin. When Megan gets married, I want her to try her luck on the first Christmas Eve. If you need traveling money, explain that to my son; it will be provided. I have a fund set aside for the cabin and any special people who may need it. No one knows about the place unless I tell them. So please keep it to yourself so it doesn't get abused. I trust you and your daughter will keep it in confidence."

"Yes," Lucia replied, "we won't tell anyone."

"Thanks, now I am going to get some rest," Lyle responded.

Lucia looked over at her daughter who was fast asleep. Turning to Lyle she asked, "Do you mind if I come and sit over next to you? I would like a window seat to watch the snow. I don't want to wake Megan."

Standing up slowly the old man replied, "Be my guest."

Lucia stepped in front of Lyle and sat down in the seat to watch the lightly falling snow.

Lyle turned and whispered, "I've been rude and doing all the talking here tonight. Tell me something about yourself.

Lucia thought for a minute and replied, "I have not done anything as exciting as you have. I got married out of college to a doctor and stayed home to raise my children until Megan got into high school. I am now a lawyer working for a firm that litigates environmental complaints against huge corporations. I guess I have things pretty well and I do a bit of traveling, nothing as adventurous as your journeys. When my family travels it seems that we always play it safe, never any real adventure seeking.

"I can really appreciate how easy I have things. You've turned on a few lights so I can see just how fortunate we are as a family. So I am just boring. I have two wonderful bright children, a great husband and a lifestyle that fills all of my most remote needs."

Lyle replied, "Trust me my life isn't as adventurous as it sounds. In the time when I was young, doing what I did was not so far off from the norm. Think of the things you did when you were young, then tell them in stories to your daughter. It will seem to her that you were the adventurous one."

"I suppose if you look at it that way you are right," Lucia responded.

"Think about it and come up with a few stories. You will be surprised with the response," Lyle said.

Lucia said nothing. Looking out the window she couldn't think of any stories that she would like to relate to her daughter. She thought maybe it best to wait so she didn't give Megan any ideas for crazy things.

Lyle sensed what was going through Lucia's head and continued, "I bet you are scared of telling your daughter some of the things you did as a teenager. Well guess what, it won't matter if you tell her what you did. Kids will think of their own crazy adventures. If you relay yours maybe she can learn from your mistakes. Tell her the stories as a learning experience. Don't preach; just relay the stories and possible outcomes. She is bright enough to figure out what is the correct outcome."

Lucia replied, "Thanks, it is something I'll have to think about and practice."

Lyle's eyes were getting heavy and his head was beginning to nod, so Lucia trailed off and soon was watching every snowflake that passed by the window. Lyle's eye closed and he fell into a sound sleep.

Soon the snow outside the window and the rocking of the car lulled Lucia to sleep. In one of those unintentional acts you do when sleep disables your senses, Lucia leaned over and snuggled into Lyle's shoulder and let her dreams take to places far away.

As Gene pulled the train into the service area of the Minot rail yard the crew flagged the train and began to fill the water in the tanks, empty the sewage and restock any supplies required. Gene finished completing his report and exchanged the controls with Greg Finley, who would bring the train to St. Cloud. The official time was still two and a half hours before midnight so Gene had made it before Christmas. It was Greg who would welcome Christmas to the Empire Builder. As soon as the crew was finished and the blue flags pulled, Greg pulled ahead to the platform and the awaiting passengers. As he sorted through the papers and looked over the previous shift report, he glanced in the mirror and noticed the snow flying. He returned to his work but quickly took another look. Many of the passengers were laughing and comically throwing snow at each other. It reminded him of the old college parties he experienced twenty years ago. He smiled and was glad that people were enjoying themselves and the trip. He was sure many would remember the snow fight for years to come.

As the "All aboard" was called, Greg closed his notebook and slid it aside to begin his journey across the North Dakota countryside on this frigid Christmas Eve night. The "Highball Amtrak" sounded over the radio so he notched the throttle up and waited for the engines to come alive and bring the train out across the yard switches and finally onto the mainline. Slowly the train began to move and he was on his way.

Once out on the mainline the activity was light. If there were no slow orders from the temperature, Greg would make some significant time. As it was, he was holding his own. The Rugby stop was insignificant, as there was not much activity at the central North Dakota station. Onward they charged. Now the terrain changed from flat to rolling hills around Devils Lake. Greg welcomed Christmas somewhere between Rugby and Devils Lake. It was a bit ironic that he welcomed the holiday celebrating the beginning of the Christian religion coming into a city named after the Devil.

Outside Devils Lake, North Dakota, the track side detector reported a temperature of minus twenty-one degrees. The engineer reported the temperature to the dispatcher and reduced his speed by ten miles per hour. In temperatures this cold, steel becomes brittle and failures can occur. To reduce the chance of failure, speed restrictions are put in place for temperature extremes. Amtrak 8 would lose more time on its trip east toward the metropolitan cities of the Midwest. Very few of the passengers were aware of the slow down. Most were asleep and dreaming of Christmas at home.

The Devils Lake stop was a bit more hectic, as more passengers boarded than departed. It took a few minutes for the attendants to get everyone situated. Greg looked across the street at the old Great Northern Hotel. The wedge-shaped building was once the palace of North Dakota. Now it's purpose was a senior living center. Though not as glamorous an occupation as in the past, it was at least restored and from the outside as beautiful as when built. Greg imagined the many stories that the building could tell, some good, others not so good. He imagined many big shots would have been brought down if the walls could talk.

The "Highball" crackled and Greg once again notched up the throttle. Soon he would come down out of the hills and into the flat Red River Valley with its fertile fields of corn, soybeans and sugar beets. It was then a short trip to Grand Forks and Minnesota.

The car lunged as it resumed its journey east. Lyle and Lucia awoke simultaneously. Looking down at his watch Lyle whispered, "Look, it's Christmas. Merry Christmas. I hope the peace I felt 64 years ago extends to you and your daughter. I had always hoped that that peace would extend throughout the world. I guess that hasn't happened yet. But an old man like me keeps hoping."

Lucia whispered back, "Merry Christmas, Lyle. I wish you would see your hopes fulfilled with peace throughout the world." With that, she reached over and gently kissed the old weather-worn cheek of the old man. Saying further, "You have given me insight and livened my trip with your stories and tales. I will remember this Christmas forever. When Megan gets married I will be sure she gets in touch with your son. I would like for her to experience that same feeling. I am afraid that her generation will miss out on so many of those pleasures in life, giving up simple pleasures for fast-paced self-gratification. Thanks again for dinner and the experience"

Lyle smiled and said, "You are welcome. It gave me extreme pleasure to please you and Megan. You have given me a very important Christmas present, your friendship. Thank you. You know you can use that cabin yourself any time you like. Just give me a call or drop a note."

Megan awoke with the same jostling as the other passengers. Looking next to her, she noticed that the seat was empty. Looking across the aisle her mother was sitting next to the old cowboy and not believing her eyes she was kissing him. The teenager rubbed her eyes and looked over once more. Her mother was now sitting back and just looking out the window. For a while Megan thought that her mother was really going to have an affair.

Lucia asked the old man if he knew where they were.

The old man replied without hesitation, "Devils Lake. There is the Great Northern Hotel. I stayed there a few times in past years. Used to be a nice place, then went into decline and now I see it looks restored. We have a little more than an hour until Grand Forks."

"Thanks," Megan replied. "Are you getting excited to see your sister?"

"Yes, it has been a while. I don't know that I'll have enough to talk about," the old man said. "I live way out there and she here in the city. But most of all I don't know how to talk to the young people any longer. Things are so different now. We don't have anything in common."

Lucia picked her book off of her lap. Turning in her seat, she looked the old man right in his eyes and began, "You have so much to tell young people. You just spent hours talking to me and Megan. Megan is impressed and intrigued; I know she would love to sit and listen to you for hours. You are very articulate. Tell your stories, relay how your feelings shaped your life, let them know that they are not the first to experience loneliness, heartache, suffering and happiness. Your experiences will help shape young lives, tell them about these experiences. In fact I think you should convince one of your younger relatives to record your experiences. This is a way of life that vanished years ago. You are lucky enough to be alive and still have the faculties to relay them to people. You told me to relay stories to my daughter; think of Jennifer as your daughter." Megan stopped and waited for a response. But there was none. The old man stared ahead and just nodded his head in agreement.

The woman reached out and took the old man's hand gently and said, "You have influenced me. Your gift to your grand niece will be more of an influence than you will ever know. Imagine if her and her husband experience the night the way you and your wife did. That will be a gift that lasts a lifetime. Keep up the good work. You still have a lot to live for. Verna would be so proud."

"Thanks," the old man replied. "You are so kind to an old man. You were patient while I flirted, and pretended I was young again. I thought I could convince you I was a worthy suitor. Take care of that daughter of yours and teach her the kindness you are so adept at. I hope your husband appreciates who you really are." With a grin he broke the seriousness saying, "If not I'll be right there. I have money and charm. Tell him to look out."

Lucia laughed out loud and said, "I'll tell him. I'm not sure he'd be too worried. We have great love for each other, even though it may be a bit unconventional. But I will tell him. But in all seriousness I may take you up on your cabin."

Outside the window the train had descended into the valley where the tracks were straight as an arrow. The snow had increased in intensity causing the lights of the Air Force base to become glowing globes in the night. Soon after passing the brightly lit base the train began to slow for the Grand Forks station.

The station was built outside of town and is fairly inconvenient for most passengers. As the train slowed, Lyle stood up to depart. He reached out a hand to shake hands with the woman and newfound friend. Lucia took the hand and clasped it gently, saying, "I'll walk you to the door."

Megan stood up and said, "It was such a pleasure meeting you and listening to your stories. Merry Christmas. I hope everyone in your family has a great holiday and the wedding goes wonderfully."

Lucia then stood as the old man stepped back and let her go first down the aisle and stairs to the door. Without a word she turned to the tall aged cowboy, gave him a big hug and a soft kiss on the cheek. As the old man bent down to accept the embrace he smiled. When the moment ended he stood up, turned, grabbed the duffel bag from the attendant and stepped through the door. Outside on the platform he turned briefly and slowly raised his left hand in a wave. Then he turned back and walked down the platform. Lucia just slightly raised her right hand in a corresponding wave, smiled and watched until the attendant closed the large stainless door. As she climbed the stairs and walked down the aisle to return to her seat, Lucia felt warm inside and remembered how the old man had appreciated her kindness and that he was not some dirty old man hitting on a younger woman for the thrill of a sexual encounter. She sat down and looked at her daughter. She would do her best to teach the things the old man had talked about. She then said softly, "I'll tell you about it sometime. Until then don't ask."

As the train pulled out of the station, Lucia looked at the group of people gathered around the cowboy in various handshakes and embraces. This was not the last she ever saw of the cowboy from Cutbank, Montana.

After the noise of the station stop subsided, Lucia returned to her seat alongside Megan, dug her book from her bag and began to read. Megan squirmed a bit, then quickly fell back asleep. Outside the window the snow blew past in gentle white clouds, distorting any scenery that may have been visible. Lucia continued to read until her eyes grew heavy and she fell asleep. Even while sleeping she kept in the back of her mind that in a half an hour they would be in Fargo and would be home for Christmas.

Outside the snow continued to fall and Greg continued on his journey toward Fargo. The freights were holed up in their sidings and he passed every signal showing green. This was the way a passenger train was supposed to operate. Keep the throttle notched out and let the locomotives do their work. Hit the schedule and keep the passengers happy. Soon the station at Fargo would come into view. After the brief stop he'd be off and running once again. It was Christmas, and he suspected he would be losing more passengers than he gained. Greg was into the rhythm of the mainline. After Fargo, two more stops, and then he'd be in St. Cloud. He'd then be off until the return trip to Minot and home.

George walked down the aisle to the sleeping women and gently touched Lucia's shoulder. Whispering he said, "Ten minutes and we'll be in Fargo. Please check to make sure you don't leave anything behind. Thanks."

Lucia rubbed her dry eyes and gently shook Megan's arm. "Come on, pumpkin, it's time to get off."

Megan rolled back in her seat, yawned, and stretched her arms over her head revealing her soft white belly. Bringing her arms down she pulled down her shirt, leaned forward, put on her shoes and sat back asking, "What time is it?"

Lucia looked at her watch squinted and replied, "I don't know."

Reaching her arm to her daughter she asked, "Can you read this thing? My eyes are so dry I can't see it without my glasses."

Reaching over and twisting her mother's arm she exclaimed, "Quarter after two."

"Good," Lucia replied. "We are on time. Make sure you have everything. Where's your book?"

"Right here," Megan explained as she stood up to check her things.

"OK," her mother replied standing and stepping into the aisle, "let's go downstairs."

Both women reached for the seat backs as the coach rolled back and forth on the rough tracks. Weaving down the aisle they descended the stairs to see George with the window open, breathing the fresh cold air. "It's snowing outside and really beautiful; take a look"

The attendant stepped back and let the women look out the open window. The scene was breathtaking, both from the cold air rushing past the window and the surreal sight of the city approaching with each streetlight surrounded by a halo of light reflected off of the falling snow. On the ground the snow reflected a perfect circle around each lamp giving the false impression that the world was flat. As they passed the flashing red lights of the crossing gate they could see the outline of the street beyond. No tire tracks. Just the straight ribbon in the snow.

Greg notched back the throttle as the conductor radioed, “I’ll spot you at the five car, Amtrak.”

“Roger, five car, Amtrak out,” Greg responded.

Within a few minutes he had pulled the throttle all the way back and was applying the air to the brakes.

The radio cut in, “Three cars, Amtrak,”

Greg applied a bit more air to slow the train. “Two more, Amtrak,” came the radio.

“One more, Amtrak,” the radio instructed. Greg let off a bit on the air so the train would roll to its designated target.

“That’ll do, when you get ’em stopped, Amtrak,” the conductor instructed.

Greg applied more air to bring the train to a gentle complete stop.

The Fargo station was deserted save for a young woman, her young son and the baby in her arms. Two women got off and the young family got on.

“Highball Amtrak,” came the signal. Two blasts of the horn and notch up the throttle. They were off into Minnesota, the fifth state on their trip. Two more to go.

Chapter 5

I Am an Engineer on the Empire Builder

From the cab of his idling locomotive, Greg watched as the crowd mingled among the snowflakes as his passengers departed at the Fargo, North Dakota, station. Since Christmas had arrived, over two hours earlier, snow had been falling steadily. This special night had turned into one of those magical Christmas scenes found on postcards. The freshly fallen snow, combined with the lack of vehicle traffic on the highway, provided a virtual blanket, covering the usual junk accumulated along the railroad right-of-way. As soon as Greg received the "Highball Amtrak" he notched up the throttle on his locomotives and pulled his train out of the station. As he passed the lowered crossing gates, the flashing red lights reflected off of the pristine snow on the byways of North Dakota. The ringing of the crossing bells made him chuckle to himself as he somehow came up with the thought that maybe St. Nick was ringing at each one with his sleigh bells. He looked in his rearview mirror and could see the clouds of snow billowing from the underside of the train. *Maybe,* the engineer thought, *I am that sleigh, delivering not the traditional toys and candy, but friends and loved ones. These would be much better presents than an X Box or an HDTV—These are the real joys in this world.* He smiled to himself in satisfaction. Sure he was missing Christmas with his wife and family, but look at all the joy he would bring between here and St. Cloud. These people were depending on him. He then decided he had better keep his mind on his job as he watched the tracks ahead of him, guiding the train east into Minnesota, toward St. Cloud, the city with the heavenly name.

Back in the coach car, George the car attendant slammed the door shut as the train began to move. He couldn't help but notice the woman who had just boarded. The short, dark-haired woman had deep dark eyes and the smile of an angel. Her long hair hung loose over her shoulders and down the front of her coat. She was carrying a bundled baby up the stairs following her six-year-old son. George pointed the boy down the aisle and said, "Sixth row back."

The young boy counted out loud, putting his hand on the back of each seat as he passed. "One—two—three—four—five—six."

With a smile he said loudly, "Here, Mama?"

The woman gently put her finger to her lips and replied softly, "Ssh, yes, that's right, good job. You sit on the inside next to the window."

The boy crawled over the seat and plopped down, drowning in the coach seat. The woman unwrapped her baby and sat down beside the boy. Reaching over, she unzipped the boy's coat and pulled it off of his shoulders. He squirmed out of the arms and twisted to allow his mother to take it off of his back.

The woman said gently, "You sit and watch out the window until I get settled here." She then took her own coat off, rolled both coats and stuffed them above in the compartment. Sitting back she took a deep breath and relaxed. It would be ten hours until they would get off.

Laura Shunt, her six-year-old son, Kyle, and the seven-month-old Shawna had traveled half the night from Wahpten, North Dakota, to catch the train in Fargo. Now that they were aboard, Laura could relax and catch her breath before reaching Columbus, Wisconsin, where they were to catch the shuttle to Madison.

This whole journey had actually started five weeks earlier when Kyle began complaining of sore legs and arms. The subsequent weeks proved to be an endless series of tests, doctors appointments, and then more tests. Last week, after a visit to St Joseph's Hospital in St. Paul, it had finally come down to the fact that Kyle had inherited a gene from Laura and his father, David, that, when switched on, triggered his autoimmune system to attack his muscles. In a sense Kyle's body was eating itself. As Laura searched the Internet looking for information, a single name kept popping up, Dr Shin Liau, a specialist in genetic disorders and stem cell research at the University Hospital in Madison, Wisconsin.

Laura contacted the clinic and made an appointment for more tests and a consult. She then scraped together enough money for the tickets by borrowing from family, jumped in the car and drove up to Fargo. She was now heading off on a desperate attempt to save her son's life.

As she sat back in her seat and closed her eyes only one thing came into view. Christmas or no Christmas, she was going to Madison and was going to do everything in her power to give her son every chance in life that he deserved.

Beside her, Kyle had his face pressed to the window watching the night world fly by in the snow. Putting her hand gently on the young boy's head she whispered, "Kyle, honey, you better sit back and try to get some sleep. There will be plenty of time to watch out the window in the daylight. Besides you will see more when it's light."

Kyle turned away from the window and flopped back into the seat. "But, Mom, I'm not tired."

"I know," his mother whispered, "but close your eyes and maybe you'll fall asleep. Tomorrow will be a really long day."

Without saying a word, Kyle closed his eyes. He still wasn't tired and was too excited to fall asleep. The entire world was passing by his window and he had to sleep. Life was not fair.

With his eyes closed, childhood thoughts passed through his mind. He was so excited to finally be on a train. The whistle sounded from the front of the train, bringing dreams of being an engineer into focus. How exciting it would be, up in that cab plowing through the snow, making all the cars stop for this speeding bullet flying down the tracks. Pulling the cord for the horn, blowing it at every road crossing, seeing mothers and their small children waving along the tracks as he passed by. Sitting tall in his seat, he'd wave and pull that cord once more tooting the horn, just for the kids. Oh, what a life, driving that locomotive into the mountains, through the great tunnels, along the flowing rivers and eventually to the sea. He'd be the best railway driver in the country. All the other kids and adults would look up to him, Kyle the engineer.

The whistle blew again up front, but the young lad was dreaming of his life on the railroad.

George helped the family settle in and then headed back up front to the crew car. The car attendant went forward on the train and descended the stairs to the crew lounge. The term lounge was a loose interpretation for the half of the sleeper car converted into the workstation for the train crew. It consisted of a normal sleeper car with half of the lower level rooms removed and an open room with two dinner-type tables in their place. As he reached the bottom of the stairs he noticed Jim the conductor was sitting at one table doing paperwork. At the other table, Mikki, another car attendant, was cradling a cup of coffee in her hands talking to Stanley, also a car attendant. Both Mikki and Stanly looked up and smiled. Mikki greeted first saying, "Hi, George, come on and sit down. Merry Christmas."

George smiled back and replied, "Thanks. Merry Christmas, Mikki. Merry Christmas, Stan."

George sat down next to Stan saying to Mikki, "What kind of bullshit is old Stan feeding you now?"

Stan, a large black man with a definite southern drawl, laughed and replied, "Now come on George, you know I don't ever dish out no bullshit."

"Oh yah," George responded, "You know this is Christmas, and you shouldn't be lying, You'll go to hell for sure."

"Well, maybe I stretch things a bit, but it's just for a story. I ain't really lying," Stan replied laughing. Stan was always laughing, either about his own jokes or someone else's. He just loved to laugh.

George turned to the good-looking, petite black woman sitting across from him and Stan. He asked politely, "Why aren't you resting? I've been covering your coach. Things are really quiet."

"I couldn't sleep. I know you can take care of things, but I am not sleepy, tired, but not sleepy," Mikki replied as she sipped her coffee from the white paper Amtrak cup.

"In twelve hours we'll all be home," Stan said

"Sure," George replied. "Have you looked outside? It's absolutely beautiful, snowing."

"Yes, I was watching from my bunk. Looks like Christmas,"

Mikki said joyfully. "I do miss this type of snow. Living in Seattle I don't get to see it. When I moved from Chicago I didn't think I would miss it."

George responded, "I was thinking yesterday how much I do like the snow in Chicago. Makes Christmas feel like it should."

"Did I ever tell you about getting my ass whooped on Christmas when I was about thirteen?" Stan interjected. "That's what I think about on Christmas."

Mikki replied, "Stan, I think you need to see a shrink if that's what you think about on Christmas."

Not even hearing the reply Stan continued, "My father was in the merchant marine so he was gone all the time. My mother was the one who done all the whooping. I only remember once my father beating my ass. Anyway, it was Christmas and we didn't have a lot, but my mom loved fried chicken. She could cook it real good too.

"As a kid, I didn't like much meat. I wasn't no vegetarian either; I just didn't like meat that much. So on this Christmas, my mom makes this big plate of fried chicken. I come into the kitchen and sit down at the table thinking, man, I don't want none of this chicken, but Mom, she's going to make me eat some. My brother was playing out in the living room and got into trouble with my sister, so Mom goes out to settle things down. Sitting there alone, I see the kitchen window open so I quickly grab the plate and throw all the chicken out the window.

"When Mom comes back into the kitchen, followed by my brother and sister, I quickly put on my best little boy face and say, 'Boy, I was sure hungry. That was the best chicken I ever tasted.'

"My mom's jaw hit the floor, yet she said calmly, 'It was that good, hah? I bet that must have been the best chicken you ever had, since you ate the bones and all.'"

Stan laughed out loud repeating his mother, "'I bet that must have been the best chicken you ever had, since you ate the bones and all.' Boy, was I dumb. I never even figured on those bones. When Mom looked out that window and saw all that hard work lying there on the ground, she burst into tears. Then she grabbed me by the collar and dragged me into the bedroom and whooped my ass good. She told me that since I ate all the food, I wasn't hungry and didn't need to eat anything else. I just sat in my room thinking how stupid I was, never even thinking about those bones." Stan laughed out loud once again.

"Them damn bones," he laughed.

Just as he finished, the conductor's radio cracked with the track side detector announcing, "No defects."

Realizing his cue, the conductor, said to the fellow car mates, "Detroit Lakes will be about fifteen minutes. We are right on time."

George got up saying to Mikki, "I'll take care of it. It is only two off and no on. I know where the luggage is. You just keep Stan here from throwing more chicken out the window."

Stan laughed a hearty laugh and Mikki replied, "I don't know, that's a pretty tall job. Maybe we need some bones since he eats them and all."

Stan began laughing so hard he ended in a cough. "You guys get to work," he said after his spasm.

Ascending the stairs he could hear Stan's voice telling another one of his usual ass-whooping stories to Joe the conductor. Turning the corner he said to Mikki, who was following, "Mikki, it's only three-thirty. You could get some rest before St. Paul. After that, it will be impossible. There will be a lot of work."

"I know," Mikki replied.

"I'll wake you up twenty minutes before we hit St. Paul. You'll have to cover for me when I sleep through Wisconsin."

"Ok," she said, "I'll go up and lie down. Don't forget to wake me up in time."

"I won't," George reassured the attendant.

Mikki slowly turned and headed to her berth, lay down and fell asleep.

As the motion of the train ceased, Laura startled awake. Shawna was sleeping gently on her lap, but there was a small whimpering cry from alongside her. She leaned over and put her hand on Kyle's forehead and asked softly, "What's wrong, honey?"

The six-year-old sobbed softly, "I hurt. My back and legs hurt."

"What can I do to make it better?" the mother asked

"I just want to lay down. It hurts," Kyle whimpered.

"Here," Laura said as she rearranged herself and the baby, "lay down across my lap and see if that helps."

The young boy leaned over and put his head on his mother's lap while she stroked his head. She bent down and kissed the top of his head and whispered, "Is that better?"

"Yes, I think so," came the soft reply from her lap. Laura continued stroking her son's head as she leaned her head back in her seat. *Thank God Shawna is being good,* she thought as she let out a sigh.

Soon the motion of the train resumed and the rocking lulled the boy and his mother back into sleep.

The snow in the headlights became lighter as the train continued on its eastward course. They had outrun the Alberta Clipper and were now at the leading edge of the storm system's front. Soon the snow diminished all together. The scene quickly changed from surreal, white beauty, glistening sparkling white, to the dirty brown of the winter, waiting, and hoping, before being cleansed by mother nature's paint brush.

St. Cloud station gleamed in the winter night as the train pulled into the station. The damp air sent chills through the departing passengers and crew. Greg backed out the door on the side of the cab and kicked the snow off of the rungs of the ladder as he descended. Reaching the ground he turned and looked down the platform to see Willie Herschaw striding toward him to take control of the Empire Builder. "Merry Christmas, Greg," Willie called from ten feet away.

"How are you doing on this fine Christmas morning?" the engineer continued.

It never ceased to amaze Greg how one man could always be so happy and jovial. He had turned his train over to Willie, routinely, for almost six years now. He couldn't recall a single night when the engineer wasn't in an outright jovial mood. "I'm doing fine." Greg replied, "Merry Christmas to you also. Just came through a bit of snow. Should be getting here shortly."

"Don't matter to me," Willie replied. "I'll be in Winona before you can break out your shovel.

"Hey, Greg, head into the office. Marlyne made some mighty good Christmas cake. Have some before the rest of the crews come in, or else you'll never get any. See you in a couple," Willie shouted as he climbed up the ladder into the cab of the waiting locomotive.

Greg walked back to the station and through the doors to the office. He did feel like some of Marlyne's cake. It had been one of those nights where you had to concentrate. Looking through the snow to see the signals and the grade crossings had made his eyes sore and his head ache. He rubbed his eyes and sat down in front of the desk with the paper plates and the dark chocolate cake with Merry Christmas in the frosting. He ate his fill and went to his motel.

Willie pulled the train out of St. Cloud and headed southeast toward the twin cities of St. Paul and Minneapolis. He chuckled at the term Twin Cities. The metropolitan area was now almost continuous from St. Cloud to Minneapolis. As he traveled the distance, the horn was almost constant. There were grade crossings practically every mile. Two long blasts, a short, and the final long blast as he hit the grade crossing. It gave the old horn a work out. A lot to watch as these city folks were none too keen on trains. Though there wasn't much traffic, he didn't need to spoil some fool's Christmas by making mince meat out of him.

He continued to watch and let the horn blast at each whistle sign along the right side of the right-of-way.

"I hurt, Mom," came the voice through the haze of sleep. With her motherly instincts kicking back in, Laura stroked her son's head. "What's wrong, honey?"

"My legs hurt really bad," came the voice again. Pretty soon there was the soft sniffling of tears being held back from public attention.

"Oh, honey, I'm sorry. I was asleep. What can I do to make it better for you?" Laura asked her son with the compassion of a mother.

Now the crying began in earnest. " I-I can't stand it. Mom, they hurt. Please make it go away."

Laura reached down rearranged the baby on her chest and put her arm under her son's arm and gently lifted him onto her lap.

"Sssh," she said, hugging him tightly, "if Mommy could make it go away I would. I just can't, honey, I just can't. Maybe this new doctor can help. Just be strong until then. Think of what an engineer would do if he was driving a train and he hurt."

"I'm trying to, Mommy. I just can't. I think I'd have to stop and let someone else drive," the boy replied between sniffles.

The tears now came to her own eyes as the compassionate mother comforted, "Mommy loves you. I would do anything to make it go away."

Sniffling she wiped her nose on her shoulder. *I'm not helping the poor guy by crying; I've got to get him through this,* she thought. She wiped her nose again and hugged Kyle once again. He was still crying but softer now. Laura picked up her son's head to see his face. Wiping his eyes with her finger she said, "Maybe it would help to lie down flat like you do at home in the living room. Come on, let me see if we can find a spot to lie down."

As Kyle crawled off of her lap she stood and gathered their coats from the overhead compartment, pushed Shawna back up on her shoulder, took Kyle by the hand and started down the aisle to the stairs. She realized the vestibule of the coach would be too busy, so she continued to the next car. Crossing through the doors, she came to the sleeper car. The long narrow hallway would not be appropriate either. Heading down the stairs she thought maybe the vestibule in this car wouldn't be as busy and would have to work. Laying the coats as a makeshift bed she told Kyle to lie down and asked if it helped. Nodding up and down he said, "Yes, I think so."

Laura sat down cross legged at his head and leaned against the bulkhead of the car. Across the space the heater kicked out plenty of heat so it wasn't too cold for the youngster, but being close to the ground, the track noise was considerable, the floor was hard, and the lights bright. It was far from comfortable. Right now she didn't have a choice and her own feelings were secondary.

Soon Kyle was asleep but now the baby was fussing. A loud sigh came from Laura. "Oh, Shawna, you've been so good," she whispered. "Momma hasn't taken care of you like she should. I'll make it up some day, I promise."

Shawna didn't care. She was hungry and Mom was here so she let her know.

Laura rocked the baby gently, pulled her hood back, grabbed a towel from her pocket, lifted her sweatshirt to offer her breast to the hungry mouth. Quickly nature took over and the baby was suckling without a care in the world. The mother sat back and let a system developed at the time of the demise of the dinosaurs take over. Soon Shawna pulled back and gave a brief cry. Laura pulled her shirt down and raised the baby above her shoulder and patted her back. After an audible burp she put her breast back in little mouth and continued the feeding. This time when the baby quit she again burped the child and rocked back and forth to comfort herself and the child.

Soon the track noise and the motion brought sleep to the youngest member of her family. Laura unfortunately couldn't find the right spot to be comfortable enough to fall asleep. The miles ticked by on this not so merry Christmas night.

Rachael Goers couldn't ignore her bladder any longer; the rocking of the top bunk would soon push her over the edge. She rolled over, fumbled with the safety harness on the edge of the bed, stuck one leg over the side and gingerly probed for the step with her left foot, found the mark and crawled down to the main floor. Unlocking the cabin door, she peered out to make sure the coast was clear before heading down the aisle to the restroom. The cold floor, the rocking of the train and the bright lights combined for a shocking experience just to relieve her bladder. More than once she rebuked herself for that last cup of tea. In the bright light of the vestibule she noticed a woman sitting with her back against the wall of the car. Not thinking too clear, she just opened the bathroom door, entered, locked the door, did her business, and returned to the hallway. More awake now, she realized something didn't seem right with the scene. The sleepy woman walked gingerly down the hallway and approached the young mother sitting on the floor.

"Are you OK?" Rachael asked politely noticing the boy stretched out on the makeshift bed.

The woman replied tiredly, "Yes and no, my son is sick and can't sit in the seats of the coach. I think he's more comfortable to be stretched out."

"God, he looks so uncomfortable, and you don't have any place to sit," Rachael said. "What can I do?"

Laura replied, "I don't know. We'll be all right."

"No, you can't stay like this. It's not right. I'll tell you what, let me go and wake my husband. You can share our room and beds. My husband is in a wheelchair so can't get out of the bed, but if you or your son wouldn't mind, you can share. Give me a second, I'll be right back," Rachael instructed. She then quickly turned and headed back down the hall to the room at the end of the car.

Laura just sat still with her head in her hands and the baby sleeping on her lap.

Waking her husband, Steve, Rachael asked, "Do you mind if we share our room with a girl and her kids? They look like they really need some help. Get up and put this shirt on. There is a young boy that needs to lie out on the bed. You can share."

Shaking off the sleep, Steve rolled over and pulled himself to a sitting position. Scooting himself back to the padded back wall, he put his arms through the long-sleeve tee shirt his wife had thrown at him and pulled it down over his belly.

"What's the problem?" Steve asked.

"I don't know, but they need some help. Don't be selfish."

"I'm not," Steve responded. "I was just asking."

After setting the assorted bags aside, Rachael passed back through the sliding door and back down the hall.

"Come on down and look to see if this would make things more comfortable," Rachael said to Laura.

Pulling herself to a standing position, her bones cracked loudly. Laura looked quickly at her sleeping son, rearranged Shawna on her shoulder, turned, and walked unsteadily down the hallway, following the tall dark-haired woman.

"You don't need to do this," Laura exclaimed.

"Don't worry about it. See if this will work," Rachael replied

As Laura reached the end of the hall, she poked her head into the room and noticed a middle-aged man with a graying beard sitting up in the bed. "Hi," she said.

Laura looked around the room and took stock of the accommodations. There was a bunk just below the window stretching the length of the room. Above at eye level was another fold-down bunk with a safety net dangling from the ceiling. On the opposite side of the car was a sink and what looked like a toilet. That side of the room was full of various pieces of luggage and bags. The man said politely, "Come on in, my name is Steve and I don't know if my wife introduced herself yet, but that's Rachael."

"Nice to meet you. It is so nice of you to offer to share your room with us," the young woman replied.

"My name is Laura, out there on the floor is my son Kyle," gesturing to the baby in her arms she continued, "here is my youngest, Shawna. Are you sure you want to do this? We'll try and be quiet so we don't disturb you"

Rachael, who had positioned herself away from the door by sitting on one of the suitcases, replied, "Don't worry about it; it is not a problem. What do you need?"

Laura looked around and said, "Kyle needs to stretch out and lie down. I can sit on the floor and Shawna doesn't really care."

Steve smiled and responded, "You will not sit on the floor. There is plenty of room. If you don't mind Kyle can sleep down by my feet. I'll stay sitting up. Rachael can sit by me, and you can have the top bunk."

"Thanks, but I can't take your bunk. I wouldn't feel right. I am younger; Rachael can sleep and I'll just sit down here," Laura directed.

"We'll see," Rachael said. "Go and get Kyle so he gets off of that cold floor. Do you need help?"

"No thanks, I'll be right back," Laura said as she turned and walked down the hall to wake up her son.

Within a minute the mother and semi-sleepwalking boy came through the door. Rachael reached over and pulled up a red wool blanket revealing the blue acrylic Amtrak blanket beneath. "Here, you just lie down right here. I'll cover you up," Rachael explained to the boy.

"Mom?" the youngster whimpered.

"It's OK, honey, I'll be sitting right beside you. These nice people are letting us share their room," the gentle mother reassured her son.

"Thank you," the boy replied half croaking, as he crawled onto the bed and stretched himself out with his head against the end of the car.

Laura asked her son, "Does that make you feel better?"

Rachael gently floated the blanket over the boy and tucked the edges around his slender delicate body.

"Yes, I'm an engineer again," came a muffled reply from under the covers.

"Good, you can get some sleep now. Don't worry about a thing; you're on the train and almost to the Cities," Laura comforted her son.

Rachael cleared off the seat of the wheelchair sitting next to the bed and motioned for the mother to sit down. Pulling here feet up onto the footrests she sat forward on her elbows and took a deep breath and exhaled loudly.

Willie, the engineer, came to a stop at the red light approaching the Northtown rail yard in Minneapolis. He got on the radio and requested permission to proceed past the signal and enter the yard. "Amtrak 8 requesting permission to pass the red flag on main one and enter the yard limit."

The response was immediate, "Amtrak 8 has permission to pass the red flag on main one and proceed at track speed through Northtown yard. BNSF Northtown dispatcher out."

"OK, Amtrak will proceed past the red flag on main one at posted track speed through Northtown yard. Amtrak out," Willie repeated.

He then notched up the engines and proceeded into the large railroad yard and past the several thousand rail cars waiting for the end of the holiday to continue on their journey. The radio crackled, "Willie, is that you? Did Marlyne make some of that Christmas cake again?"

Willie opened the channel and replied with a chuckle, "She sure did, but guess what, it's up in St. Cloud."

The response, "You old pack rat, why didn't you bring some down?"

"I didn't know you were going to be here," the engineer replied. "I'll tell you what, I'll be coming back through on Thursday. I'll have Marlyne make a fresh one and bring it along. You going to be here?"

"Should be," came the reply. "See you then"

Willie signed off, "See you Thursday, Amtrak out."

He continued through the yard and out onto a side track leading to the St. Paul station stop. Soon he saw the familiar blue and white station with its covered platforms. He pulled to the end of the platform and stopped the train. Now he could take a break, since they wouldn't leave for twenty minutes.

Back in the sleeper car, Steve asked the young mother, "Where are you heading?"

"Columbus, Wisconsin," came the reply. "You?"

"We're getting off two stations sooner, in Wisconsin Dells." Rachael said, "Where are you from?"

"We're from Wahpten, North Dakota," Laura replied and then continued talking about her life, growing up in South Dakota on a grain farm, going to school in Fargo for nursing and her rotation in Minneapolis. She then went on explaining how she met her husband and moved to Wahpeten, North Dakota. Now after her second child it seemed that things had fallen apart. She explained how she caught her husband having an affair, tried to make amends, which failed, and now kicked him out of the house. On top of all this Kyle suddenly came up with this gene malfunction. She told of all the trips to the doctors who couldn't find answers, the endless tests on poor Kyle and the many sleepless nights between that first appointment and tonight.

With the listening ears it just seemed such a decompression to let it all out. She continued to explain how, if it hadn't been for her aunt, she would not have been able to afford this trip. And in fact, her ex-husband-to-be's parents even chipped in some money. After fifteen minutes of releasing all the pent up feelings and emotions the young dark-eyed woman sat back in the wheelchair and sighed

Steve smiled and asked, the young woman, "Why are you going to Columbus?"

Laura's face changed slightly from matter of fact to sad. She then began slowly, "We are on our way to Madison. Our only hope is in one of the doctors at the University Hospital there

"I originally planned on driving but the only thing that helps Kyle's pain is to stretch out. His body is fighting itself so he has a lot of pain. Also he just loves trains and dreams of being an engineer. I thought it might be the last time he would get a chance to ride a real train."

"Oh no," Rachael exclaimed. "How old is he?"

"He just turned six in October," Laura replied. "It was only two weeks later we started the testing. We've spent almost two months running from one test and doctor to another. I am really hoping we can do something here."

Rachael added, "That's too bad. Where are you staying in Madison?"

"Well, first off I'm staying at a Ramada Inn. They are picking me up at the station in Columbus. After that, I am going to try get a room somewhere so I don't have to take a taxi across town," Laura said

Steve entered into the conversation saying, "What about the Ronald McDonald House? They would probably let you stay."

Laura turned to the man and said, "I don't know anything about that. This is all so sudden, I really didn't have much time to prepare."

Steve asked, "When is your appointment?

The young woman responded, "The 27th at eleven fifteen."

Steve then looked at his wife and half asked half stated, "Why don't we have Laura and the kids stay at our house? She can use the van to get back and forth. Or since we are both off all week, we can take her and the kids down."

Laura looked puzzled at the offer and how this whole scene evolved. The older couple recognized the bewilderment and picked up the conversation. Rachael going first, "We have a large house with three bedrooms upstairs that we don't use. There is also a bathroom on the second floor. It would be like an apartment without a kitchen. We've had students live with us and never really noticed they were there. We would love to have you stay."

Steve added, laughing, "We probably never told you where we live, so you're wondering what we are talking about. Well we live in Mauston, Wisconsin, about an hour and a half north of Madison. We both went to school in Madison and Rachael worked there for years. I actually did my rehab at the UW Hospital way back when. We really would like to help. Besides you are talking to a huge rail fan. I, or we, could give Kyle a really great Christmas. I have a model railroad layout, a miniature railroad museum in my office and we only live a hundred yards from the Canadian Pacific mainline. You couldn't ask for more."

Rachael rolled her eyes and said lightheartedly, "I'm not sure you'd want to expose your son to a railroad nut." She then asked, "But seriously, you guys spent Christmas Eve on the road. What did you tell Kyle?"

"I told him Santa would have presents for him at the hospital," Laura replied. "I really didn't even have time to do any shopping for the poor guy. I was hoping Madison would have some places I could pick up a few things."

"You will stay at our house, at least tonight and tomorrow night." Rachael said sternly, "We will make sure you and your kids have the best Christmas ever. Then we'll take you to Madison and get you set up at the Ronald McDonald House if you want."

Laura was still in shock and said meekly, "Are you sure? I don't want to impose."

Steve replied quickly, "You are not imposing. We would think of it as a Christmas gift. Of course, Rachael, the poor woman doesn't know if we are some sort of ax murderers. We could show her the house as we pass. From the window she could see that at least she is not staying in some dump somewhere."

Rachael rolled her eyes at Steve.

Laura responded by saying, "I trust you. Obviously I wouldn't have to worry about running away from you, Steve, unless you are some speed racer, which I can see you are not."

Steve laughed and pretended to be hurt by the racer reference. "Oh, you say you can see I no racer. Boy, I am disappointed."

Rachael broke in saying, "Oh cut it out." Turning to Laura she said, "Don't mind him; he's always full of B.S. Do you think you might stay?"

"If you really don't mind, I think Kyle would really like it, and to be honest, I could use a break myself. I don't want to put you out. I can pay you for what a hotel would cost and for food," Laura said politely.

Rachael replied with no uncertainty in her voice, "You will not pay us a cent. This will be our Christmas treat, and besides it doesn't cost us anything to have you stay. You are welcome as long as like."

"Thanks. What do I do about the tickets and hotel reservations?" Laura asked, wondering aloud. With the force and honesty of the older couple, Laura was accepting Steve and Rachael as parent figures. With the fatigue and stress of the past several months she was relaxing her brain and allowing some decisions to be made by someone else. It felt good.

"Don't worry," Steve said. "The conductor will let you get off early, and it is still early so you can probably cancel the hotel without penalty. Give them a call."

The young woman shook her head and smiled. "I'll give it a shot. I can't lose anything by calling. Will my phone work from the train?"

Steve replied, "It should; mine does."

Laura handed Shawna to Rachael, who gladly accepted the infant, and began shuffling through the fanny pack around her waist. As she dug, she thanked the older couple saying, "You guys don't have to do this. I can stay in Madison. But I do know that Kyle will enjoy having some sort of Christmas." The woman found the paper she was looking for and her mobile phone. Stepping back through the door she walked to the middle of the car and made her phone calls.

Willie watched as the passengers strolled up and down the

platform in the damp December air. Nothing seemed to cut through a body like the cold wind blowing around the buildings of a city. The open country wind blew hard and cut like a knife, but the city wind twisted and turned as it followed the streets and picked up the moisture and grime of the alleys. This wind acted more like sandpaper on your body, rasping, getting under your clothes, up your pant legs and down your neck as it scraped at your body, sucking the warmth out little by little. The hint of snow was in the air and the grime of the rail yard beckoned for a fresh coat to renew its vitality. The engineer just waited and soon the conductor came on the radio and called for the two blasts of the horn signaling the "All aboard." The platform cleared, as the "Highball Amtrak" sounded and as Amtrak 8 pulled out of St. Paul, the first few flakes of snow drifted down on the city that was the home of the Empire Builder.

Up on Summit Avenue, across from the St. Paul Cathedral, The Hill mansion lay deserted on this Christmas morning. A historical monument, it no longer held the laughter and celebrations of years gone by. James J. Hill, the Empire Builder only lived on in spirit. The red sandstone walls stood overlooking the Mississippi River and the town that played the pivotal role in developing the Great Northern Railway and the empire around it. Amtrak 8 passed below the hill where the mansion stood and only Steve noticed the home of the namesake of the train they were riding. Willie kept his eye on the signals and the track ahead and rest the passengers didn't look up at the massive red stone structure.

As the train came down the hill it began following the Mississippi River. They would not leave sight of the historic transportation artery for almost three hours. The experienced engineer guided his train down the tracks, soon reaching the edge of the metropolitan area, and for the first time since leaving Seattle, he left the BNSF tracks. Now the Empire Builder entered the property of the Canadian Pacific Railway.

As they left St. Paul, George closed the coach door and climbed the stairs to look after his passengers. He looked at his manifest and figured it was about time to head down to room H and see if his handicapped couple wanted breakfast. Since wheelchair access to the diner was impossible, it was his duty to bring the meals to the room for the occupants.

Walking steadily on the rocking coach he reached into his pocket, checked to see that the menu and a pencil were there, proceeded up to the sleeper car. As he approached the end room he noticed the pretty woman sitting in the wheelchair facing the door. He recognized the good-looking woman and saw the young boy sleeping at the foot of the bed. Suspect at first, he then quickly realized the room occupants and the woman were involved in conversation. Poking his head into the room he greeted everyone, "Merry Christmas," turning to Rachael and asked, "Mrs. G do you want any breakfast on this fine morning?"

"Sure," Rachael replied, "I've been thinking about it for a bit. I'll have the two eggs scrambled, with sausage."

George began writing on his notepad and asked, "Do you want toast or a biscuit? What about something to drink?"

Rachael wrinkled her brow in thought and replied, "I'll have the biscuit and a coffee."

"All righty," George said as he turned toward the bed where Steve was waiting. "How about you Mr. G?"

"I'll have oatmeal with a biscuit and a glass of milk. Can I have a cup of coffee also?" the man answered leaning forward.

George finished writing and replied, "Sure, cream or sugar?"

"No thanks," Steve answered

Turning to Laura, George asked, "Do you need anything miss?"

"No thanks," Laura replied with a smile. Continuing she asked the attendant, "Is it a good Christmas for you?"

"It sure is," George responded, " in eight hours I'll be home and I'll be with my wife and kids. Can't have a much better Christmas than that."

"I guess not," Laura said. "Merry Christmas."

George turned and started down the hall saying, "Thanks, merry Christmas to you. I'll be right back with your breakfast."

Steve asked, "Don't you want something to eat? Or a cup of coffee? We'd be happy to get it for you. Our meals are included in our ticket but we'd buy you breakfast if you want."

Sitting forward in the wheelchair Laura said, "No thanks, I'm not much of a breakfast eater, and I'm not big on coffee."

The train crossed the switch entering the Canadian Pacific rails causing the car to jump slightly and sway. Kyle blinked his eyes several times rolled over and asked, "Mommy?"

Laura replied gently without even thinking, "Right here, honey."

The young boy sat up and looked around briefly asking, "Where are we?"

"These people are kind enough to share their room with us." Laura told her son, "This is Rachael and Steve."

"No, I mean where are we outside?" Kyle asked impatiently as he crawled forward to see out the large window.

Laura raised her eyebrows in question. Steve noticed and quickly responded, "We are just south of the Twin Cities. You can see the Mississippi River right over there."

Laura said to Kyle, "Be careful; don't hurt Steve's legs. He can't feel anything. Don't move around too much; you might hurt him."

Steve replied to both the young boy and his mother, "I'll be OK. He's pretty light. But thanks."

Turning back to Kyle Laura asked, "Steve and Rachael invited us to their house for Christmas. Your appointment isn't until Tuesday so we don't have to be in Madison until then. Would you like to stay with them? Steve knows a lot about trains and even has a model train set."

Looking apprehensively at his mother the boy asked, "Really/"

"Yes. They have extra room and are willing to share. They live right along the railroad tracks and you could sit and watch trains all day," the mother comforted, making the sell to the child. Deep in her heart she really didn't look forward to the hotel. The thought of staying in a real home, with friendly people, just sounded good at this point.

"Can I play with the train set?" Kyle asked, pondering the situation.

Steve answered before the mother could speak, "You sure can. It isn't just a train set I'll have you know," Steve said teasing. "It's a layout with lots of trees, houses, a barn and tiny people."

"Really?" the boy asked again. "I can run the train? How fast does it go? I want to be an engineer when I grow up."

Steve smiled and shaking his head said, "Yes, you can run the train. It can go pretty fast but a good engineer will make it go slow so it doesn't come off of the tracks and get wrecked. We'll get you running that train like a real engineer in no time."

Laura smiled at Steve and realized that the deal was cinched. Asking Kyle, "What do you say? Do you want to stay there until Tuesday?"

"Sure, if I can play with the trains," came a quick response.

"Now, honey, there will be more to do than play with the trains. You'll help Rachael and Steve around the house too. Right?" Laura told Kyle in her motherly tone.

As his face fell Kyle responded, "I suppose so. Do engineers have to help around the house?"

Steve replied with a smile, "Engineers have homes and wives. They certainly have to help. But we won't make you do too much. I'll help you learn all about trains and engineers."

Laura interrupted, teaching, "Steve is in a wheelchair so we'll all need to learn what to do to help and we must make sure we are respectful of both of them. Right?"

"OK, Mom," Kyle said looking at Steve and then at his mother asking, "Where is his wheelchair? How did he get into bed?"

"I'm sitting in his chair, and he hopped into bed like you do," Laura instructed.

"Can I sit in it?" the boy asked as he recognized the chair beneath his mother.

"No, you just stay where you are. It is not a toy," the mother said firmly.

Kyle looked disappointed but quickly returned to looking out the window at the passing scenery.

George came down the hallway carrying two large trays and whistling "Jingle Bells."

"I hope you are hungry, Mr. and Mrs G., because I've got a lot of food here."

Handing the top tray to Rachael, he reached toward Steve with the second. Steve asked Laura quickly, "Can you grab that? I can't."

Quickly Laura lifted the heavy tray from the attendant's outstretched arms saying, "Sorry. Where do you want it?"

"You can set it here on my lap," Steve replied, straightening the blankets covering his legs.

Handing the paper cups to Laura, George said, "Can I get you folks anything else?"

Steve grabbed one cup and set it on the small shelf under the window saying, "I'm good. Thanks."

Rachael standing now, took the other cup and set it on the edge of the sink with her tray. "Thanks, I think I've got everything."

Turning to Laura George asked, "You sure I can't get something for you?"

With her long hair waving she shook her head side to side saying,"No. Thanks again."

George smiled politely and said, "OK enjoy," as he left down the hall and back to his duties.

Willie watched the parallel steel rails stretching out in front of him. *These are the lifeline of the country*, he thought. Not the same artery that existed in the early part of the 20th century but still an important artery all the same. Out in the distance a bright light appeared on the horizon. A freight was approaching on the parallel track. The priority freight was heading north, and as it blasted past, there seemed to be an endless string of auto racks trailing behind. Friendly competition, the automobile pulled the passengers away from the railroad and the railroad delivers more cars to the lot. Just a business.

Willie waved to the freight engineer and kept his eyes on the signal light ahead. It remained green so the seasoned engineer kept the throttle up as he rumbled across the switch, and headed south toward Red Wing, Minnesota. Off to the left the river was a mosaic of ice and open water. Where the current kept the water moving the ice was reluctant to form. Where the water stood still, the ever-opportunistic ice quickly engulfed the surface, creating the playground for the ice fisherman and winter sportsmen. Willie smiled as he passed the shanties on the frozen backwaters. This was not his idea of fishing. Way too cold.

George, Stan and Mikki sat down in the crew car to share stories and a cup of coffee. Stan had been in the middle of instructing Mikki on a computer problem when George joined the group. As soon as Stan finished, George asked, "Stanley, how many computers do you have?"

Stan thought for a minute staring at he ceiling and counting, "I've got five. Not all of them running mind you, but I could use all of them. I like tinkering with them."

"Five?" George gasped, "Where do you keep them all? What can you ever do with all those machines?"

"I've got two in my bedroom, two in the office and one downstairs in the basement," Stan replied. "Like I said, not all of them run. I just like playing with them. Figuring out how they work and all. Did I ever tell you about the time I took apart my brother's radio?"

George rolled his eyes and replied, "No and I bet you will right now."

Without even listening for a response, Stan launched into his story. "When I was about ten, my brother and I had these transistor radios. Well I liked to take things apart, so I took his radio apart and tried to figure out how the thing worked. Of course I couldn't get it back together right, so it looked good from the outside, but it never played again. My brother knew right away I'd been messing with it, but couldn't prove a thing. My mom just accused him of breaking it and laying the blame on me. So my brother takes my radio and cuts off the cord to get even.

We had to go without radios for a while. One night I was watching TV, and *McGyver* is on, you know the guy who could get out of any situation by inventing something out of junk. Well this night he gets out of a locked room by cutting the cord off of a lamp, dumping water on the floor, sticking the cord in the water and getting his captors to walk through it—therefore electrocuting them. I developed a scheme to take the cord from my radio and hook it to the shower door when my brother was taking a shower. When he was done, he would grab the door and get a good shock.

When my brother was in the shower, I wired the cord to the door and plugged it in. Of course every fuse in the house blew. My brother screamed bloody murder, my mother flew up the stairs, and I almost peed in my pants. I thought I had killed my brother. Turns out the only thing he screamed about was that it got dark in the shower. That was another time my mother really whooped my ass. I didn't sit for a week."

George and Mikki both sat there and shook their heads in disbelief. "Stan, it's amazing you never ended up in jail," George said.

Stan laughed in his hearty deep laugh, "Well I should've once. The time I burned down the gas station."

Mikki stood up and asked George if she could get past. George stood following Mikki's lead saying, "I gotta get back to work. Maybe next time, Stan."

Mikki followed George out, smiling at Stan she said, "Next time, Stan."

Stan smiled, stood up, and followed the other two car attendants. I suppose I'd better get to work too," he muttered to himself.

Steve pulled the cover off of the tray sitting on his lap revealing a bowl of oatmeal, several packs of sugar and two light brown biscuits. Opening the sealed plastic bag containing his spoon and fork he asked Laura, "Do you or Kyle want my biscuits?"

Laura turned to her son giving the nonverbal cue that it was OK if he wanted the fresh roll. Kyle responded by nodding his head up and down.

"Butter or honey?" Steve asked, handing the youngster one of the biscuits from his plate.

Laura reached over and took the biscuit from Kyle's hand and said, "If you don't mind, I'll butter it for you."

Steve quickly handed the woman the sealed containers of butter and honey, which she spread delicately on the biscuit. Handing the other warm roll to Laura he said, "Here have this one too. Here's more butter and honey."

"Thanks," Laura said as she spread the butter and took a bite herself.

Kyle was looking out the window chewing as Steve handed him a napkin. "Thank you," the young boy said without missing a beat.

"Hey, you guys mind if I turn on the scanner and see what's happening out there?" Steve asked excitedly. Rachael shook her head in disgust, but said, "Go ahead. Kyle would like to know what things are like on the railroad. But keep it quiet so you don't disturb everyone."

The bearded man reached forward and picked up what looked like an over-sized walkie talkie. Sticking out the top of the black radio was a rubber antenna, on the front a small display and some buttons. Steve turned a knob on the top and leaned forward to talk to Kyle. "This is a radio scanner. I can listen to what the engineer and other railroad people are saying." Just then there was a burst of static and some voices saying,. "CP 4350 to Amtrak 8, you're looking good."

Kyle's eyes lit up. "Who is that?" he asked.

"Wait," Steve instructed.

"Thanks, 4350. You're flashing red back here. Amtrak out"

Steve quickly explained to Kyle, "That was the engineer of the passing freight telling the engineer of our train that everything looked good as he passed us."

"Wow, Mommy, we can hear the engineers," the boy exclaimed.

In a couple of minutes the scanner came alive again

"Amtrak portable to the head end."

"Go ahead, portable," came the reply.

"I'll spot the seventh car, Amtrak."

"Roger, Amtrak out."

"Portable out."

The scanner was quiet. Steve said to Kyle, "That was our engineer and the conductor. The conductor told the engineer where he wanted him to stop the train in Red Wing. They will be stopping the seventh car in front of the station."

There was silence as the entire group ate their breakfast. As soon as Kyle finished the biscuit he asked, "Why can't we hear them now?"

"They aren't talking on their radios. Wait until we get to the station and there will be more chatter," Steve instructed.

Steve finished his oatmeal before the train reached the Red Wing station. Kyle was glued to the scanner, reminiscent of the golden age of radio, where the children just stared at the glowing dial of the crackling squawk boxes.

As the train slowed the scanner came alive once again with the familiar, "Three cars, Amtrak. Two cars, Amtrak," and finally the "That'll do, Amtrak."

With each burst of the scanner, the older man explained and the child listened, to the working of a passenger railroad. Soon the consist was back up to track speed heading toward Winona, Minnesota, and the final crew change.

After finishing their breakfast, Steve and Rachael asked if they could have some privacy to get dressed and get ready for the day. Laura and her family took the occasion to walk back up to their coach seats and gather up all of their belongings.

Upon their return to the lower level cabin they found the door open, the lower bunk neatly converted into two booth-type seats with Steve sitting in the seat closest door looking out the window. Kyle was the first through the door as he ran and hopped onto the seat opposite the door, sat forward and glued his eyes to the window.

"Anything happen?" the boy asked referring to the radio.

"No, pretty quiet," Steve replied.

Rachael, who was rearranging the luggage on the floor, stood up, yawned and announced, "If you guys don't mind, I am going to take a nap."

"Go ahead," Steve replied. "We've got a few hours before getting off."

Laura, who was standing in the doorway with Shawna over her shoulder said, "Don't stay up on account of us. I don't mind."

Rachael climbed up onto the top bunk and lay down. Steve

instructed Laura, "Come in and sit down. I am not going to get up into my chair until we get to Sparta. If I get up for a while it seems to lessen some of the vertigo when we get off."

As the short dark-haired woman sat down next to her son, she asked Steve, "Where are we at?"

Steve responded, "Between Red Wing and Winona. A little more than two hours until we get off. I am looking forward to having you stay at our house for Christmas. I hope you like it and things go well."

"We are so glad you are willing to share. It sure beats a hotel room on Christmas night. I can't think of any place more depressing. Maybe it will help get my mind off of the next few days also," the woman answered as she shifted the baby from one shoulder to the other.

Willie pulled the train into the station at Winona right on schedule. Gathering his papers and stuffing them into the black briefcase he had practically worn out, he grabbed his empty Thermos and opened the cab door. Looking out the door he spotted Rich Johnson approaching on the platform. Smiling he called out, "Hiya, Rich, merry Christmas. How do you like it that I brought number eight in on time?"

The short, blond-haired, slightly built Rich Johnson replied with a smile, "Hey, Willie, merry Christmas. Don't try and tell me you were 100 percent responsible for getting here on time. I've seen the mainline and it sure isn't very crowded today. But I am happy. Maybe I'll get home to the old lady and kids for a bit of Christmas cheer this afternoon. You know when you got a tool like mine the old lady needs some of it every night."

Willie groaned and slung it right back, "You ain't got nothing. Last week when I was doing your old lady, she told me she wished you were half as good as me."

Rich slapped Willie on the back and responded, "You wish you could have my old lady. Shit, you wouldn't know what end was up. She'd have your pecker tied in knots before she was through."

Willie responded quickly, "So that's why your dick is so short, you've got a knot in it."

Both men laughed heartily as Rich climbed into the cab. "You have a merry Christmas, Willie. I'll see you on the return," Rich exclaimed warmly.

Willie waved and said, "Same to you. Give Linda and the kids my regards."

Rich and Willie had known each other for over ten years now. Each time they exchanged shift, the banter was pretty much the same: always bragging about each other's manhood. In reality both were as loyal to their wives as a greyhound to its master. But in the railroad circle, talk is king.

As soon as Rich received the "Highball" he headed the train out of the station and down river to La Crosse. He wanted to make sure he arrived home in time to help his wife make Christmas supper. He hoped the five hours would fly by and the shift would be over before he knew it.

Back in the sleeper car Steve helped the young, budding engineer learn some more of the basics of railroading. Not wanting to destroy the poor child's dreams, he left out the reality of the long hours away from home, the waiting at the signals and the dangers of heavy equipment.

The scanner remained quiet as the rail traffic was light and things were going smoothly. Soon the rocking of the car had Kyle's eyes drooping and his head bobbing. Laura put her arm out and drew him to her side. Within minutes he was asleep.

Steve reached forward and turned off the scanner. Laura smiled thankfully.

Steve asked in a whisper, "Are you going back right after the appointment?"

Laura whispered back, "I don't know, depends on what the doctor says. I don't have a return ticket. Things are up in the air."

Steve replied softly, "You must be exhausted. Make sure you rest when you get to our house. We can help take care of some things for you. Rachael is a pro at these kind of things. You make sure you maintain your health for Kyle."

"Thanks, I will," she responded. "I don't know what I would ever do if this doesn't work. He is so precious; it is not fair for him to be sick, and not me."

Steve remained silent as the young mother continued, "I've always tried to be the best mom I could. Now I feel like I am failing. There is nothing I can do."

With a smile, the fatherly figure reached out and put his hand on hers. "You are doing more than most other mothers. You've sacrificed everything right now to make this trip. A poor mother would have given up hope and stayed in her comfortable home and hoped for the best. You are out here doing the best you can for your son."

There were now tears in Laura's as she said, "Thanks. All I hope is that this is all worth it."

"It is worth it," Steve exclaimed. "No matter what the outcome, it is worth it: you gave him the best opportunity you can. It is now out of your hands."

Wiping her eyes Laura said, "Don't make it sound so final. Maybe there is more I can still do."

Steve replied, "Oh, don't get me wrong, see what the doctor says. If there is more to do, please share some of the burden with us. You can't continue alone."

"Thanks. You two are too kind," the mother replied.

Steve wiped a tear from his eye, leaned forward and hugged the young woman as she burst into a full-fledged cry. Rocking forward, he patted her gently on the back saying, "We'll help do whatever we can. You just take it easy and relax for now."

Letting go and sitting back both people sniffled and wiped their eyes. Now was not the time for more conversation so they let the wheels sing and the car rock. Christmas was here and things were going to be OK.

The room remained quiet until the train stopped at the approach to the Mississippi River bridge. In a minute, the motion resumed and the car clanked and rumbled across the swing bridge that the old Milwaukee Road built so many years ago. After crossing a second bridge, which crossed the Black River, the Empire Builder entered Wisconsin, and the city of La Crosse.

The change in motion from the bridge crossing and the station stop proved too much for the sleeping child. Blinking his eyes he squirmed out from under his mother's arm and returned to watching out the window

Steve reached forward turning the scanner back on saying, "We are in Wisconsin. One more hour until we get off."

With a sound of disappointment the youngster said, "So soon, I missed so much."

"There'll be lots more," his mother confided.

"I dreamed again that I was an engineer," Kyle said happily. "I was driving the Empire Builder. You and Daddy were riding and I got to show you what a good driver I was. I didn't go too fast so I made sure the train stayed on the tracks. We passed lots of other trains and went through lots of cities. My legs were hurting but I kept driving. Finally we got to a big city where a doctor made the pain go away. He reached down and put a machine on my legs and they got better. Then I got back in my engine and drove home. I could really become an engineer, right, Steve?"

With a tear in his eye he leaned forward to Laura and motioned to the far side of the car. On top of a large black suitcase was a black baseball cap with a bright orange bill and florescent orange BNSF lettering. "Could you please get that hat please?" Steve asked

The woman got up putting the baby down on the seat. Reaching the hat she handed it to the railroad junkie.

As the mother sat back down he asked politely, "If you don't mind a used hat..."

Sensing what was going on she smiled and shook her head yes.

Steve then placed the hat on the young boy's head. Falling forward the too-large hat covered the boy's eyes. He quickly pushed it back with his left hand.

Steve then said, "Since you are such a good engineer, you can have this cap. This is a real BNSF hat that real engineers wear. Your mom can tighten it up for you and you can wear it whenever you feel like driving a locomotive."

The boy's eyes lit up and sparkled with joy. If his mouth smiled any wider Steve thought his face would split. "Really, this is a real engineer's cap?

"Yes, I bought it from the railroad, where their employees buy their things," Steve replied

The mother kicked in and Laura asked her son, "What do you tell Steve?"

"Thank you! Sorry I forgot," the boy exclaimed. "I'll take really good care of it and won't loose it."

Smiling, Steve replied, "I know you will."

"Why don't you give Steve a hug," Laura said

The small boy bounced forward, practically jumping on the man's lap. He wrapped his thin arms around his neck and gave a great bear hug.

Steve wrapped his arms around the boy and said, "My, you've got the hug of a bear."

Quickly the boy slid back losing his hat in the process. He picked it up immediately and handed it to his mother instructing her to tighten it up so it wouldn't fall off. Laura tightened the cap off and then unpacked some lunch for herself and Kyle while she and Steve were talking, The sandwich and cookies disappeared quickly and soon Shawna decided it was time for her lunch also.

Laura politely asked, "Do you mind if Shawna nurses?"

Steve replied, "No, I don't mind. Why should I mind?"

The woman turned a bit red and replied, "I just never know. I figured I'd better ask before I whipped out a boob and startled everyone."

Steve replied comforting, "It is a shame that you even need to be worried. It is one of the most primal acts in nature. We've become so anal that we can't even accept each other's bodies."

The young woman pulled her sweatshirt up and revealed her ample breast and moving Shawna closer, guided her nipple into the baby's mouth. Taking no pains to cover herself she continued to nurse the child. After a bit, Shawna began fussing. Laura boosted her up above her shoulder and began burping the baby. After a few seconds and a large burp, she repositioned the hungry mouth back on the nipple.

Steve watched the whole process paying particular attention not to stare at the exposed breast. The woman didn't notice, or pretended not to notice, and began another segment of her story. She wasn't sure what she was going to do after she got Kyle cured and back to Fergus Falls. She supposed she would stay working at the local hospital and put Shawna in daycare.

Once again the baby fussed and the mother repeated the burping process. This time she smiled at the man sitting across from her and said, "I hope I'm not embarrassing you, or making you feel uncomfortable."

"Oh no," Steve replied getting warm in the face. "To tell you the truth, I was admiring your breasts. I guess I never tire of seeing nice boobs."

"Thanks, I feel like I'm some old cow, not very sexy. I keep thinking that is why my husband had to find another woman," Laura replied

"Oh my gosh," Steve exclaimed. "You are pretty, and very attractive, and mind you, you are the furthest thing from some cow. And I know, I grew up on a dairy farm."

Smiling, Laura said again, "Thanks."

She then lifted Shawna up, pulled down her shirt and said to the young girl, "You've had enough there, young lady. Mommy doesn't have any more for you. Come on let's get that last burp so you'll feel better."

She then proceeded to burp the girl and rock her gently from side to side.

The scanner picked up intensity as the dispatcher began putting Amtrak into the siding to allow an empty coal train to pass. Kyle listened intently as Steve explained how Amtrak has priority over freight trains, and that if possible the dispatcher should put the freights in the siding, and allow Amtrak to pass. This is not always possible since some trains are too long for the closest siding and the dispatcher's main job is to keep the railroad running. It wouldn't do anyone any good to have a coal train or Amtrak back up for miles to find a suitable siding.

The passenger train stopped and in a few minutes the roar and whoosh of the passing train flashed by the window. Steve said to Kyle, "Count the cars."

The boy quickly counted, "One, two, three, four, I can't, they are going too fast."

"That's OK, Kyle," Steve explained. "They are definitely going too fast; I can't count them either."

As the motion of the train resumed there was a noise from the top bunk. Rachael asked sleepily, "Where are we?"

"We are almost to Sparta. You'd better get up."

Soon one leg flopped down over the side of the upper bunk, followed by another. Steve reached over and grabbed one foot and guided it to the step alongside the door. Rachael quickly stepped down and rubbed her eyes. "Come on," she said, "let's get you up."

Steve slid himself over to the edge of the seat while Rachael positioned the wheelchair alongside. Reaching behind him and grabbing his belt, she counted to three and helped pull the man into his chair.

Laura, said, "It looks like you guys really have a system there. How long have you been in a chair if you don't mind me asking?"

"I've been in a chair for 23 years," Steve said as he wiggled himself back in the seat. Then continued saying, "I don't mind telling people about it. I was in an automobile accident and broke my neck."

"Wow, you are certainly doing well. What level are you?" Laura asked.

Steve replied, "I am a C-5—C-6 complete," referring to the vertebrae in his neck where his spinal cord was severed.

"You are a quad then," Laura continued. "You don't look like a quadriplegic."

Steve replied smiling, "Thanks, I guess, I'm wired screwy. I am technically a quad since I can't move my fingers, though I do have full use of my arms."

Laura replied, "In nursing school, I worked a rotation at Sister Kenny Rehab Center in the Twin Cities. I got to know quite a few spinal cord patients. You certainly do all right for yourself."

"Rachael helps a lot," Steve replied. "She keeps me in line."

Rachael laughed from her seat across the room, "He does most everything himself, but he can be a pain in the ass once in a while," she joked. "Did you ask the conductor about your tickets?"

"No. Do you think I need to?" Laura replied.

"It probably wouldn't hurt. It will help keep their records straight," Steve said.

Rachael instructed Steve to push the yellow call button behind him. In a few minutes George appeared in the doorway. As Rachael explained the situation, George realized that this was a situation for the conductor, and it would be best to have him come up to the room. Excusing himself, the car attendant promised that he would be right back.

Soon a short man in a dark blue suit and blue conductor hat knocked on the door and announced that he was the conductor and would be happy to help.

Rachael got up and walked through the door and asked the conductor to follow to the center of the car. After a brief conversation the conductor came back and asked for Laura and Kyle's tickets. After brief examination he handed them back and told them everything was clear and they would be getting off in Wisconsin Dells.

As the conductor turned and left the room the scanner crackled and came alive, "Amtrak portable to the head end."

"Go ahead," came the reply

"Rich, can you give me a call on the cell?" the conductor asked

"Sure, Amtrak out," the engineer responded

Kyle looked at Steve with a puzzled look and asked what that meant.

Steve shrugged his shoulders, replied that he didn't know and that there must be something confidential going on.

Two minutes later the conductor appeared at the doorway once again saying, "Ma'am can I speak to you in private?"

Laura became noticeably alarmed and replied, "Of course."

She then stood up, handed the baby to Rachael, and followed the conductor down the hall. Kyle watched intently as his mother disappeared through the door. As quickly as she departed she appeared, this time with a smile on her face and a tear in her eye.

Grabbing her son's coat, she instructed the boy to get ready as they were going to get off at the next stop. First, he had better use the bathroom and then she would put on his coat.

With his face fallen, and a sad look in his eye the youngster sniffled, "The trip is over already?"

"Not quite, but we are getting off," Laura responded, as she led the boy down the hall and opened the bathroom door. "Hurry up in there. We don't have much time."

Steve looked at Rachael in disbelief. Why were they getting off? This was Tomah, Wisconsin Dells wasn't until the next stop, forty minutes away.

Rachael looked back at Steve and said firmly, "Don't ask, and don't say a word."

"But," Steve started, but the look from his wife put an end to his sentence. He would keep quiet. Suddenly, the car became engulfed in blackness and the sound of the train became muffled, like being in a tin can. They were in the tunnel. Kyle came out of the washroom and looked surprised at the darkness. The light from behind him illuminated everything in front, but the rest of the car was dark. Steve quickly told the boy of the tunnel in central Wisconsin, the only tunnel east of the continental divide that the Empire Builder passed through.

In a couple if minutes the train came back out into the light. Shortly thereafter the conductor appeared once more. "You ready ma'am?"

Laura shook her head yes.

"We only have three minutes, so we'll have to make it quick."

"OK, what do you want me to do?" Laura asked

"You just follow me," the conductor replied

The man then stepped over to the door, opened the window and stuck his head out, pressing the radio button on his shoulder. He spoke into the microphone, "Five cars, Amtrak—Four, Amtrak" Waiting a few more seconds, he then continued, " Two cars, Amtrak—one more—That'll do when you get 'em stopped, Amtrak. You ready, Rich?"

The engineer replied quickly, "Let's do it."

Quickly the conductor opened the large door, stepped out and helped the woman and boy to the platform. "Follow me," he said, as he turned and walked briskly toward the front of the train. As the trio approached, Rich, the engineer, stuck his head out of the cab door.

"Mommy, where are we going?" Kyle asked half running to keep up with his mother.

"Kyle, the engineer has agreed to let you look up in the engine. He doesn't have much time, so we have to hurry," Laura replied half dragging the six-year-old down the platform.

Now the boy's legs sped up. Did he hear his mother right? Or was he dreaming? The closer they got to the engine the more real it became. He was going inside the engine, and for the first time in his life would be a real engineer. His legs pumped harder. Now he was actually passing his mother. Time was of the essence. If he didn't hurry, he might wake up, and the dream would vanish. It did not. They reached the ladder of the locomotive. Without a pause, the conductor reached under the small boy's arms and whisked him high in the air and right into the arms of the waiting engineer. In less than a second Kyle was transformed from a small frail child into a superhero locomotive engineer.

In shock, Kyle just stood frozen in the middle of the brown cab. Unable to speak, he just looked at the computer screens under the front windshield and the levers on the desk in front of the engineer's chair.

"What da ya think, buddy?" came a voice through the haze of shock. Blinking twice, he brought himself around, and located the source of the sound. Rich, the blond engineer, was crouching alongside to be at eye level with the young boy. "You like trains, buddy?"

Just shaking his head up and down, Kyle croaked a soft "Yes, I want to be an engineer."

"OK, buddy, we don't have much time. You stay right here," Rich instructed, as he headed for the door and climbed down the ladder.

Kyle remained motionless, but gradually became aware of his surroundings as the numbing shock released his senses.

Soon the engineer climbed through the doorway and closed the door behind him. "You ready to drive, Buddy?" Rich asked

By now Kyle was fully free from the blanket of shock and embraced the situation, replying confidently, "Sure am."

Rich sat down in the engineer's seat and said, "Come on over and sit here on my lap. I'll show you how it's done."

Kyle quickly crawled up on the man's lap and studied the controls and computer screen in front of him. "It looks like a video game," the young boy exclaimed.

"Kinda," the engineer agreed. Pointing to the brown T-handle, he explained the throttle, then the brakes, just as the "Highball Amtrak" came over the radio.

Rich instructed Kyle to put his hand on the throttle and gently placing his larger hand over the top helped the young boy push the lever to notch one. The big diesels came alive and whined with anticipation to get up and go. In what seemed like eternity, but was actually only a second, the train started to move. Rich again helped the small hand move the throttle to notch two. More power behind them, more speed in front. Kyle was holding his breath in excitement, but now he had to take a breath. Notch three—now the trees began to blur as they passed the window. All the way up to notch six, Rich kept his hand over Kyle's. He removed his hand and said, "OK, buddy, move it one more notch."

Kyle gave a gentle push; the lever moved ahead and clicked into the next location. Rich then said proudly, "Let's sit back and enjoy the ride."

Kyle settled back as he sat between Rich's legs in the seat of a full-blown Amtrak engineer. Watching the trees, houses, barns and sheds fly by at 79 miles an hour, Kyle pictured himself carrying sick boys to be cured in faraway cities, bringing lonesome mothers to meet long lost daddies as he stopped at the stations. Here is where he belonged. He didn't need legs to carry him from place to place, not when he had this magnificent machine under his control. Those poor people waiting in those puny cars had to stop when he passed by. That is what power the engineer had. This is where he had to be.

He crossed a bridge over a small creek; no creek was going to stop him and this silver bullet. Soon a headlight appeared in the distance, another freight. This one stopped in the siding, just to let him by. He flew by the freight locomotive, waving as he passed. Of course they would wait for him: he was the best engineer on the planet. No one could stop him from keeping his schedule. This is what made him Kyle, the locomotive engineer.

Rich broke into his dream, "You want to blow the horn?"

Since he was so entranced in throttling up the locomotive, the budding engineer didn't even notice that Rich was pushing the horn button at each grade crossing.

"Here push this button; I'll help. Two longs—one short—and a long. Remember that, two longs—a short—and then a long."

Putting his hand over the button, Kyle pushed down. Above him, outside the cab, the powerful air horns erupted in their signature song. Rich said quickly, "OK, now again a long."

Kyle pushed once more. Then a short and another long as they crossed the road in front of two stopped cars.

Kyle almost burst with pride. He could do it; he could be an engineer. Rich said quickly, "OK, let's do it again, do you remember?"

"Yes, two longs—a short—and a long," Kyle responded proudly.

"Start when we pass that white sign with the 'W.' See it?"

Kyle spotted the sign and pushed the horn as he flew past the sign. Two longs—a short—and a last long.

"Good job, buddy. Do you know how fast we are going? Look there at the screen, 79 miles an hour. Now see that yellow sign ahead. That means we have to slow down to 69 miles an hour through this town. Let's pull the throttle back one notch. I'll keep track of the horn"

The young hand reached forward and gently pulled the throttle back. The diesels eased back on their strain and the train slowed a bit.

A few miles ahead a yellow signal displayed on the mast alongside the tracks.

Back in the sleeper car, George descended the stairs and walked toward the end cabin. Rachael was busy packing last-minute items into a red backpack and Steve was zipping his jacket.

"We're just about ready," Rachael said to the car attendant. She dug into her fanny pack and pulled out a twenty dollar bill. "Thanks so much for all your help," she said as she handed it to the attendant.

"Well thank you, Mrs. G. What do you want me to bring out for you?" the attendant asked.

Handing the man a large black suitcase, she thanked the attendant, and handed the red pack to Steve.

Laura fretted outside the door in the hallway, clearly worried about her son. Steve clipped the scanner to a front breast pocket on his coat and adjusted the volume.

The scanner then reported,"Yellow Flag, Amtrak."

Soon the train began to slow. Again the scanner came alive, "CP Wisconsin dispatcher to Amtrak 8."

"Go ahead, dispatcher," Rich answered

The dispatcher then gave the following instructions, "You are running a bit ahead of schedule so I am going to put you off to the side at Mile Creek. I am going to let priority 7003 go by."

Rich answered, "OK, dispatcher, Amtrak out."

The dispatcher signed off, "CP Wisconsin, dispatcher out."

Steve wheeled out to the vestibule in the center of the car and announced to the two women that they were going to stop and wouldn't be getting off for a while. Soon the train slowed to a crawl, bounced over a switch and came to a stop. Rachael sat down on one of the bags and Laura just looked out the window in the door. Suddenly the scanner came alive with a faint voice in the background, "You can go ahead and talk now."

Then suddenly a loud voice came on, "Mommy, I'm an engineer. I'm driving."

The radio quickly silenced.

The three people waiting to depart, looked at each other, burst into laughter and then just as suddenly came the tears. All three reached out for each other and combined into a group hug.

An odd lot they were, a young woman carrying a baby, a man in a wheelchair and a tall dark-haired woman wrapped in a convoluted hug. All with tears of sadness and joy flowing freely down their cheeks.

The train jerked slightly as it once again came into motion. A passing freight whooshed by.

Slowly the train made its way toward the end of the siding where it would merge with the mainline and continue east. The three entwined passengers had visions of the courageous, six-year-old boy sitting in the engineer's chair, controlling the six thousand horsepower locomotives as they delivered the world's most precious cargo. This was a Christmas never to be duplicated.

Kyle watched intently as the freight passed and the train approached the end of the siding. Fearful they would proceed too fast and hit the passing freight, he told Rich to keep it slow. Smiling, Rich replied, "OK, buddy, notch it back one more."

Kyle quickly grabbed the throttle and pulled it back so the train slowed back down. Suddenly the last double stack car whizzed by. The passing freight was gone.

"Wait for the light to turn green," Rich instructed

In a few seconds, the red light blacked and the green appeared. Rich instructed the new engineer, "When I push the radio button you say Green Flag, Amtrak. Got that?"

Shaking his head yes he counted one-two-three. Rich pushed the radio button and Kyle said loudly, "Green flag, Amtrak"

Rich released the button and told Kyle to notch up the throttle.

Feeling back in control of the rushing locomotives, Kyle was again flying. Across the highways, through the towns and over the bridges, the silver bullet was flying. He knew how proud his mom was going to be of him. He could drive the train and keep it on the tracks. In a few minutes, Rich informed Kyle that the trip was coming to an end. Turning a bit sideways he moved his leg to allow the boy to slip off the seat and stand in the middle of the cab. As he slowed the train to a stop at the brick station in Wisconsin Dells, he turned and lifted his dark blue Amtrak engineer hat off of its hook. Removing the BNSF hat from the boy's head, he placed the Amtrak hat proudly on the boy.

"You are now an Amtrak engineer, buddy. This BNSF hat is for freight hauling. You are a passenger engineer."

He stood up, walked to the far side of the cab and opened the door. As the conductor stood underneath, Rich swung the boy out and down into the conductor's arms. In a continuous motion he placed the boy firmly on the ground.

Handing her baby to Rachael, Laura threw her luggage aside and ran the length of the train. Her young son hit the ground running toward his mother. The two met at the end of the second locomotive. The woman bent slightly as the young boy made a flying leap into her open arms, the Amtrak hat flying to the ground. Spinning half to absorb the force of the flying leap and half in excitement, she danced, hugging, crying and laughing. "You did wonderful. I heard you on the radio. Honey, I am so proud of you."

Kyle just hugged his mother, pulled his head back and said, "My hat, get my hat."

Rich had climbed down and walked to the reunited family. Picking up his hat and placing it on the boy's head, he told Laura, "He did wonderful. Good luck. I have a seven-year-old at home. I can't imagine. Here is my card; let me know how things work out."

Turning to Kyle, still in her arms, she said, "What do you say?"

"Thank you," Kyle said as the engineer turned and walked back to his waiting train. Hiding a tear, he climbed back up the ladder and continued his duties. He may have to face disciplinary charges tomorrow, but today he made a young boy's life more memorable.

Laura set the boy back on the ground as they started back toward the waiting, Steve and Rachael.

Just as they reached the waiting couple, Amtrak 8 pulled out of the station, when all that was left was the flashing red light in the distance, Kyle announced proudly, "I am the Engineer on the Empire Builder."

Chapter 6
City Boy in the Country

Rich received the "Highball Amtrak" and notched the throttle up. Glancing in the outside mirror he watched the boy and his family as they walked down the platform. He thought with a smile, *There goes one happy kid. I hope this helps with his fight for life.* The diesels groaned as they brought the train into motion. As he gained some speed, Rich pulled the throttle back and could still feel the fragile hand that had helped him a few minutes past. Staring ahead he rounded the bend as he headed out of town and into the Wisconsin countryside. He hoped the kid rounded the bend and that his road to recovery was straight and downhill from here. He let his mind drift to his own home and his son waiting for him on this Christmas day. He would be so excited to show off his presents. Rich said out loud to no one, "I've got it good."

As Craig Wrightman boarded the coach car he watched as a small child was swung out of the locomotive cab. George the car attendant took his bag saying, "Merry Christmas. You staying with us to Chicago?

"Yes, I'm heading back home. Merry Christmas to you also," replied the tall, broad-shouldered man.

George smiled and instructed the man, "Head on up the stairs and your seat will be on the left six rows back."

"Thanks," Craig replied as he started up the narrow stairs. Once at the top he noticed the car was only three quarters full, so he counted the rows and sat down in his seat. He quickly settled in and glued himself to the window and checked out the scenery as it rolled on by. He sat watching, recalling with delight his visit with his mother and brothers around the kitchen table of the old farm house.

The thoughts cascaded into thoughts of all those meals and all those chats around that same kitchen table in that same old farm house. Oh what memories.

A few minutes had passed when a short overweight man with a green plaid shirt loomed above Craig's right shoulder and boomed arrogantly, "Excuse me, you are sitting in my seat."

Turning from the window almost in shock Craig quickly replied, "Pardon me?"

The round faced man repeated himself with even more arrogance, "YOU are sitting in my seat."

Craig looked at the man in disbelief. "I'm sorry, I thought the attendant told me to sit in the sixth row back."

The fat man shook his head so his jowls wiggled side to side, "This is row five and this is my seat. Yours is the next one back."

"Sorry," Craig replied as he stood and squeezed past the man blocking the aisle.

As he stepped into his proper seat Craig opened his mouth to tell the man to take a chill pill, but on further thought, stopped himself and decided not to stoop to his level. He then thought of wishing him a Merry Christmas, but figured that too would escalate the situation. So finally he just decided to observe the day of peace and sat down quietly. To ease his own tensions he put the picture of the man shaking his jowls back into his head. He then superimposed the face of one the hogs he had back on the farm over the man's own face. This brought a smile to his face. At least his hogs weren't so arrogant.

Soon Craig was watching the rolling Wisconsin landscape pass by the window in the muted winter sunshine. The bright red barns and tall concrete silos stood fast against the cold winter air. The hills were various shades of brown and the remnants of previous snows littered the fence rows between fields. Occasionally a herd of the signature black and white Holsteins dotted the landscape, but it was winter and most of the cows were nestled in their barns chewing their cuds and snoozing. Craig again brought back memories of all those years of working around the farm. The hard work followed by the feelings of accomplishment and physical exhaustion. He just smiled and continued to watch as the train followed the Wisconsin River southeastward across the middle of its namesake state.

Rich kept the locomotives notched up as he followed the level valley toward Portage and his next station stop. He could not keep his mind off of the small boy that had sat in front of him and piloted this huge locomotive, with his frail fingers he was able to operate this highly complex piece of technology. Fifty years ago such a feat would not have been possible. The old steam locomotives required real men to operate. A boy's greatest dream would be to sit in the seat and operate the whistle. Times change.

Soon the train passed under the highway overpass and Rich piloted his locomotives and train into the Portage yards. He pulled to a stop in front of the old station house and watched the six people depart and walk toward their cars and waiting friends and relatives.

As the motion ceased in the coach car, Craig stopped George the car attendant and asked, "Is the diner car still open? Can I get something to eat?"

George replied with a smile, "Sure is, I can check to see if there is a waiting list."

"Thanks, I would appreciate that," Craig replied.

George quickly walked down the aisle, through two cars and came upon the dining car attendant. "You got room in there yet?"

"Sure, George, you hungry? I'll buy," Stan replied.

"Thanks, Stan, but I can't eat right now. This is for a passenger," George responded. "How about we eat in twenty minutes? I'll let you buy if you promise not to tell any more of your terrible stories."

"Hey, You know I can't promise nothing like that. They just come out," Stan said half laughing.

George quickly replied, "Yeah, like diarrhea."

Both men broke out in laughter and Stan quickly slapped George on the back and said, "Go get your passenger so we can eat."

George quickly returned to Craig's seat and told him of the opening for lunch and where to find the car.

Thanking the attendant, Craig stood up and started for the aisle. Looking forward toward the man seated in the row ahead of him,

Craig studied the overweight man who was just sitting and staring out the window. Taking a chance, Craig leaned forward and said politely, "Excuse me, I am going to have some lunch in the dining car. Since I am all alone on this Christmas I was wondering if you would like to join me. I would like to buy you Christmas lunch."

The man looked away from the window not believing anyone was talking to him. Blinking his eyes to adjust to the change in light. he replied, "Pardon me. I was daydreaming and didn't comprehend what you were saying. Sorry."

Craig smiled and repeated himself, "I was just wondering if you would like to join me for lunch in the dining car. My treat. I would like the company."

"I-I guess. Sure, I am kind of hungry. But you don't have to buy," the man said as he used the seat in front of him to pull himself up.

"No, this is my treat. It's Christmas and I'd be delighted to share lunch with a stranger. By the way my name is Craig Wrightman," Craig said as he stuck his right hand out in a friendly gesture.

"Brian Clark," the man said as he grasped Craig's hand and shook it in a tight grip.

Craig turned as he said, "The diner is this way two cars back. I'm sorry I almost stole your seat. I guess I need to go back to kindergarten and learn to count."

"No problem," Brian replied. "I'll follow."

As the pair reached the dining car Stan showed them to a table and seated them across from each other next to the window. Since the car was not busy they had a nice quiet spot.

Brian was the first to speak after sitting down, "Where are you taking the train to, Craig?"

"I'm going all the way to Chicago. I live in Elk Grove Village, but grew up on a farm near here, outside a town called Randolph," Craig replied and then followed with a question, "Where are you heading for on Christmas?"

"Same place as you," Brian replied without looking up from his menu. "I live in Round Lake, Illinois. I'm on my way home. I just came up here to Wisconsin Dells because my wife's aunt passed away and I had to take care of liquidating the estate. A real pain in the ass. She didn't have anything prepared when she died, so I've been running back and forth for the past three months. Thank God I finally got everything cleared up and this is the last trip up here. Boy, the lawyers in this town are a bunch of small town bozos. I first made a bunch of phone calls to arrange things. Then I drive all the way up here only to find they didn't get the paperwork finished. So I start over. I make more phone calls, arrange all the appointments and drive up again. This time it seems the woman attorney decides to have her baby and wouldn't be in for a couple of months. You'd think she would have known she was pregnant and had a replacement or something. I guess the third time's a charm and I got everything cleared and settled."

Craig just smiled and replied politely, "I'm glad you got everything taken care of. Too bad that I hadn't met you three months ago, I could have helped you out. I know the area and some of the people."

Without acknowledging the offer and goodwill, Brian just asked, "What's good on the menu?"

Craig responded, "I like all of it. I think all the food on the train is very good. It's not only the food; I just think of it as a whole experience. Eating a good meal traveling 79 miles per hour. Just can't get much better. Is this the first time on the train?"

Brian smiled and nodded his head. "Yes. Except for the ride up here I mean. I had been driving but my wife's car is in for service. I've never eaten on a train though."

"Oh, that's the fun of riding the train. Don't think of it as moving from point 'A' to point 'B.' Use it as an experience. Look out the window; enjoy the scenery. Indulge in a meal and a glass of wine. Relax a bit. When the train gets to your final station, you will join the rest of the world. But in this seat, you are in a world where time stands still. You don't have to worry about anything," Craig said as he sat back in his chair and watched as the brown rolling hills and bare trees rushed by the window.

"What do you do for a living Brian?" Craig asked, breaking the introspective mood.

Brian looked up and folded the menu as he set it to the side, "I'm a CPA for a small firm in Round Lake. We do mostly small business accounting and tax preparation. I try to stay away from private returns. Too many headaches."

Craig thought to himself, *No wonder he stays away from private accounts. He probably couldn't hold any.* But he smiled and said aloud, " I suppose there would be a lot of hassles."

Stan, the waiter appeared out of nowhere and asked if both men were ready to order.

Craig looked up from his thoughts. "What do you feel like, Brian? I'm having the chicken sandwich. The regular hamburger is great also."

Looking at Stan, Brian said, "The hamburger sounds good. I'll have a Pepsi to drink."

The waiter jotted down the order and asked if he wanted all the trimmings.

"Sure, sounds good," Brian replied

As the waiter turned, Craig started, "I'll have the chicken sandwich with everything. You can keep the chips, Stan. I'll also have a glass of milk and a cup of coffee."

"OK, Craig. I'll be right back," Stan the waiter replied

As Stan turned and rustled down the aisle, Craig leaned forward and said, "Check out the window, Brian."

Brian leaned his large frame forward and looked to see what his new companion was pointing to.

"See that farm over there with that long red barn and huge white sausage-looking things behind them?" Craig pointed out.

Brian replied, "Yes. Looks like typical Wisconsin farm."

Craig said, "That's where I grew up. Of course it didn't look like that when I was still on the farm. My brothers run it now. It's more of a corporate farm than a family farm but it still is home."

Brian looked surprised and said, "I never would have pictured you as a farmer. You must have moved away quite a while ago."

Craig leaned back away from the window trying to decipher what his travel mate had just said. He looked across the table at Brian's eyes and realized that he really didn't mean any harm; he was just sheltered and probably considered farmers some separate species like the ones in his childhood books. Craig didn't have time to respond as Brian broke the silence first.

"You know, I never understood how you farmers just reminisce about the good old days and get so attached to a place," Brian said, and then continued as he sat back from the window. "My family moved three times when I was living at home. Never once did I look back at our old house. I was always excited to get a new bedroom, furniture and house to explore. It was an exciting event not a time of reminiscence."

Craig sat forward and asked, "Really? Didn't you ever miss your friends? Your neighborhood? Your old room?"

"Not really. We didn't move that far. As far as friends, we always seemed to stay in the same school district," Brian responded

"You never missed the neighborhood and your usual haunts?" Craig asked

"No, not really. I didn't hang out in the neighborhood much. That was for the poor kids. I always had things at school or I'd go to camp in the summer," Brian responded.

Craig sat back and thought for a second. "Do you have any brothers or sisters? Didn't you do things in the yard with them? Didn't you have secret hideouts in the neighborhood, secret clubs, like you see in the movies?"

Brian looked back out the window, "No, it is not like that. I only had a sister who was five years older. We didn't do much together. Life was all so planned, sports, school, band, clubs. Everything was laid out. You just had to be sure you were there on time."

"Maybe that's why you didn't care about moving. You really didn't have any roots in the neighborhood," Craig said as he put his face in the palms of his hands. He was trying to understand this man. There just seemed to be something missing. It was all so alien to not spend your childhood exploring the outdoors and the world around.

So Craig continued probing, "What did you do for fun?"

Brian smiled and asked, "What is this 20 questions on what makes Brian tick?"

Embarrassed Craig quickly said, "Oh no, I just always wondered what it was like to grow up in the city. When we were kids we spent almost all of our time around the farm. We knew where every tree, rock, gully, gopher hole and even where the ant hills were on the entire one hundred and twenty acres. I can't imagine not being rooted in an area."

Brian cut in, "We had free time. I spent a lot of it reading, watching TV or building model cars, and like I said in the summer we went to camp, where we'd go and explore every free second we had. I suppose being on a farm would be like summer camp to us."

Craig replied slowly, "Well yes and no. Yes in the fact that we would explore every second we had the chance. But no in the fact that it was all fun and games. With the risk of sounding like a stereotypical grandfather, we had to work. I remember having chores to do when I was in first grade. We always did chores before we went to school in the morning. I'm not talking about some Depression-era farm. This was in the late '60s early '70s."

Brian looked surprised and just muttered, "Really?"

Craig continued, "Sure, my brothers did this into the '80s. Didn't you have at least house-type chores?"

"Sure, you know, cleaning my room, helping Dad clean the garage, or sometimes running errands. But never anything that interfered with school," Brian responded

"We never had anything that interfered with school. All of our chores were done around school," Craig said

"I thought you said that you did chores before you went to school. You went to school late, right?" Brian replied.

Craig smiled and shook his head, "No, we got up at five and were done by seven so we had time to eat breakfast and get to school by eight twenty."

The smell of food preceded Stan down the aisle as he carried the plates to the two gentlemen. Setting the plates down he said, "Here you go, hamburger for you and chicken sandwich for you, Craig. I'll be right back with your drinks."

Brian looked down at his sandwich as Craig replied to the waiter, "Thanks, Stan."

No one spoke as each performed his own ritual of preparing the sandwich for eating. Craig took his fingers, piled the tomato and lettuce on the open bun, ripped open the packet of mustard and spread it across the top of the lettuce. After everything was in place, he put the top bun on the pile and smashed it down with the palm of his hand. He then picked up the whole assembly and took a large wholesome bite.

Meanwhile Brian removed the lettuce and taking his fork placed the tomato on top of the meat patty. After opening his ketchup packet spread a thin layer carefully over the entire surface with his knife. Laying the top bun in place, he wrapped his large hands around and took a small bite.

Craig watched while he was chewing and wondered how a man could get so large eating so gingerly. Stan set the Styrofoam cups in front of each diner and asked, "Is there anything else I can get you?"

Brian shook his head no and Craig swallowed and replied, "No thanks, Stan."

Craig took another a bite from his sandwich as Brian asked, "What do you do now? You still in agriculture?"

As he finished chewing Craig responded, "No, I got out of agriculture when I went to school. I am actually a steel salesman. I travel a three-state region selling steel to manufacturing companies. It's a good job. I meet a lot of people but I spend a lot of time on the road.

"Do you get out of Round Lake much? You know travel and such?" Craig asked.

Brian took a bite and looked out the window as he chewed. He could see where this conversation was going and really wasn't sure he wanted to go there. No, he didn't get out much. He was happily married, had two grown children and liked his sheltered life, or so he tried to convince himself. Turning back to face his new companion he decided to jump in. "No, I suppose I don't get out too much. My wife and I are happy to stay in our house in the city. I have a son and daughter at Northwestern University so they are close."

Craig smiled a bit and said, "That's fine. People are different. I love to travel and meet new people and see new places. Even for vacations, my wife and I travel. You would think I spend enough time on the road I'd want to stat home. I just like exploring and meeting people. I guess that's why I'm in the line of work I do. Aren't you ever curious to see what's outside your life?"

"Sure, I'm not a hermit or anything. Just because I don't travel, doesn't mean I am not curious," Brian responded with dignity.

"Oh, I'm sorry, I wasn't implying that you aren't," Craig replied quickly. "I just know how I look at things. I like to study people and their way of life and thinking."

"So do I," Brian responded as he turned back toward the window. "I just do it from the comfort of my house and armchair. There is such comfort in my house and settled lifestyle. I don't like to put myself in harm's way. Don't you ever get scared out there by yourself? There is just so much going on now days," Brian asked

Craig smiled broadly. "It's not like I am some wilderness explorer. For my work I have a route all laid out and for the most part see the same customers. When my wife and I travel for vacation we just head off the beaten path whenever we can. We don't take unnecessary risks. We just want to see what other people live like."

"Yes, but even in your job, living on the road, you could have an accident and no one would know you or you could get mugged somewhere," Brian stated

"So what?" Craig replied. "Things will turn out. If I am mugged, I give them my money and go on my way. I really don't worry about it. Life's too short. I suppose some of the self-reliance comes from living on the farm. You are raised learning that you need to be prepared for what you can control and the rest you have to deal with as it is pitched at you."

There was a long pause in the conversation. Both men continued eating, pensive in their own thoughts. It was not an awkward silence but a welcomed reprieve where each man could reflect on his opinions. Outside the Wisconsin countryside rolled on.

Up front in the locomotives, Rich got the car spotting instructions for the Columbus stop. As he approached the small brick station he mused that it was a sure cry from the Nina, Pinta or Santa Maria, but he was bringing his passengers to their destination half a world away.

"Three cars, Amtrak," the radio barked. "Two cars, Amtrak." Again the radio. And finally, "That'll do, Amtrak."

Rich set the brakes and waited for the highball. This was going to be a quick one and then in an hour he'd be in Milwaukee, turn south and head down into Chicago and home.

"Highball Amtrak."

Rich finally got his instruction to get his train into motion and do what it did best: pass over those ties at 79 miles an hour, make those steel wheels sing on the rails. Quickly the speed indicator was holding at 79. Rich sat back and watched each grade crossing, whistling at each one. Farm fields rolled by and occasionally a small village broke the monotony. The Empire Builder was heading into the final stretch. Like a race horse stretching its neck and getting a second wind, the diesels roared behind the engineer and the electric motors kept those steel wheels singing on the cold steel rails.

At the far end of the diner, George and Stan sat enjoying a quick meal before reaching the end of their duties as Amtrak attendants. Stan sat facing the car so he could keep a watchful eye on his guests halfway down the car.

"What'd you get your girlfriend for Christmas?" George asked.

Stan replied with a smile as he reached down and grabbed his crotch, "I'm giving her the best present in the world."

George just shook his head. "Spare me, Stan. We all know about your sex life."

Getting more serious Stan replied, "I got her a new laptop computer. She needs one for her job and is running around with an old piece of shit she bought a couple of years ago. It was junk then, and didn't get any better with age."

George asked, "Stan, you know a lot about computers. Why do you keep working for Amtrak?"

Stan replied, "Ain't no money in fixing computers. Besides I like traveling and I like the people. Sure sometimes they can be a pain in the ass. But mostly they are good and decent folks. I really miss talking when I'm off. How about you? Why do you stay?"

"I guess the same as you." George replied, "I've been on this same route for some time now and it gets a bit boring, but there are advantages to having familiarity. Yet, like you said I love the people."

Stan then grinned from ear to ear and said, "Plus this job gives your wife a chance to get rid of you, so she can go out and have a real man for five days. She only has to put up with your little weenie for them five days you're home." Stan broke into laughter as he stood up and slapped George on the back. "I see my guests are about done over there. I'll be right back."

George shook his head and said, "Stanley, I don't know why I even listen to you."

Stan had already walked out of earshot and was standing in front of Craig and Brian's table. "Can I get you two gentlemen anything else," Stan asked.

"No thanks, I'm fine," Brian said. "How about you, Craig?"

"I'm good," Craig replied in amazement. This was the first act of courtesy he'd seen from Brian. The two had pretty much finished their meal with small talk and not really engaged each other. Craig said to the waiter, "I'll take the check."

Stan looked down the aisle toward the kitchen and said softly, "Tell you what. Merry Christmas. This one's on Amtrak. We're not too busy so we'll get this one."

Craig replied as he handed the man a five-dollar bill, "Well thanks, Stan, Merry Christmas."

Brian reached into his pocket and also pulled out a five-dollar bill and handed it to Stan saying, "Merry Christmas. I think I'm learning a few things on this trip."

"What's that, sir?" Stan asked Brian.

Brian looked at Craig and then back at Stan, "Craig here thinks that maybe I've lived a bit of a sheltered life and don't get out to explore and meet people. Maybe he's right. I just met two fine gentlemen in the last couple of hours. If I had driven or stayed home I would not have had the experience."

Stan replied, "Good for you. George over there and I were just talking about how we liked the people we meet on the train. Basically they are mostly good folks. You just have to talk to them and find out. Or else you just assume the worst and you get yourself in a downward spiral. Eventually you never get out at all. My uncle did that. I don't ever want to be like him."

"I could see that happening. But not everyone is like you and Craig," Brian said with a smile.

Craig was the first to respond, "How do you know until you talk to them?"

Brian replied, "That's the point. I've learned that I need to get to know people before passing judgment. If I would have known before hand that you grew up a farmer, I would have assumed you for a country hick. But you forced me to talk to you. I now know you are not. Stan, just because you are a car attendant I could assume you a Pullman porter from the 1940s. You are not. Thanks, guys, for showing me that I need to explore, not just my surroundings but my surrounding people."

Stan looked at his watch and said to the two seated men, "I'd let you sit here and talk for the rest of the trip, but I gotta get closed up and started cleaning by the time we hit Milwaukee. That'll be about ten minutes."

"That's okay, Stan. We'll head back to our seats," Craig said

"I don't mean to rush you," the waiter said as Brian and Craig stood up and squeezed toward the aisle.

Brian reached his chubby hand toward the waiter and when Stan grasped it Brian shook it heartily.

"You have a very Merry Christmas and thanks for the service and the meal. Maybe I'll catch you again on this train," Brian said

Turning to Craig, Brian said, "Craig, why don't you sit in the seat next to me. It's not taken and I want to learn more about traveling and the farm."

Craig turned to Stan, shook his hand and said, "Merry Christmas, Stan. Be good and have a happy New Year."

Stan looked around the car to be sure no one was watching and then grabbed his crotch once again and replied, "I'm always good, just ask Carmine."

Craig just laughed and responded saying, "Dream on, Stan."

Then he followed Brian out of the diner, back to the coach car and their seats.

Outside the train, the rural countryside had become more scarce and the usual urban track side elements could be seen. The businesses had changed from agricultural to industrial. The streets came more frequently and backyards lined the right of way instead of pastures and farm fields. Rich watched the signals and smiled with delight as he passed each green without delay.

Rich sat back and kept a close eye on the grade crossings, which were becoming more numerous as they entered into one of the more populated regions of the state. In the back of his mind he, as did every engineer, feared the sight of a vehicle approaching at the crossings. There was always the possibility of it not stopping. Just the thought brought back the memory of three years ago, at the crossing outside of Milwaukee, where the teenage girl took her life using his train. He winced as he thought of the night and he could still see the girl's face through the windshield as she stopped that car on the tracks. The helpless feeling as he pushed the emergency stop button, knowing he would not come to a halt for a half a mile. The crunching, tearing noise as the locomotives completely ripped the automobile in half and spewed it out along the tracks for several hundred yards. He remembered the feeling of disgust within himself for not wanting to get out of the locomotive; he didn't even want to check on the state of the vehicle or the driver. Inside he knew the outcome. Then there was the bewildered feeling as he climbed down from the cab; he didn't even know which side of the tracks to look on for the girl. He felt helpless and disgusted with the whole scene and how he couldn't do anything. It was the conductor who came across the girl's body first, or what remained of it. Gene remembered crossing behind the train and seeing the conductor vomiting between the tracks from the horrible sight. Between spasms, he told Gene not to go over to the wreckage as nothing would be gained. Gene obliged, so the two sat down on the rail and wept before the emergency crew arrived. It was two weeks before Gene could sleep at night and now three years later he still had visions of the girl crossing in front of his train. Gene knew that it was these visions that caused many a good engineer to give up his job and the love of railroading for a desk job.

Shaking his head to remove the memories, Rich wound through suburban Milwaukee and eventually made his way down into the Menomonie River Valley. It was here that, with the heavy industry and stoic, German, Italian and Polish workers, much of the equipment used in mining the steel, digging the earth and grading the paths of the modern-day railroads was forged. Names like Bucyres Erie, P&H, and Rexnord became synonymous to earth moving. Allen Bradley to electronics, and of course Milwaukee's most famous commodity, beer.

Rich looked off to his right where the old Milwaukee Road railroad yards once covered acres of this valley. All were gone now. The once flourishing transcontinental Milwaukee Road outspent its coffers and now existed in memory only. Since leaving St. Paul The Empire Builder had been traveling on the old Milwaukee Road right of way. Now Canadian Pacific owned the route retaining the last vestiges of this once-proud railroad.

Soon the dated, white, Milwaukee, Amtrak station came into view. Here Rich would make a quick stop as passengers could only depart the train. Any people traveling from Milwaukee to Chicago would take the intercity Hiawatha. As he checked his watch he realized he was ten minutes early. He would have time to make a quick toilet break before heading to Chicago. As soon as he got the train stopped and tied down he headed for the small toilet in the cab.

George helped Stan clean the table before heading back to the coach car. As the train came to a halt, George helped a family of three off the train wishing each traveler a Merry Christmas. The car attendant quickly realized that the air was not so cold, but damp. Close proximity to Lake Michigan brought the moist winter chill into the city. The hazy sunshine did little to temper the dampness as he walked up and down the platform watching the city move around him on this Christmas day. He looked down impatiently at his watch, muttering to himself, "Come on let's go."

Just an hour and a half and he'd be in Chicago and soon afterward on his way home. The conductor yelled the "All aboard" bringing relief to the car attendant. Climbing back into the coach he quickly slammed the door shut, as if it would get things moving sooner. As he turned and headed for the stairs, there was a pounding in the steel door. George quickly turned back and pulled down on the latch swinging the door open. There stood the conductor without a smile on his face; he quickly hopped aboard and pushed his radio button attached to his collar. "Highball Amtrak."

Turning to George he scolded, "You're pretty quick on the door today George."

"Sorry," the car attendant said, "my head's not with it this afternoon. My kids are at home waiting for me so they can open their presents."

"No problem, I know the feeling. I've got a three-year-old waiting at home," the conductor said as he bent his head closer to the microphone, pushed the button and said, "Amtrak, thirteen off, 2:01 and 2:13. Amtrak out."

The conductor then said to George, "Merry Christmas, George. I'll see you in Chicago." He then turned and climbed the stairs

George stood and watched out the window as the bleak city junk passed by along the tracks. Soon they were out of the old section of town and heading down the lake shore to the Windy City and home. George shook off his fatigue and headed back to his work. Still more rooms to clean and passengers to check on.

Brian squeezed his large frame into the window seat as Craig followed and sat in the aisle seat. Craig spoke first treading on neutral ground by asking, "How come things were so tough with the estate settlement?"

Brian answered, "I don't know. My aunt didn't have a will or anything in place for her death. She was 86 years old but I guess ignored the fact that she was going to die. So I had to jump through the legal hoops to settle everything properly."

"Did you know her very well?" Craig asked

Brian replied, "Not really. I met her at our wedding, but never really talked to her. My wife's mother and her were not on speaking terms. Some stupid family feud I've heard."

Brian thought for a bit and then continued, "You know I suppose it goes back to not being afraid to talk to people. The feud, I mean. If my mother-in-law would have been bold enough to attack the issue head on, it probably would have been solved within minutes. But now my mother-in-law has to live the rest of her life regretting not saying goodbye to her sister."

Craig replied, "Yes, it is a shame. Brian, I still can't figure you out. You were so, oh I don't know, don't take this personally, but an asshole, when I got on the train. What happened?"

Brian turned and smiled at Craig. "It's Christmas. You ignored my pig headedness and in spite of my manners invited me to lunch. You talked to me and gently pried open my inner self revealing to me what I may be missing. I am sure this won't be *A Christmas Carol*-type transformation, but I want to try to see the world the way you do. I want to travel, meet different people, take a chance or two. Live in a life of what comes what may."

Craig smiled broadly, slapped Brian on the back and said, "Hold on there, buddy. Don't change the world overnight."

"Y'ah don't worry. I've got to convince my wife first," Brian replied.

Craig turned and said, "Why don't you start by coming over to my house next weekend? I'll make arrangements with my wife."

Brian thought for a second and replied with disappointment, "Next weekend is New Years; we have plans."

"Oh y'ah. How about the next weekend? Then once spring gets here and the weather turns nice, why don't you come up and visit the farm? I can show you around the Wisconsin Dells so you can join the rest of Chicago on vacation," Craig said

Brian responded, "I'd like that. I want to learn about rural areas. Tell me about the farm and growing up. I've read books and seen movies of the hardships and the joys. Was it really like that?"

Craig looked straight ahead in thought before beginning, "I suppose. It is a matter of perspective. At the time it was neither. Just way of life, one day came after the next and you faced one problem at a time. We were certainly not a family of means, but we weren't poor either. My parents always made sure we had what was necessary, not what we wanted, but what was necessary. Do you know what I mean?"

Brian replied, "I think so."

Continuing Craig said, "I don't remember the work so much or the bad times. The good times stick in my head, exploring new sections of the farm, finding special rocks in the rock piles along the fences, sledding in the winter. These are the things that made a young life memorable. The good part is that all these things are still part of the farm. I can go back and find the tall hickory tree where we spent hours as a kid gathering nuts. The big red granite rock that served as a pirate ship is still at the edge of the field. Though not as huge as I remember, it is still there. These are the roots I talked about earlier. Things that I couldn't imagine moving away from."

Brian asked thoughtfully, "I would like to see those places. Will you share them?"

"Sure. They won't be as grand as I remember, but they'll be there," Craig replied.

As the train passed a farm, Brian pointed out the window and asked, "You have a farm background and something has been bugging me for the past several years. What the heck are those long white, worm-looking things I see beside so many farms now?'

Craig laughed and replied, "Those are feed. Farmers pack feed into long plastic bags to preserve feed for the winter. They used to fill those big blue or concrete silos for the winter. But now with the larger farms it's proving too expensive to build the structures and fill them. So farmers either fill pits or stuff feed into those long sausage-looking bags."

Brian shook his head. "I've often wondered. Thanks for clearing that up. See another reason to talk to people. I would not have gotten my question answered sitting at home reading."

Craig just replied, "I suppose so."

Brian turned to Craig and asked once again, "Can I bring my kids up to the farm?"

Craig replied, "I suppose. Do you think college kids want to trudge around on a farm for the weekend when there are parties and friends to be enjoyed?"

"Doesn't matter. I'll make them come along. I don't want them to turn out like me and have to wait until they are middle aged to realize there is a whole world out there," Brian replied.

Craig said with a smile, "Boy, I need to offer to buy lunch for more people. If they have a second coming like you, I could become famous."

Both men laughed and sat back in silence. The skyline had changed and Chicago loomed in the distance. Both men knew that once they left the train it would be different. Even if they kept up as close friends, they wouldn't have these intimate conversations. They had explored each other and now that phase was complete. They would go back to their lives, meet each other, talk, but it would never be Christmas on the Empire Builder.

The hazy sun disappeared and foretold of the coming snowfall. The Empire Builder was returning home. With every green signal, every parked freight they passed, the closer to the real Christmas they came. Friends and families reunited at the last minute to celebrate each other's love, companionship and presence. This is what the Empire Builder delivers. Not passengers, not employees, but human beings, people, wives, lovers, friends, mothers, dads, grandparents, brothers and sisters. Since 1929 the cargo has been the same. Times may change but the human heart does not. When Rich pulled his train up to the platform, one could imagine the scene in 1929, 1939, 1969, or 2009. The cloths change and the faces change, but the heart remains the same.

George opened the door for the final time as the train stopped in Chicago. He had everything he could do to contain himself from running off and heading home. Brian and Craig stepped off the train, wished George a Merry Christmas, exchanged business cards, shook hands and headed for home in separate directions. Stan finished his last chores and cleaned his room, packing as he did so. He then stepped off the train. Seeing George, he yelled a Merry Christmas and Happy New Year before heading for his car parked in the lot.

Rich backed out the door, grabbed his bag and climbed down the ladder. Obtaining his land legs he walked slowly toward the station door. One more shift completed, one more train brought home safely. All that was left was to finish his paperwork and head for home. There his son and wife would be waiting. It would be a new beginning.

Meanwhile the cleaning crews scrubbed the floors and made sure the train was ready for the trip to New Orleans as Amtrak's *City of New Orleans*. That trip would depart on Christmas night with a whole new set of stories. The Christmas Empire Builder trip is now history and will live only in memories.